His eyes teased her again

Then he drew her back into the circle of his arms. She was warm and secure and naked against him beneath the blankets.

"This is the best part," Adrian whispered. "The afterglow." His voice grew sleepy and low, his hands lazily stroking her. "The time when we just hold each other, when we feel for each other and think about each other."

Sandy closed her eyes, content with the sound of his voice, the security of his embrace, the lingering warmth of their coming together, which was like a glow that would never fade, that would light her life forever.

Yes, she thought. It was the best part.

Books by Rebecca Flanders

These books may be available at your local bookseller.

Don't miss any of our special offers. Write to us at the following address for information on our newest releases.

Harlequin Reader Service
P.O. Box 52040, Phoenix, AZ 85072-2040
Canadian address: P.O. Box 2800, Postal Station A,
5170 Yonge St., Willowdale, Ont. M2N 6J3

Afterglow
REBECCA FLANDERS

Harlequin Books

TORONTO • NEW YORK • LONDON
AMSTERDAM • PARIS • SYDNEY • HAMBURG
STOCKHOLM • ATHENS • TOKYO • MILAN

Published September 1985

First printing July 1985

ISBN 0-373-15999-4

Printed in Canada

Chapter One

It was the end of November. There was forty-two inches of fresh powder in Vail. The International Music Festival was in full swing in Belgium, and everyone who was anyone would make it a point to stop by for a few days. In Waikiki it was eighty-two degrees, and the beaches were filled with Beautiful People. Father Noel was spreading his good cheer throughout the villages and provinces of rural France, and the Gem Exchange in Tokyo was bustling. But in Philadelphia the day was cold and rainy and unforgiving, and there was nothing to do but wait.

The young man who stood at the window of the stately Wesley mansion was tall and blond and classically beautiful, and sometimes passersby, rushing along through the rain, would glance up and be struck by the figure he made, silhouetted by golden lamplight against the background of the elegantly furnished room. But he was oblivious of any attention he might have attracted. He simply stood there, long, delicate fingers shoved into the pockets of his woolen slacks, his slim figure lounging with unconscious grace against the window frame, and stared blankly out. His name was Adrian Alexander Wesley III, and he felt, at that moment, as though he were the only living being left in the world.

Wes, as he had been known to everyone but teachers and employees since he was two, was twenty-seven years old, and he hadn't been home for the holidays more than twice in the past fifteen years. There was always something better to do: skiing in St. Moritz, a cruise in the Mediterranean, big-game hunting in Kenya, enjoying a love affair that simply couldn't be interrupted for familial amenities. He had always *intended* to make it home, and the year was filled with promises. "See you at Thanksgiving, Dad..." "This Christmas for sure..." "We'll have a big blowout on New Year's Eve, okay?" But by summer the enthusiasm for plan-making had waned; by fall it was forgotten. His father never seemed to mind—after all, he was a busy man, too—but Wes knew he was always a little disappointed that the two of them could never seem to get together for Christmas.

Well, Dad, he thought now, dully, *here I am. Where are you?*

The funeral had been yesterday. It had rained, of course. A week ago Wes had been in California, making plans for a deep-sea fishing expedition down the coast of Mexico, and suddenly he was here, back in this house, talking about funerals and protocol and open stock....

Alex Wesley had been one of an almost extinct breed— that rare blend of old wealth, high culture and unabashed class snobbery that was almost unheard of in American society. He could trace his ancestry back to European royalty—and not so many generations removed, either—and had maintained that legacy of superiority, refinement and taste with a sense of noblesse oblige that was the natural order of things for centuries untold. He had never worked a day in his life, or concerned himself with the management of the enormous financial empire that had been his birthright. He was gentle, scholarly and generous; he was fun-loving, adventuresome and sometimes even a little mischievous. He was Wes's best friend in the world.

I loved you, Dad, Wes thought now, bleakly. *If only I could have told you that one more time....*

Quickly, Wes focused his eyes on the scene outside to forestall the tears that threatened to choke him once again. He had cried too much these past days, alone and silently. He wasn't going to begin again.

Wes's grandfather had built the magnificent twenty-room mansion in which both Wes and his father had been raised. It stood, with the exception of some minor remodeling and modernization, exactly as it had then, on a piece of prime downtown property, a monument to the old money of the ruling class that had built Philadelphia into the international city it was today. There had been good times in this house, and Wes's face softened as he thought about them: sitting upon his father's shoulders at this very window, watching his first snowfall, trying to reach his chubby hand through the glass to catch the flakes; sliding down the sweeping mahogany banister into his father's waiting arms; playing make-believe polo in the marble foyer; beating his dad at pool in the elaborate game room....

During the later years, Wes had not been back to this house much. His mother had died before he was three, and in Wes's formative years his father had felt it important to establish a stable home environment. After Wes went away to school at age twelve, however, home lost its sentimental value and became just a place to go to when he and his father couldn't get together any other place. And there were lots of other places. London, Cannes, Vienna, Martinique, Honolulu...wherever there was fun to be had, Alex Wesley and his son could find it. Alex used to tease him about that—why one of the most eligible playboys in the world would want to spend most of his time with his old man—to which Wes would toss back an impertinent demand as to why one of the most eligible playboys in the world would want to spend his time with his son. Then Alex would threaten to teach him a little respect for his elders and they both would laugh, because neither of them could think of anyone else he would rather spend time with.

Twenty-seven years, Wes thought now, and there was a sense of finality in the realization that heralded the last, bittersweet resignation. *We had that, and I'm glad. It's more than a lot of people get. It's more than I had with my mom. I wish it could have been more, but...* But nothing could ever take away the specialness of his dad, the memories he had, the gift of all those years. Now it was over; it wasn't fair and Wes hated it, but his best friend was gone and there was nothing to do but say goodbye and move on.

The problem was, Wes didn't know where to go from here. His father would have been furious to know Wes was moping about the house so aimlessly and so disconsolately when there was a whole world waiting out there to be explored, but the truth was Wes could not think of anything he wanted to do. The coast of Mexico had lost its appeal; skiing in Switzerland required entirely too much energy; the Caribbean seemed unsettled and, besides, Wes wasn't entirely sure he wanted to be with people right now. The only thing he was sure of was that he didn't want to be here.

Unfortunately, here was exactly where he had to be for at least another couple of weeks. His father's estimable firm of Wilkins, Wilcox and Wilkins had informed him that there were a few matters of business to clear up before formal execution of the estate could begin, and had requested a meeting with Wes for the fifteenth of December. Wes hoped it wasn't going to be anything too complicated—he knew even less about matters of business and finance than his father did—but the lawyers seemed to think it would be helpful if Wes stayed in town for a while, in case they needed signatures or approval. Wes had nothing better to do, so he agreed. He only hoped the eminent attorneys didn't have any questions for him that required the skills of third-year algebra, which he had failed.

A small, dry smile tugged at the corner of Wes's lips, shading his face for a moment with a sad beauty that was as arresting as it was heartbreaking. There was a line his father was fond of, from some obscure short story by a long-forgotten author: "If I had known it would be this much trouble to die, I never would have done it." *You don't know the half of it, Dad,* Wes thought, and the smile faded.

Wes turned at the sound of footsteps crossing the room. Mitchell, in silent running shoes, baggy jeans and a Golden Gloves sweatshirt that had seen its last serviceable day in 1952, had somehow entered the room, set the lunch table before the fire, and had almost departed again before Wes noticed. The perfect, soundless servant.

Wes smiled and pushed himself lazily away from the window, crossing over to the fire. "Not staying for lunch, Mitch?" he invited carelessly.

Mitchell detested having his name shortened; it under-minded his dignity and showed an insulting lack of respect. Wes did it purely because Mitchell refused to address him by his nickname, and persisted in calling him "Master Adrian" and "Sir," despite Wes's most strenuous objections and constant efforts to persuade him to do otherwise. It was, like most of their relationship, a running battle between them.

Mitchell did not consider Wes's question worthy of a reply, so he merely gave his young employer his best impassive-servant look and said, "Will there be anything else, sir?"

Wes looked at the luncheon table, elaborately set for one with white linen, china, silver and even a white candle in a silver tulip holder, and he had to smile. Mitch did like to do things up right.

Mitch—né Roy N. Mitchell, as Wes had discovered on one secret, and highly dangerous, foray into Mitch's private quarters—had been with Alex Wesley for as long as Wes could remember. Rumor had it that he had once served with Wes's father in the army—rank, sergeant; assignment, cook—but he had first joined Alex's staff as a bodyguard when Alex was living in Italy and bodyguards were almost a necessity. Over the years his position had evolved into one of personal servant and cook, household manager, head of security, chauffeur, mechanic, companion and general right-hand man.

Alex never made a move without Mitch, and the six-foot-two, two-hundred-fifty-pound ex-prizefighter and army sergeant's devotion to Alex Wesley and all that was his was complete and unshakable. He gloried in his position in the Wesley household, and there was never any doubt as to who was in charge. Mitch took care of everything. Mitch had always been and would always be. And for Alex Wesley or his offspring, Mitch would have cheerfully gone to his death.

Wes realized suddenly that Mitch's own grief must be devastating. As controlled and orderly as ever, Mitch had quietly and efficiently gone about making the funeral arrangements, notifying the press, making travel arrangements for the huge entourage of friends and acquaintances, making sure, in his steadfast and unobtrusive manner, that Wes lacked for nothing and that the smooth flow of the household organization was not interrupted. He had never once displayed any sign of loss, or grief. Until this moment it had not occurred to Wes to look for it. Mitch was such a steadfast, unchanging part of the household that one never thought of the great man as having feelings, or needs.

But Mitch had lost more than an employer. He had lost a central part of his life. And Wes did not have to wonder how Mitch felt; he knew. He only cursed himself for not noticing sooner.

He said suddenly, "Did you ever think about it, Mitch?" He swept a hand around the room. "How archaic we are?"

"I haven't lost much sleep over the matter lately," Mitch admitted tolerantly, lapsing back into his conversational tone now that the matter of names was dismissed. "Will there be anything else?"

"No, really," Wes insisted. "You and I—nobody has butlers anymore. The whole servant-master thing is outdated. We should have lived in another century. This house should have been a castle, I should have been a marquis—"

"Only a marquis?" interrupted Mitchell dryly, and Wes shrugged.

"Okay, an earl," he conceded. "You should have been my trusty knight-at-arms and the garage should have been filled with white stallions instead of Bentleys and Rolls-Royces, and all those people out there—" he gestured toward the window "—should have been my serfs. At this very moment we should be planning a gala Christmas feast for all the peasants of the village, with roast lamb and wassail and a pig with an apple in its mouth."

"Whatever your lordship says," murmured Mitch, and bent to remove the cover from a dish of hot lobster salad. The touch of sarcasm in his tone was intentional, but the quirk of amusement at his mouth was not.

Wes, however, was satisfied. His own grief he could bear, but not that of other people, and he had succeeded, for the moment, in touching Mitch's well-disguised sense of humor. He felt better, but only marginally. He could joke, and he could tease; he and Mitch could assume the roles with which they felt most comfortable—Wes trying to irritate and Mitch getting the upper hand—they could pretend everything was the same, but in the end they knew nothing was the same, and there were just some things they had to deal with.

Wes looked at Mitch, who was fussing over the lunch table, and a sudden thickness came into his throat. He had to clear it before he could speak. He was the master now, the employer, responsible for all that his father had left behind. It was an uncomfortable role, one he was not at all sure he would ever get used to. Wes said, "Ah, Mitch. Listen, I don't know whether you've given any thought to..." Absently, he picked up a carrot stick from the platter and let it drop again, not meeting Mitch's eyes. "What I mean is, you know that you have a job here as long as..."

"I'll stay as long as you need me," Mitch said in his usual terse manner, dismissing the obvious and freeing Wes from the awkward business of being an employer. "Are you going to eat or not?"

Wes's eyes roamed restlessly from the elegance of the table to the crackling fire to the rain-fogged window, and he barely suppressed a sigh. Wouldn't it ever snow, he wondered. If only it would snow, things might not be so bad. But this weepy, cold, constant rain, the sound of it against the window, the sputter of it from the eaves, the bone-chilling damp that crept into every corner of the big old house... If he stayed in the house one more minute he would go mad, Wes knew without a doubt, and he said now to Mitch, "Would it break your heart if I skipped lunch?"

"I should no doubt sob into my pillow all night," Mitch responded dryly. He was already beginning to cover the dishes.

"I think I'll go out for a while," Wes said, trying to muster enthusiasm for the prospect. "Window-shop or something."

"Shall I bring the Rolls around?"

"No, I'll take the Austin." That thought cheered him somewhat. He loved driving the Austin. Then he paused. "You have kept it up for me, haven't you?"

Mitch looked insulted. "Of course."

Wes started for the hallway to get his coat.

Mitch called out patiently, "Will you be dining here tonight, sir?"

Wes's usual reply to that was a grinning "Not if I get lucky." But at the door he paused and glanced at the window one more time. It looked cold, wet and miserable, and he really didn't want to go out at all. Suddenly he had lost enthusiasm for everything, even teasing Mitch. He shrugged and answered without much interest, "Probably." Then he went, at a greatly slowed step, to get his coat.

SANDY GARRET HESITATED for a moment beneath the eaves of the office building before plunging out into the rain, shivering and turning up the collar of her coat. Wouldn't it ever snow, she wondered dismally. Three days of this mess was enough to give anyone a case of the blues.

Sandy had more than enough cause for depression without the rain, but she knew there was no point in mourning her situation. She had had over a year to prepare for it, and the doctor's pronouncement today had come as no surprise to her. She was an athlete; her body kept no secrets from her. She knew exactly what she was and was not capable of doing, and the doctor's professional opinion had only confirmed her own: that it was high time she started thinking about going into another line of work.

It was only the day after Thanksgiving—the biggest shopping day of the year—and already the Christmas decorations were up. Sandy found that mildly irritating. Red-and-silver tinsel garlands wrapped the signposts, small plastic evergreens looked like battered feather dusters in the rain. Multicolored lights blinked fuzzily from the storefronts across the street and were reflected in the puddles on the asphalt. Already some poor soul was standing on a corner ringing a bell, and every elevator in the city was piping in "The Twelve Days of Christmas." *Another month of this,* thought Sandy with a stifled groan, and she stepped out into the rain, hurrying toward the parking lot and the shelter of her brother's car.

Being one of six siblings was a mixed blessing. The advantages were free rent, a choice of whichever one of her relatives' automobiles that was not being currently used, dinner at a different house every day of the week if she so desired and an endless array of job offers. The disadvantages were a constant stream of helpful advice, a lack of privacy and the simple fact that not once in her entire life had Sandy been allowed to make a major decision on her own.

It had taken all her skill and powers of subterfuge to keep today's appointment from her family's prying eyes. They had been waiting over a year for this final pronouncement, encouraging, hopeful, hiding their own anxiety behind a constant screen of optimism. Each and every one of them had learned the rudiments of physical therapy and had patiently guided Sandy through the rehabilitation program, reminding her to do her exercises, insisting that she keep her muscles in shape, watching her diet, preparing her for that day when, they naively believed, she would take to the slopes again. Now Sandy had to tell them they could stop worrying. It was all over.

Sandy Garret had been skiing since she was five. She had been in competition since she was twelve, and from that time there was no doubt in any member of her family's mind that she was on her way to an Olympic championship. Every day of her life for the past fifteen years, since she was nine, had been spent in training. From September to May she was on the slopes, from May to September she was preparing to be there. Regional and divisional contests, Olympic training camps, exhibitions and practice runs—she knew no other life and had never once even thought whether or not she would like to know another.

She had made the last Olympic team, but even her coach did not try to build up false hopes about her chances for a medal. She didn't care; just being there was the achievement of a lifetime. She didn't place, but her family had been more disappointed in that fact than Sandy was. Those who could afford it had traveled to be with her at the events; those who couldn't offered support and generous excuses via long distance about the condition of the snow and the wind factor and the unfair competition. Her father, beaming through his disappointment, had assured her that a medal was hers next time, but Sandy shared neither his disappointment nor his confidence. She had skied with the best in the world, and she had held her own. That to her was enough. She was not looking for new horizons.

At the beginning of the season last year a freak accident on the slopes had put an end to whatever ambition she had ever had. After knee surgery there was a three-month recuperative period, and Sandy knew she had lost too much training time to make up that year. Then there was more surgery, more physical therapy and an awful lot of time to think.

For the first time in her life Sandy was not on the slopes, not training for competition, not looking forward to the next meet or looking back at the last; it was a frightening feeling. It was like being suspended in midair with nothing below, nothing before and nothing behind. It was, quite simply, losing all sense of identity.

Sandy still felt that occasional sense of emptiness, of confusion, of floating in midair without purpose or direction, and perhaps she always would. But during the past year she had come to realize something else: it didn't matter. Those around her—her coach, her family, her teammates—looked at her and saw a young woman who was struggling with the loss of her hopes and dreams, her life's ambition. But all Sandy had really lost was something to do.

It was over, and she didn't really care. She wondered if she ever had.

She also wondered, as she unlocked the door to her brother's VW with wet, frozen fingers, how she would have felt if the doctor had told her today that she could return to the slopes tomorrow with nothing but time lost. She smiled to herself a little as she realized she would probably have been disappointed. She liked the way her life was now, the open ends, the uncertainty, the endless adventure of the future that had never been hers to explore before. The final medical verdict had been only the turning of the key that opened a door on vistas so wide she had not yet begun to comprehend their significance. But of course she would never be able to explain that to her family.

She sobered a little as she turned the starter on Rick's bug and it chugged reluctantly to life. The damage to the cartilage of her knee had been extensive; reconstructive surgery had resulted in a loss of flexibility and stability. There was simply no way she would ever be able to ski competitively again; she was fortunate to be able to walk without a limp. Her family could understand that; in the backs of their minds, they must have been prepared for it all along. What they would not be able to understand was Sandy's apparent apathy to the entire situation. What they would want to know was what she intended to do with her life now. And Sandy had no answer to that.

She turned on the windshield wipers and shivered at the blast of cold air from the heater, wiping away the fog from the window as she prepared to make the turn into Christmas traffic. She would not be back to this office again, and what awaited her out there was new and exciting—and a little scary. It wasn't regret she felt, exactly, nor was it quite anticipation. Things would be different from now on, and it wasn't necessarily a bad thing.

But, she decided as she eased the little car out into the dismal, rain-soaked street, and with the first real pang of pathos she had felt all day, she would miss the snow.

Chapter Two

The entrance to the mall was guarded by a swarm of plastic reindeer; traffic was being directed by orange-coated policemen. Candy-striped poles marked the parking lot, and every tree on every median was strung with white lights. The effect was ridiculous now—all those naked deciduous trees decked out in Christmas lights—but Sandy grudgingly admitted the sight could be quite spectacular after dark. On top of the front building a huge live spruce, glittering with flashing red, blue and yellow lights and topped with an elaborate laser-lit star, swayed unsettlingly in the wind and collected raindrops. And everywhere people rushed to and from their cars, loaded down with bags and boxes, dragging children or chasing them, braving wind and rain and dark of night for the Great Sale. Sandy steeled herself for the coming hours.

Of course Sandy had to park at the far end of the lot, and she was soaked and chilled to the bone by the time she reached the mall. She moved with as great a speed as possible through the milling crowd, hardly glancing at the huge first-floor display in which children boarded a miniature choo-choo for a ride through a cotton-candy wonderland to meet Santa Claus, or the second-story centerpiece in which robotized elves endlessly loaded a red velvet bag with toys beneath a silver Christmas tree. Every store window had its own tree, or "Merry Christmas" written in plastic snow on front. Muzak was playing "The Twelve Days of Christmas."

Sandy hardly paused to grimace at the huge crowd inside her sister's little shop, but she edged her way past as gracefully as possible, explaining breathlessly at the counter to a harried Linda, "Sorry! Traffic!" even as she pulled off her coat and moved toward the back room to hang it up.

"Thank goodness you're here!" Linda was beside her, having grabbed another hapless assistant to take over the checkout. "I've been going crazy! Your costume is right here. We must have twenty children in the store! I don't believe the nerve of some parents! What do they think this is, free baby-sitting? They just walk right off and leave them—"

Sandy understood the references to children and thoughtless parents—the mall was conducting a "Santa's Helper" afternoon in which parents could leave their children with designated sales personnel who would help them shop for gifts for mommy and daddy while mommy and daddy themselves were free to go off and shop elsewhere. Linda, who had participated in the event last year, considered it totally insane, and had voted loudly to discontinue the practice, but had been overruled. Sandy, who considered the entire Christmas frenzy utter madness from the word go, did not think this idea was any crazier than, say, beginning Christmas advertising on Halloween. It was all merchandising, pure and simple, and though Sandy wouldn't exactly say her heart was in it, she was ready to assume her role as Santa's helper. But at the word "costume" she balked.

"Wait a minute." She stopped at the entrance to the cluttered back room, turning a formidable glare upon her older sister. "If you think for one second that you're going to dress me up in a little green elf suit..."

"Not elf," insisted Linda impatiently, pushing a strand of ash-blond hair away from her stylish tortoiseshell glasses. "*Helper*. And it's not green, it's red. Here, you're going to look adorable." She grabbed Sandy's wrist and pulled her into the room, tossing her wet coat over the garment rack in the same motion. "Put it on, you'll love it. And hurry. I've got a store full of screaming kids and a half-dozen impatient parents and a crazy old Santa who keeps wandering in and out looking for his reindeer, and I really have to get back out there. You know the kind of shoplifting that goes on this time of year."

Sandy took the bundle of red flannel and white fur Linda thrust at her and held it up dubiously. Except for the trim and the piece of plastic mistletoe pinned to the shoulder, it could have been a pair of thermal underwear. "No way," she pronounced flatly, and shoved the costume back into her sister's hands. "There is absolutely no way I'm going to go parading around the mall in a pair of Dr. Dentons. I'll stay dressed just the way I am, thank you."

For a moment the two women faced each other down, and the mutual stubbornness in their eyes was the only thing that gave any hint they were sisters. Johnny Garret was proud of the fact that each one of his six children was "an original, not a copy in the bunch." But the lack of family resemblance was most pronounced in the two sisters, Sandy and Linda, who were separated in age by three years, in appearance and personality by more than that.

Sandy was the shorter of the two, her body firm and hard from years of athletic regimen. Her dark hair was shorn into a crop of careless curls, her eyes wide and brown and fringed by velvet lashes. Her round face and small, slightly up-turned nose gave her a pixie look that would have been perfect casting in the elf costume, but the rigid definition of her jaw when she went into her stubborn mode quickly erased any impression of gullibility the rest of her features might have given.

Linda was tall and willowy, and although the blond hair may not have been precisely nature's choice, it matched her fair complexion and tawny eyes perfectly. Her cheekbones were high and carefully enhanced by makeup; her lips, full and pouty. Linda had an innate sense of style and fashion; Sandy threw on whatever she happened to grab from her closet. The result was that Linda looked like a high-fashion model; Sandy looked, most of the time, like a street urchin. Linda never raised her voice; Sandy did not hesitate to screech if the occasion or her temper called for it. But both women were used to getting their own way, and it looked for a moment as though this contest of wills would be a draw.

Then Linda, who really did not have time to worry about any of this, decided on an effective compromise. "Just wear the hat," she pleaded. "How else are the children going to know who you are?"

Sandy picked up the fur-trimmed Santa's hat with its rather bedraggled looking fur ball at the point and decided she could contribute that much to the Christmas spirit. "All right," she agreed, not entirely ungraciously, and plopped it on top of her rain-flattened curls with a flourish. "How do I look?"

Linda took in the plaid skirt, the tweed sweater, the rumpled navy leg warmers above the tops of Sandy's flat-heeled boots, the whole topped by a crooked Santa's hat, and she shook her head helplessly. "Ridiculous," she answered. "But no more than usual, I suppose. Now could we get to work?"

Sandy made a face at her sister's retreating back as she followed her out of the room, but she was inwardly grateful that the first shopping day of the season had kept Linda so preoccupied she had forgotten to ask where Sandy had been that afternoon.

When Sandy had first gotten out of the hospital, she had gone home to her parents' three-bedroom suburban house to recuperate. Her brother, Rick, and his wife and children were also living there, waiting for their new house to be completed, as well as her younger sister Midge, who was in her first year of college. Her middle brother, O.J., was home on leave from the navy, and the small house was, to say the least, crowded. As soon as she was physically capable of doing so, Sandy started looking for a place of her own.

Her oldest brother, Bill, who had always come closer to understanding Sandy than anyone else, appreciated the fact that the emotional trauma Sandy was undergoing was not in any way enhanced by the well-meaning cheerfulness of a house filled with relatives, and moved her into a furnished one-bedroom flat in a small apartment complex he owned. For the first month Sandy accepted it rent free, but as soon as she was able to work she paid her own rent—which, she guessed but could not prove, was only a fraction of the amount Bill usually charged.

Her brothers and sisters fought over who had the best part-time job for Sandy, one that would not be too strenuous on her injured knee, one that afforded her plenty of mental stimulation but did not require much concentration, one that allowed her plenty of time to keep up her therapy regimen and rejoin her training program, one whose hours were flexible and not too demanding—with the result that Sandy had to rotate her services among all of them. She had worked for a while at Bill's real-estate office; kept the books for her father's business at home, answered phones in her sister-in-law Judy's office, helped her mother take orders for the Christmastime business. The only member of her family in Philadelphia who did not offer her employment was her brother, Rick, who was a cop. His wife, Judy, however, was more than happy to employ Sandy's baby-sitting services for their three active children on that rare occasion when she had an evening to spend alone with her husband. Sandy was now working for her sister, Linda, who owned and operated a very successful boutique in Wesley Mall called Collectibles. And it was, of course, the busiest time of the year.

Collectibles was a charming shop that featured hand-made crafts from all over the country, one-of-a-kind imports and hard-to-find items of every description. It was the best place in town to find that special gift for someone who has everything, and it did a booming business all year round. During the Christmas season it was absolute madness, and to deal with the overflow crowds Linda stocked standard gifts like cheese platters, imported jellies and cookies, boxed toiletries and monogrammed silk handkerchiefs and ties. It was to this section that Sandy tried to direct the children, but it was difficult to keep their attention from straying to the display of Johnny Garret's handmade toys.

One thing could be said of Sandy's family without fear of contradiction: they were definitely into Christmas. Once, when Sandy was assigned the task of sending out the hundreds of Christmas cards, she had mischievously signed each and every one "Mr. and Mrs. Claus and Elves," and it was an appellation that stuck. Never had there been a single family for whom it was more appropriate, for Sandy doubted that even the flurry of activity at the North Pole could compare with what went on at the Garret house once the holiday season was rung in.

Linda spent all year stocking her store for the thirty shopping days before Christmas. From October to just before Christmas, Sandy's mother operated a "Letter from Santa" business in what was, during calmer times, her basement sewing room. From January to August, Johnny Garret was one of the most sought-after renovation specialists and contractors in the state, but on September first, come what may, he put down his slide rule, set up his drawing board, and turned his workshop into an assembly line for hand-carved wooden toys.

Every member of the family was enlisted in the business of Christmas in one way or another—the daughters helping to answer their mother's hundreds of letters to Santa until their fingers cramped and their eyes blurred, often into the wee hours of the morning; the sons cutting patterns of wood and gluing and sanding and lacquering until their shoulders ached and their fingers grew numb. In previous years, Sandy had been excused from duty because of a rigorous training schedule that allowed her to be home only for a couple of days at Christmastime; this year she was trying to stay busy enough that her services would not be required.

It was hard to be enthusiastic about Christmas when the season lasted half the year, and besides, she thought her parents were crazy for putting so much effort into a business that returned so little. Her mother answered all those letters by hand on specially designed stationery practically for nothing. And her father...Johnny Garret's wooden toys were works of art and in demand all over the country. Sandy was convinced he could be a rich man if he devoted his full energy to the project, but he only replied that going full-time would take all the fun out of Christmas, and insisted upon retailing his handcrafted originals for less than half what they were worth.

Sandy was trying to distract an enthusiastic six-year-old from one of Johnny's wooden freight trains—the young boy was apparently bent on determining for himself whether the toy was as indestructible as it was advertised to be—when someone tapped her on the shoulder.

"Excuse me, are you Santa's helper?"

Sandy had been working for three hours by then, and her first instinct was to hide the Santa cap in her pocket, smile pleasantly and tell the woman she was in the wrong store.

But the little boy's mother came to collect him just then, with much scolding and shaking of the finger, and all Sandy could do was rescue the freight train before it was tossed onto the floor in a fit of temper, take a deep breath and turn to greet her next customer.

"Merry Christmas," she said. "May I help you?"

The woman pushed a little blond girl forward, obviously eager to dispose of the child and be on about her business. "This is Kerry," she said. "She has fifteen dollars—show the nice lady, Kerry—and she wants to buy her mommy a Christmas present." She absently patted the child's head with a smirk. "Such a sweet girl. Her daddy is just outside the store—" she gestured toward a man in a beige overcoat who stood with his back to the window "—so just send her out when she's finished. Go with Santa's helper, Kerry. There's a good girl." And in an aside to Sandy, she whispered, "Pick out something nice, will you? Last year she gave me a goldfish."

But before Sandy could even reply, the woman had given the child another absent pat on the head and was threading her way toward the door.

"Well, Kerry," Sandy said brightly, extending her hand, "what do you think Mommy would like for Christmas?"

The little girl looked up at her with grave blue eyes, not smiling, and not unclenching her chubby little fist from the red purse she held. Sandy let her own hand drop. "Well," she tried again. "How about some nice pretty-smelling soap? I think Mommy would like that, don't you? Come on, let's look at it...."

But as she turned to escort her young charge up the aisle, Linda came shoulder-to-shoulder with her. "There he is again," she said sotto voce, and her eyes were fixed on the doorway.

Sandy turned just in time to see the owner of the reverberating "Ho-ho-ho!" that rang through the store, and she stifled a grin. It was the kooky Santa again, and surely there had never been a sorrier specimen in the history of Saint Nick.

He was tall, skinny and altogther quite bedraggled-looking. His beard was scraggly and scruffy, thready-looking in some places and bristly in others, but it was at least white—and obviously his own. A ruff of hair began just above his ears and encircled his otherwise bald head, straggling down to his shoulders in back, but it, too, was white. The red suit hung on his undernourished frame and had obviously seen better days; it was threadbare and stained, the white fur dingy and matted. His rheumy eyes and red nose were those of a street wino, and from his appearance and demeanor Sandy suspected that what he carried in the knapsack slung over his shoulder was about ninety proof. Whoever had hired this joker for the mall was no doubt looking for other employment by now.

"I don't know why they let him just wander around like this," Linda complained, still eyeing him warily. "Looks like security would have picked him up by now. He's scaring the kids."

This was the third time Santa had wandered into Collectibles and Sandy had not noticed any frightened children. All the guy did was shout a few ho-ho-hos and Merry Christmases before wandering off in search of his mythical reindeer again, and the children gave him no more than a cursory glance before turning back to the more interesting diversion of seeing how much damage they could do to the shop in how short a time. Raised in a commercial age, they were not about to be fooled by a skinny Santa in a dirty suit.

Sandy shrugged. "He's not doing any harm." She turned back to young Kerry. "How about a pretty pair of slippers? We've got some with butterflies on them."

"I'm going to keep an eye on him," Linda muttered suspiciously. "There's something creepy about that guy."

"What kind of slippers?" inquired Kerry, and Sandy, relieved that she was not going to have to deal with another six-year-old who miraculously lost her power of speech when it came time to make a decision, guided Kerry toward the minimally priced gift items.

Twenty minutes later Sandy was trying to explain to an obstreperous Kerry that her mother's goldfish would *not* enjoy swimming around in a two-hundred-dollar Oriental bowl and that, in all likelihood, a meerschaum pipe would not be a practical alternative.

"Then I want *that*," insisted Kerry stubbornly, pointing again to the blue-and-white porcelain bowl that was displayed on a top shelf, safely out of the reach of clumsy fingers.

Never again, thought Sandy grimly. *Never again do I work for any member of this family at Christmastime.* "No, Kerry," she began again patiently, "I told you before, your goldfish—"

"*Mommy's* goldfish," interrupted the child belligerently.

"*Mommy's* goldfish would not be happy in that bowl. He couldn't see where he was swimming. Goldfish like glass bowls."

"What does he need to see for?" scoffed Kerry. "All he can see is water anyway."

It was impossible to argue with that kind of logic, so Sandy tried a different tactic. "Look, here's a pretty candle. It smells like Christmas, doesn't it? Wouldn't your mom like that?"

"No." The child thrust out her jaw in a purposeful imitation of the adult she would one day become. "Mommy would like the bowl."

"But you don't have enough money to buy the bowl!" Sandy explained a little desperately.

"I do too!" The child's voice became shrill, and she obstinately thrust the little red purse toward Sandy. "I've got

plenty of money! And you know what else! I don't think
you know Santa Claus at all! I think you're just a mean old
lady and I'm gonna tell my daddy!''

The time for diplomacy was long since past. Sandy replaced the candle with utmost care, counting to ten, then
turned and sank down on her heels, at eye level with her
adversary. "Look, kid." Her voice was low and her eyes
grim; hers was the face of a woman who would brook no
further argument. "You're not getting the bowl and you're
not getting the pipe. I'm going to wrap up a scarf and you're
going to give me your money and you're going to walk out
of here happy, have you got that?''

The kid was no fool. She had seen the very same look on
her father's face right after she had drawn crayon suns all
over his brand-new Buick. She swallowed once and nodded.

"Good." Sandy got to her feet with a curt nod of satisfaction and strode over to the counter. "Let's get to it."

She was just passing the wrapped present and three dollars in change to a now-meek child when Linda whispered
triumphantly in her ear, "I knew it! That creepy Santa has
been ripping me off!''

Sandy gave her a puzzled, half-skeptical look. *"What?"*

"I've been watching him," Linda said excitedly, and
nodded toward the vagabond Santa, who, as far as Sandy
could tell, was doing nothing more than browsing. "So far
he's slipped a pair of kid gloves, a porcelain ashtray and a
box of Belgian chocolates in that knapsack of his. I've already called security," she pronounced on a note of satisfaction. "They'll be here any minute."

Sandy looked again at the raggedy Santa, and then at her
sister. "Are you sure?''

Linda nodded grimly. "I knew there was something
wrong with that character the minute I saw him."

There was a bloodthirsty look in Linda's eyes that Sandy
found oddly inappropriate in her delicate-appearing sister,

and she had to suppress a smile. Christmastime brought out the worst in everybody, she supposed.

Sandy would have liked to follow up on the tale of the delinquent Santa Claus, but first she had the matter of the six-year-old tyrant to dispose of. After three hours she was in total agreement with Linda on the folly of the "Santa's Helper" program, and utterly amazed by the carelessness of parents who allowed their children to participate. What kind of people just walked off and left their kids in the care of an unknown salesperson in one of the busiest malls in the city? All kinds. And even though Sandy's responsibility ended when the purchase was made, she was not about to have any irate parents suing her for negligence after their child wandered off and became lost—or worse—in the mall. She always delivered her charges personally into the hands of the parents.

"Okay, Kerry," she said, coming around the counter. "Where's your daddy?"

The child looked around the store once, very slowly, and then twice, and Sandy began to despair. One more minute with this kid... And then, to Sandy's very great relief, Kerry lifted her arm and pointed toward the door.

The man was tall, slim and elegant looking. He was wearing a camel-colored coat that was probably cashmere and most definitely hand tailored. It was unbuttoned over gray wool slacks and a white sweater that also appeared to be cashmere—the real thing, not an imitation blend. His blond hair was styled to sweep back from his forehead and drift over his ears, just brushing the collar in the back. It was a pure blond, the kind of color Linda was constantly trying to achieve from a bottle, but was almost never seen on anyone over four years old. He had the most beautiful face Sandy had ever seen. There was an aristocratic delicacy about the perfect construction of the nose, the cheekbones, the heavily lidded eyes. But the broad forehead, the well-defined jawline, the perfectly shaped mouth with just the tiniest of clefts above it were distinctly, and quite strikingly, masculine. It was a face that looked as if it belonged on a Greek coin.

"Wow," Sandy said softly. "Lucky kid." And she proceeded to follow her young customer toward the front of the store.

WES HAD BEEN WANDERING around the mall all afternoon, buying nothing, not really noticing much. He enjoyed the feeling of being anonymous in a crowd, and all the lights and gaiety were distracting. Another time he would have found the novelty of it all immensely enjoyable, but now he found it hard to concentrate on anything—even the absurdities of life's little vignettes that went on around him— so mostly he just walked. He had come into Collectibles because it looked like a frontispiece from a Dickens novel, and he stood now, absently examining a magnificently carved wooden soldier. He looked up when a cheerful voice said, "Well, here she is."

The elfin-looking young woman in the Santa's hat appeared to be addressing him. Beside her stood a sober-eyed, blond-haired little girl to whom he gave a cursory glance before returning his eyes to the woman.

She was not beautiful in the accepted sense—certainly not in comparison with the women Wes usually aligned himself with—but she had a certain pixie charm that struck in him the first real note of interest he had felt all day. She was not tall, not svelte, not alluring; she was, in fact, rather frumpy and, with that absurd little Santa's hat, delightfully comical. A flutter of burnished mahogany curls framed a face that was creamy smooth and softly shaped, and that seemed to hold a guileless good humor that Wes found fascinating. Her eyes were rich brown and sparkled with a smile, and they seemed to be expecting something from him. So Wes obliged.

His lips curved upward into a friendly though somewhat puzzled smile, and he said, "Hello."

He had a wonderful smile, and his eyes were as blue as Kerry's. Sandy could certainly tell where Kerry had gotten her good looks. *Too bad,* she thought. "Well, Kerry is finished with her shopping. I think you'll be pleased. Here's the receipt."

The puzzled look Sandy had only half noticed before deepened, and he did not take the receipt. "Who's Kerry?"

Had she not been quite so fascinated by the man's incredible good looks, his smile, the grace of his long, perfectly manicured fingers as he moved to replace the toy soldier he'd been examining—in short, if Sandy had been paying more attention to her job, the obvious would no doubt have occurred to her much sooner. But as it was, all she felt was a mild confusion, and she said, "Why...Kerry. Your wife left her here to Christmas-shop, and—"

"I'm not married," Wes said, but he wasn't particularly anxious to find the solution to the puzzle. This conversation was the most distracting thing that had happened to him all day, and he was enjoying it.

"You're not..." And then Sandy understood. Her spirits sank, though she did not know whether it was from embarrassment, concern or relief. "Then I don't suppose you're Kerry's father," she said in a rather small voice.

"I'm afraid not," he replied cheerfully, and tucked his fingers casually into the pockets of his slacks. "Is she missing one?"

Kerry began to cry.

Sandy, looking in distraction from the softly weeping child to the handsome young man in the cashmere coat, berated herself mercilessly for the mistake. This was all she needed, a crying child and a missing father. She should have known. She didn't know *how* she should have known, but she should have. This man didn't look like anyone's father.

"I'm terribly sorry," she began. "She pointed at you, and I thought—you must have looked like her father from where she was standing. I think his coat was the same color as yours..." Kerry cried louder, and Sandy looked around the mall distractedly. "I can't imagine where he could be...."

Wes, moved to sympathy for the young woman's plight, offered helpfully, "I'm sure he wouldn't just walk off and leave her. He's around here somewhere. What does he look like?"

"I—I'm not sure," Sandy admitted, and she winced as Kerry began to sob "Daddy-daddy-daddy!" quite loudly. Heads were beginning to turn.

It was obvious the situation was on the border of slipping out of control. Wes didn't know what he could do to help, but it seemed to him the first order of business was to quiet all the distressing noise the child was making, and then perhaps he and the cute little shop assistant could get on with their conversation. His fingers touched a roll of breath mints in his pocket, and on inspiration, he drew them out.

"Look, little girl, candy." He knelt beside her and offered the breath mints, slipping a comforting arm around her shoulders. "Do you want some candy?"

It all happened at once. Kerry went rigid, she screwed up her face and opened her mouth, and from her lungs issued the most heart-stopping scream Sandy had ever heard—more along the proportions of an air-raid siren than the cry of a six-year-old girl. Wes sprang back in astonishment, dropping the mints and getting to his feet, his hands going involuntarily to his ears as the shrill wail went on and on and everyone turned to stare. From the corner of her eye Sandy saw the hurried approach of two uniformed security guards and someone—Linda, she thought—cried out, "That's him! Grab him before he gets away!"

A man in a beige overcoat came running up, and Kerry began to scream, "Daddy! Daddy! He touched me, that man touched me! Daddy!"

The security guards hesitated only a moment, then bore down on Wes, each of them grabbing one of his arms and pinning it behind his back while Kerry jumped up and down screaming, "He touched me, Daddy, he touched me!" Wes, speechless, only stared.

The man in the beige overcoat swept up his daughter, demanding, "What did he do, darling? Are you all right?" and one of the security guards whipped out his walkie-talkie to radio for the police, never releasing his grip on Wes, who by now had found the presence of mind to begin a startled protest.

But before he had uttered more than "Wait a minute, I—" the irate father released his daughter and got to his feet, lunging at Wes.

"You filthy scum!" he yelled. "I ought to take your face apart with my bare hands! Why they let creeps like you out on the street I don't know! What did you do to her, you—"

One of the security guards had to release Wes to hold off the berserk father, and Sandy, at last galvanized into action, cried, "Wait a minute! He didn't do anything, he was only—"

And then Linda came pushing through the curious and shocked crowd, demanding in alarm, "What is going on here? You're going to let him get away! Over there…" She tugged at the arm of the guard who held Wes. "That guy in the Santa suit—he's robbing me blind! Stop him!"

The guard who held the still-struggling father tried to calm him. "Just take it easy, sir. We know how to handle these creeps. The police are on their way." Then he turned to his partner. "Sam, better call for reinforcements. What's this about a shoplifter?"

"Pervert!" shouted the father. "Child molester!"

Child molester. Wes paled abruptly. This situation had ceased to be amusing, if indeed it had ever been. He began to struggle in earnest. "Let me go! You've made a mistake, I tell you! Do you have any idea who I am?" He gave his arm one mighty wrench and was rewarded with a pain that shot through his shoulder and actually took his breath away. These fellows were serious. He jerked his head in Sandy's direction, rather desperately. "Ask her—she'll tell you who I am. This is absurd! I was just standing here, minding my own business..."

Sandy looked at him helplessly. "But I—I don't know who you are," she stammered. Then, seeing the look of angry despair come over his face, she added quickly to the guard, "But he's right—you have made a mistake.... I was standing here all the time. It's really kind of my fault...."

"There! There, you see!" Wes gave another experimental tug at his arm. "Will you let me go? You have no idea what you've let yourself in for—"

"Arrest him!" demanded Linda, and Sandy turned on her in angry amazement only to see that she was trying to pull the guard away from Wes and toward Santa. "Hurry, before he gets out of the store!"

Santa Claus was edging discreetly toward the door, another team of guards was approaching, a red-faced father was trying to get at Wes, Wes was furiously protesting his innocence, Kerry was sobbing, and it all went downhill from there. The second team of security guards apprehended Santa Claus, a hysterical mother joined the foray and scooped up her daughter, telling her she was a good, *good* girl, all the while stridently demanding to know what was going on from her husband. Customers began to press close, trying to get in on the action, and the arrival of the police only a few minutes later did nothing to alleviate the confusion. Sandy tried to soothe the customers, reason with the irate parents, explain the situation to the police, but her words were lost in the melee.

"Unhand me, you villains! I'll have you know that you're interfering with my sworn mission, held in sacred trust for hundreds of years! Thousands of children are depending upon me to make my rounds—what have you done with my reindeer?"

"Insane! If you'd just give me a chance to explain...."

"Only went across the mall to the drugstore for a minute, and when my back was turned this—this *slime*..."

"What a good girl, Kerry, for remembering to scream. She's been trained to scream whenever a stranger touches her. We learned it in the child-safety program at the police station...."

"Check his knapsack! He's got over a hundred dollars worth of merchandise in it and *no* sales receipt. I knew from the minute I laid eyes on him...."

"Mommy, are they taking Santa to jail?"

"This was supposed to be a very *exclusive* shop!"

"Tell them, Sandy. Tell them how we stood right here and watched that phony Santa—"

"Lady, will you *tell* them? I'm just an innocent bystander. All I was trying to do was help! I can't believe this is actually happening. Will you please tell them?"

Sandy looked from her sister to the somewhat frantic young man who was only one step away from police custody, and she knew where the greatest urgency lay.

"He's right," she insisted, finally succeeding in capturing the attention of one young police officer, who looked vaguely familiar. "There's been a terrible mistake. Look, I'm Rick Garret's sister—do you know him?"

The officer looked up from the pad he was scribbling on, a look of pleasant surprise coming over his face. "Sure, I know Rick. Hey, you must be the youngest—the skier, right?"

"No, not the youngest, the middle sister, but I am a skier. Was, that is. But that's not the point...."

"Well, imagine that." The officer grinned, enjoying the break in the routine. "Rick'll get a kick out of this. How's it going, anyway? We watched you on TV last year, you know, down at the precinct. Now that you told me, you do look familiar...."

Wes threw his head back with a weary sigh of despair. He could not believe this was happening to him. A comedy of errors, that's what it was, and he was playing straight man. It was incredible. Purely incredible. "Look," he interrupted tersely. "I don't mean to break up old home week, but if we could get on with the business at hand..." He shrugged his shoulders to indicate his own hands, which were still being held behind him by a cooperative security guard.

"You just watch your mouth, mister," snapped Kerry's father, who had calmed only marginally while giving his statement to the officer. "You dirty, lowdown—"

"He's *right*," insisted Sandy for what must have been the tenth time, turning on the father. "You made a mistake. Will you just shut up for a minute and listen?"

"You watch who you're telling to shut up, sister! This is all your fault anyway! If we hadn't trusted you to take care of our little girl—"

"Will you let the lady talk?" demanded Wes somewhat frantically.

The police officer agreed gallantly, "Yeah, let's all just calm down here...."

Sandy took a deep breath, torn between anger at the father who had the temerity to accuse *her* of carelessness, guilt over the fact that he was partially right, and incredulity at how terribly, terribly out of hand the entire situation had gotten. "Look," she said to the officer, turning her back on both Kerry and her parents, "it was all very simple. The little girl mistook this man here—" she gestured to Wes, who relaxed visibly "—for her father. As you can see, they do look something alike from the back, and they're wearing the same color coat...." A six-year-old, she reasoned, could not possibly know the difference between cashmere and a wool blend. "I brought her over to him, and when she realized her mistake she started crying. All he did was put his arm around her to comfort her, and she started screaming bloody murder and—" she shrugged "—all hell broke loose."

The officer nodded thoughtfully. "Sounds reasonable to me." He got down on his knees beside Kerry. "Is that about the way it happened, Kerry?"

"He gave me candy," replied Kerry self-righteously, proud of her importance. "Mommy says only bad men give you candy."

Kerry's mother tossed a triumphant look at the officer, and he got to his feet. "Look," he said, turning back to Sandy, "I'm sure this is all a big misunderstanding, but if they want to press charges..." He looked inquiringly at the parents.

"Damn right we do!" asserted the father, drawing Kerry protectively against his leg. "It's about time someone did something to put filth like this behind bars!"

I don't believe this, thought Wes with a kind of weary hysteria. *Nothing in the world is going to make me believe this....*

"Okay, Sam, I'm ready to go." The other officer came up, escorting a handcuffed and indignantly protesting Santa by the elbow. "He had the stuff on him. What about you?"

The young officer looked apologetically at Sandy. "I'm afraid this is all going to have to be straightened out at the station. It might be helpful if you came along."

Sheer panic shot through Wes as the police officer took his arm. "Wait a minute—you can't do this! You can't arrest me!"

"You're not under arrest, sir," explained the officer patiently. "You're just coming along with us for questioning." He glanced over his shoulder at the parents. "If you want to sign a complaint, you'll have to follow us."

Wes, frantic, turned his wrath on Sandy. "You're not just going to stand by and let them do this, are you?" he demanded furiously. "This is all your fault—but *my* life is on the line! You can't just—"

Sandy was quite certain that, had she been in his position, she would have been given to bursts of irrational anger, too, but on top of everything else she resented the fact that he was yelling at her. She glared at him. "They're not going to execute you for giving candy to a child!"

But then the anger in his eyes turned to despair, and she got her first real glimpse of what a truly horrifying thing this could turn out to be. "Child molesting," he said in a pained undertone. "Do you really think it's a laughing matter to have something like that on record?"

"I've got to go down and sign a complaint against this jerk," Linda said brusquely, pulling on her gloves as she moved past. "Keep an eye on the shop, will you?"

Sandy looked from Wes to her sister. "But I—"

"I say, young lady," protested Santa indignantly, "you have no idea what forces you are reckoning with. I can see right now I can mark *one* stop off my list!"

"Come on, old man." The officer gave Santa's arm an ungracious tug. "Let's get the paperwork started. Let's go, Carl," he said to his fellow officer, then added, muttering, "This time of year brings out all the crazies."

Sandy took one last look at the desperation in the cloudy blue eyes of one of the most beautiful faces she had ever seen, and she made up her mind. "I'll be right down," she promised. The officer began leading him away, and she called after him, "Don't worry, we'll get it all straightened out, and—I'm sorry!"

"*You*'re sorry!" he shouted back, and Sandy winced. "You should be in my shoes!"

Quickly, she turned to give instructions to the remaining clerks about operating the shop, then hurried to the back to get her coat and purse. As she rushed out into the dark and the rain, she couldn't help thinking in wry incredulity, *And only twenty-five shopping days to go....*

Chapter Three

Wes had never been inside a police station before. On what occasion would a person with the last name Wesley have to do so? But this precinct was small and in a relatively upper-class neighborhood, and there was none of the inner-city squalor and filth that Wes had expected. The atmosphere was quiet and orderly, the officers courteous and friendly. The building itself was clean and quite new, and there was a small plastic Christmas tree decorated with miniature flashing lights and candy canes on the reception desk.

Wes sat at a table in what they called the squad room, smoking a pack of stale cigarettes he had found in his coat pocket. Wes smoked rarely, but when he did it was with a vengeance. He could easily consume a pack every two or three hours for a couple of days, followed by weeks, or even months, in which he did not think of a cigarette once. Before tonight, Wes hadn't smoked in six months. This had seemed like the perfect time to start again.

He had given his statement to the officer who had brought him in, and now, presumably, statements were being taken from the parents in another room. There was nothing for Wes to do but wait.

There were three desks in the spacious room, at which two policewomen and one male detective were working; other officers wandered in and out, chatting about anything and everything except business. One of them even offered Wes a cup of coffee, which he drank despite the fact that it would probably leave a foul taste in his mouth for days. At the table next to him Santa Claus was being interrogated, and Wes amused himself for a time by eavesdropping on that conversation. Now that the worst was over, his natural good humor was beginning to find its balance again and there was nothing to do but relax.

He thought about calling his attorney, but the vision of the good Mr. Wilkins interrupting his dinner hour to hear the news that Adrian Wesley was being held at a local station house for child molesting almost caused Wes to choke on his coffee. The poor man would probably have a stroke before he even hung up the phone. As for actually coming down to a police station to get a client out of jail... The very thought made Wes shudder. It simply was not done, not by the firm of Wilkins, Wilcox and Wilkins. Wes wondered briefly which of the state's very fine criminal lawyers came most highly recommended these days, and hoped that, if the occasion arose, Mr. Wilkins would be able to restrain his horror long enough to refer him.

Chairs scraped as the two officers who were interviewing Santa Claus got up and left the room, presumably to have the complaint signed. Santa himself, after looking around aimlessly for a time, got up and ambled over to Wes. Wes wondered in amusement if he was going to try to make a break for it.

But, instead, Santa pulled up a chair and sat down beside him.

"How's it going, old-timer?" Wes greeted him easily, lighting another cigarette.

"Shameful, just shameful." Santa shook his head mournfully. "No one believes anymore. Now, I ask you, sonny—" he fixed Wes with his rheumy blue eyes "—what kind of justice is this? My elves can't do *everything*, you know. Why, the things children want for Christmas these days. Computers!" he exclaimed. "Have you ever heard of an elf who could make computers? Of course not!" He gave Wes a scornful look and a dismissing snap of his bony fingers. "So where am I to get them except at a computer store? And why should anyone complain? It's not for myself, you know, certainly not. It's all for the children."

Wes, feeling a bubble of laughter creeping to the surface, stared at the man. "You ripped off computers, too?"

Santa drew himself up with all the dignity inherent in his stature. "I did not 'rip off.' I merely collected. It's all for the same purpose, whether it comes from the North Pole or a Philadelphia retail store, don't you see? It all ends up under the right tree, eventually. It's simply a matter of middlemen, and I'm only doing my job. Why should anyone object to that?"

Wes could no longer restrain a grin, and he brought the cigarette to his lips to hide it. "Things are rough all over," he agreed.

The vagabond Santa beamed at him, the dirty beard rippling with the wrinkles that formed on his sallow face as he did so. "Now, *you're* a sensible boy. Have I got your name on my list?" He began to pat his pockets searchingly. "My list...my list. I'm sure it's here somewhere...." His brow crinkled with concern. "Now what could I have done with..."

"Okay, Kris," the arresting officer had returned, this time with the pretty blond woman from the store who had made the complaint. Wes wondered briefly what had become of his own eyewitness, or if she ever intended to show up at all. And if she didn't, what would happen to him? The officer tapped Santa on the shoulder and jerked his head toward the other table. "Let's finish up the paperwork and find you a room for the night."

"I'm sure your name is on my list," Santa assured Wes as he got to his feet. He was still patting his pockets absently. "As soon as I find it..." And he wandered off with the officer and the blonde, still muttering and searching.

Wes considered calling Mitch, but that idea was even more repellent than the thought of calling his lawyer. It actually made his stomach turn, imagining the look of supercilious disappointment in Mitch's eyes as he came down to the police station to drive Alex Wesley's only son home. Not only would Mitch never let him live it down, but the genuine shock that he knew Mitch—the man who had guided his every step from kindergarten through college—would experience was just too much for Wes to think about. No, he couldn't involve Mitch. He didn't dare call his lawyer. This was one thing he would have to handle on his own.

Wes had never handled anything in his life entirely on his own. It was more than a little scary.

The officer who had questioned Wes had been gone a long time. Wes hoped that was a good sign. Maybe they were beginning to unravel this whole thing. Maybe the kid had finally told the truth. Maybe the young woman from the store had shown up after all and had gotten someone to listen to her. Wes moved restlessly in his chair, trying not to think about what would happen if that woman didn't show up, if the kid stuck to her story, if the parents were as crazy as they had seemed. He lit another cigarette and tried to figure out how this could possibly have happened to him, Adrian Alexander Wesley III. Surely they must have figured by now how insane it was to try to hold him. If they let him go home within the next five minutes, Wes decided generously, and with quite a bit of bravado, he wouldn't sue. But if he missed dinner over this thing...

He glanced toward the open door just then, and the sweep of relief that went through him was overwhelming. It was the woman from the shop. She had come, after all, and everything was going to be all right.

UNTIL FIVE MINUTES AGO, Sandy herself hadn't been at all convinced everything was going to be all right. She had given her statement; she had talked to the parents; she had talked to Kerry. The parents were adamant. It had become more a matter of pride to them, Sandy suspected, than any real interest in seeing justice served, and it was hard to keep her temper with them. Of course, Sandy realized that the matter was not really her responsibility, and it really should be left to the police to straighten out the tangle, but she could not help remembering the panic in the young man's eyes just before he had been escorted out of the store. And she *had* been the one to bring Kerry over to him. She just couldn't allow such an ugly thing to get on a perfectly innocent man's record, but try as she would, she could not persuade Kerry's parents to the same conviction.

It was Rick who finally saved the day. He came into the visitors' waiting room, chuckling, and said, "I might have known if I looked hard enough I would find you at the bottom of this. I just saw Linda, and she was raving like a lunatic about some Santa who's wandered from the straight and narrow, then I look through the window and who should be sitting here but you? What're you guys trying to do, bring the whole Garret clan down on my head?"

"This is not a laughing matter, Rick," Sandy told him tersely, then, in a few quick phrases, explained the situation to him. After he recovered from his hilarity over the part Santa Claus had played in the fiasco, Rick agreed that the potential consequences of Sandy's problem were not amusing at all, and he promised to do what he could. Though a patrolman by assignment, Rick was well recognized in the department for his talents as a diplomat, and he had been called upon to negotiate trickier situations than this. Not ten minutes had passed before he returned with a "not guilty" verdict.

"They didn't exactly apologize," he told Sandy, shrugging off her effusive thanks, "but they agreed it might be a mistake to press charges." And he grinned. "It might have been the mention of the phrase 'slander suit' that did it. This Wesley character could build a pretty good case if he wanted to, you know."

Sandy shuddered. "I hope he doesn't think of it. I'll probably be named codefendant."

"Ah, come on, kid, it wasn't your fault." Rick flung a companionable arm around her shoulder. "And you did try to help the guy out, didn't you? He can hardly be mad at you."

Sandy looked up at him. "Could I see him now? Maybe tell him the good news?" she inquired hopefully. Part of her was thinking that it couldn't hurt to let him know what part she had played in his release, just in case he did decide to sue, another part simply wanted to see him again.

"Sure," Rick agreed, and the twinkle in his eye let her know that he suspected that her interest in the young man was far more than that of an ordinary citizen doing her duty. That was the curse of having three older brothers—no secrets.

She saw Wes lounging at the table, smoking a cigarette, looking as though he didn't have a care in the world, and she felt an immediate and totally irrational resentment that all her worry on his behalf had apparently been for nothing. In this environment he looked even more confident and self-contained than he had in the store, and she wondered how she had ever allowed herself to feel so sorry for him. What had happened had been an unfortunate thing, granted, but what could a man with a Harvard accent and a cashmere coat possibly need with her help?

His casual greeting and the lazy way he got to his feet when they approached only reinforced Sandy's feeling of awkwardness. How had she imagined he would be glad to see her? He probably had a high-priced lawyer on his way down at this very minute, and all her effort had been for nothing.

"Mr. Wesley," Rick said, greeting him with a friendly handclasp. "I'm sorry for all the trouble, but you're free to go now. We've got everything straightened out, and there are going to be no charges."

"Good." Wes stubbed out the cigarette with a nonchalance he was far from feeling, and he did not glance up. His heart had doubled its rhythm the moment he looked up and saw salvation in the form of a pixie in a Santa's hat standing at the door, and he suddenly became aware that he was perspiring heavily beneath his coat. "There'll be no record of this, I presume."

"No, of course not. Again, we apologize for the inconvenience."

Wes barely restrained the huge sigh of relief that swept through him. Instead he smiled pleasantly and rather absently, the way he had trained himself to do when he wanted to disassociate himself from an unpleasant situation. He was not aware that the smile came off as condescending. "No matter. I had an evening to waste anyway, and I can't think of a better way to do it. Is that all?"

"That's it." Rick gave Sandy's shoulders a squeeze. "Got to get back to work, babe. Try to stay out of trouble from now on, huh?"

Sandy grimaced at him and thanked him for his help, and then she was left alone with the man Rick had referred to as Mr. Wesley.

Wes had followed the interchange between brother and sister with more than a flicker of interest, and now he commented casually, "Must be helpful to have a boyfriend in the police department."

"Brother," corrected Sandy automatically, and because she seemed to be having a hard time finding something intelligent to say to him, she let her eyes stray to the next table, where another member of her family was apparently doing her best to persecute Santa Claus.

Wes was not entirely conscious of the relief he felt upon learning the nature of her relationship with the policeman, but it drew a smile to his lips that was relaxed and natural. He wondered if she had any idea how ridiculous she looked, standing there in her quilted coat and boots and Santa hat, or how terribly, terribly glad he was to see her. "Do I thank you or your brother for my timely rescue?" he inquired politely. "Or perhaps it was our justice system at work. Did the child finally break under the bright lights and rubber hoses?"

Sandy didn't know whether to smile or frown at the unexpected impertinence. What an unusual man he was! He looked so perfectly at ease standing there, his long body sculpted gracefully in cashmere and virgin wool, all golden hair and blue eyes, elegance and refinement. Perfectly contained, perfectly in control, perfectly aloof—everything Sandy wasn't.

She said, somewhat awkwardly, "Listen, I'm really sorry..."

He lifted one elegant shoulder in smooth dismissal. "Someday we'll all laugh about this." And then, dubiously, "I'm sure."

For a moment longer Sandy stood there, not knowing what to say. It was one thing to conduct a casual conversation in her sister's shop with a man she thought was the father of a customer, one thing to come to the rescue of a distraught young man in trouble, but this—this was entirely different. She couldn't remember why she had even wanted to be taken back to him. She thought with absolute irrelevance that his hairstyle alone probably cost more than she made in a week.

"Well," she said brightly, "you seem to be taking this all very well. Glad to see there are no permanent scars."

"Are you kidding?" He laughed rather weakly, then ran a long-boned hand through his gold- and silver-toned hair, ruffling it beautifully. "I'll probably have nightmares for years. I'm still shaking. Believe me, lady," he assured her with a rueful downward twist of his lips, "this is not my idea of a fun night on the town."

Then Sandy really didn't know what to say. It was impossible to believe that this perfect specimen of Madison Avenue manhood, with his aristocratic drawl and his dry humor, could ever be unsettled by anything. It was impossible to believe now, but an hour ago, when they had taken him out of the store, the story had been quite different. He had been frightened then, and very vulnerable, his self-assurance and charm completely absent. Suddenly Sandy didn't feel quite so awkward around him anymore, and she thought she really might like to get to know him better.

Sandy might have found a way to continue the conversation, but she wasn't given a chance. At that moment they were both distracted by the indignant assertions of Santa Claus at the next table. "This is unconscionable! I will *not* be thrown in jail like a common criminal! You can't arrest me; that's absurd!"

"But that's exactly what you are, Mr. Kringle," said the officer patiently, tugging at his arm. "A common criminal. Now just come along quietly."

A small struggle ensued in which Santa grabbed hold of the table with both hands, planted his booted feet firmly and refused to budge. When the officer grabbed Santa by the waist and tried to pry him loose, someone called out, "Be careful there! Those old bones are like tissue paper. We don't want a brutality suit!'' A second officer came to assist, grabbing Santa's feet. The two of them lifted him like a doll and prepared to carry him to his cell.

"Your tax dollars at work,'' murmured Wes.

"Oh, for goodness' sake!'' exclaimed Sandy in exasperation. "Wait just a minute,'' she called to the officers, who were more than glad to pause in their rather breathless struggle to keep the obstreperous Santa Claus airborne. "Put him down!'' She strode over to Linda. "What are you trying to do? Are you serious? Are you really going to put that poor old man in jail?''

"Sandy! What on earth are you doing here?'' Linda demanded. "Who's watching the shop?''

"Never mind that now,'' Sandy said impatiently. She had had about all she could handle for one day; watching her own sister send a helpless old wino off to jail was more than she could take. "Are you crazy? You're not really pressing charges against that old man, are you?''

Linda drew herself righteously up. "I most certainly am! He stole—''

"A cheese tray and a box of handkerchiefs—''

"One hundred and two dollars' worth of merchandise!''

"At your inflated prices! Thirty dollars' worth of merchandise in real value, if that much!''

The two officers, sensing the development of a lengthy discussion, set Santa on his feet, where he began to brush off his costume with all proper disdain for his crude handling.

A faint color stained Linda's cheeks. "What do you want me to do? We can't just let criminals roam the streets!''

Sandy released an angry hiss. "If I hear that one more time tonight! I've just spent almost an hour trying to convince a pair of outraged parents not to send an innocent man to jail and that was the only argument they had against him, too. I've had it up to here with concerned citizens. For crying out loud, Linda,'' she insisted, casting a glance in the direction of the hapless Saint Nick and lowering her voice a fraction, "the poor old guy's got to be pushing ninety and nutty as a fruitcake. It's not like he's a mass murderer or anything. What are you trying to do to him?"

Linda did not like to think of herself as a person who lacked compassion. She did not, in fact, like anyone to think anything of her that was less than flattering, ever. Sandy could see her resolve begin to waver. "What difference does it make to you?" she demanded, a little sullenly.

Sandy sighed. Good question. She had had enough trouble tonight without borrowing it from her sister. "None," she said, losing patience. "None except that I'm tired and I want to go home. And," she added on an inspiration, "I'm not looking forward to the publicity when this gets out. 'Local Shopkeeper Prosecutes Santa Claus for Shoplifting.' The press will be down on the shop like locusts, as if we didn't have enough to do this time of year."

That persuaded her. Linda looked uncertainly toward the arresting officer. "It's up to you, miss," he said. "But I've got to tell you, we get pretty crowded up here this time of year, and the chances are, since this guy has no previous record and you've recovered your merchandise, the judge will let him off with a reprimand. Of course, if you go ahead with the complaint, you'll have to go to court…"

"Oh, all right." Impatience with herself and Sandy and the entire situation was bitter in Linda's voice. "I've got a business to run, I don't have time for this nonsense. Let him go, but if I ever see him in my shop again…"

"I wouldn't dream of visiting your establishment again, young lady," asserted Santa with dignity. "I assure you, from now on, I will do my shopping elsewhere."

Linda glared at him, long and hard, and then turned and strode from the room, head held high. Sandy barely restrained a giggle.

"Well, well," said Wes at her elbow. "Two good deeds in one night. I'm impressed."

Sandy shrugged and grimaced slightly. "The Christmas spirit."

Santa paused before her on his way out and gave her an old-fashioned bow. "My humble thanks, my dear. It would have been most inconvenient to be incarcerated at this time of year, you know. I still have to find my reindeer."

Sandy grinned at him. He was a pathetic old character, with his rumpled suit and stained teeth and dirty beard, and she hoped she had done the right thing by talking Linda out of pressing charges. She wondered if he even had a place to sleep tonight. "Anytime, Santa," she said.

"Don't forget to hang your stocking now," he said as he turned to go, then winked. "There'll be something special in it for you this year."

He wandered off, inquiring at each desk he passed as to the whereabouts of his reindeer, and Wes and Sandy stood there together for a moment, watching him and grinning. Then, when Santa finally made it through the door and everyone returned to work, Sandy glanced at Wes, hesitating for a moment before saying good-night. The bizarre evening was over and she was glad of it, but she wasn't particularly anxious to part company with this beautiful young stranger who had played such an important part in it.

But he forestalled whatever awkward attempt she might have made at saying good-night by inquiring, "Was that your boss, or is it the other way around?"

"Linda? She's my sister. And my boss," she amended with a grin. "Although sometimes I think even she's not too sure of that."

Wes lifted a cryptic eyebrow. "You have a—er—interesting family. They do seem to be everywhere, don't they?" And then, reflectively, he added, "She's a beautiful woman."

Of course. She should have known. Sandy was ashamed of the small stab of disappointment she felt—or was it jealousy for her long-legged, blond-haired sister?—and she said, shortly, "She's also married." She hitched her purse more securely over her shoulder, painted a deliberately pleasant smile on her face and said, "Well, I'm glad everything worked out for you, Mr....Wesley." She remembered the name. "And again, I'm sorry for the trouble. Good night."

She started toward the door, suddenly very, very tired. It wasn't every day, after all, that she lost her career, had an innocent man accused of child molestation and rescued Santa Claus from a life of crime. She still had to deal with telling her family about the doctor's decision on her skiing career, but the very thought almost pushed her fatigue over the border. And as for the young Adonis in cashmere...well, he wasn't her type anyway. And given a choice between herself and Linda, any reasonably normal man would, of course, be attracted to Linda. Not that it mattered. Given the consequences of his last visit to the shop, neither she nor Linda was very likely to see that particular young man again.

Sandy was halfway to the door when she heard running footsteps behind her. "Wait!"

She turned, surprised, as Wes drew up beside her. "Are you going back to the mall?" he asked.

The mall. What a depressing thought. But it was not quite seven, and Collectibles was open until nine. She still had a job to do. "I guess so," Sandy admitted reluctantly.

"Do you think..." He looked momentarily embarrassed. "That is, I don't exactly have my car with me. Would you give me ride back?"

There was absolutely no cause for the almost imperceptible lift of Sandy's spirits that simple request caused. It was only logical, after all. Whom else was he going to ask? But

Sandy didn't feel nearly as tired as she had before, and she answered casually, "Sure. No problem." She would, in fact, be glad of the company. More than glad.

One final incident crowned Wes's memorable first visit to a police station. As they were exiting, an officer was entering with a teenage prisoner who was not taking his arrest very well. Obviously intoxicated, he was struggling and swearing loudly, and refusing to relinquish his hold on a half-full bottle of Jack Daniels. Just as Sandy and Wes came abreast of them, the teenager broke the officer's hold long enough to draw back his arm and throw the bottle. It grazed Wes's ear, missing his shoulder by inches, and crashed against the wall behind him, spraying glass and bourbon all over the side of his coat.

Wes and Sandy sprang back, shocked and staring; someone shouted, "Are you all right?" The arresting officer got his charge under control, and in a moment Wes, beginning to brush futilely at his stained coat, recovered enough to assure them that he was all right. The desk sergeant said philosophically, "Well, there goes the evidence."

But the arresting officer assured him cheerfully, "Nope. Most of it's still in the suspect." Then he pushed the boy against the desk, with a firm hold on him this time.

Sandy didn't know whether to laugh or cry. She looked at Wes sympathetically, not knowing what comfort she could offer, but feeling somehow as though she should apologize. "I guess this just isn't your day," she ventured, after a moment.

Wes succeeded in picking the last piece of glass off the fine weave of his coat, then decided that the stains—and the odor—were irreparable, at least for the time being. The corners of his lips turned down dryly, and he shrugged. "'Tis the season to be jolly," he murmured, and pushed open the door for her.

Sandy tried not to grin.

It was fully dark when they stepped outside, and the rain was coming down in a light but steady sheet. The temperature was that raw-boned cold that kept the precipitation hovering just on the border between sleet, snow and rain, refusing to budge even the half a degree that would turn it into something more solid. They paused beneath the shelter of the eaves, Wes pulling on his gloves, Sandy searching for her car keys, both of them taking in the state of the weather with disappointment and reluctance.

"If only it would snow," they both said out loud, and then looked at each other startled. Wes smiled at her and Sandy smiled back, and in that very strange moment standing on the steps of the police station in the midst of one of the most miserable nights of the year, Sandy felt his smile go through her and meet something within her; she felt warmed. She didn't understand it, she couldn't analyze it and afterward she would not adequately be able to describe the sensation even to herself, but in that very fleeting moment she felt as though she had found a friend. And she was very, very glad she had met him.

But it was all too strange; she couldn't maintain the eye contact. She found her keys and turning up the collar of her coat, rushed out into the rain, with Wes following.

Rick's VW had a yellow-and-black-striped bumblebee on the back and a bumper sticker that said, "The Mercedes is in the shop." About three months ago Rick had decided a bug with a bumblebee painted on the back did not precisely fit the image of the macho cop he was trying to project, so he had invested his anticipated cost-of-living raise in a six-year-old Camaro with red racing stripes. Since the net worth of the VW was something under three hundred dollars, he had taken no great loss by turning it over to Sandy to use as long as she liked. Sandy, who had never considered automobiles as status symbols, had never understood why Rick would want to give away a perfectly good—if somewhat shabby—car in favor of a racier model. Until now. There was something a little bit embarrassing about inviting this elegantly clad man to sit in such a ramshackle little vehicle.

"Be careful," she warned as she unlocked the passenger door. "Rick left some tools on the seat this weekend when he was working on the car. Just move those books on the floor to the back seat.... The window leaks a little on that side, too, so don't sit too close to the door."

Wes stood there, looking at the car and the funny little pixie in the Santa hat, and he began to chuckle, shaking his head a little in disbelief. "I was just thinking," he explained at Sandy's questioning—and somewhat challenging—look, "about all the times I've complained of being bored." Then he bent and obediently began to remove the books and the tools to the back seat, where they joined a basket of laundry and a pair of old shoes. "I'll never do so again," he assured himself gravely.

Sandy hurried around to her own side of the car and out of the rain.

Wes thought of removing his bourbon-scented coat, but changed his mind when Sandy informed him the heater didn't work. "Just don't go through any red lights," he advised her. "I smell like a distillery, and if we get pulled over we'll both probably end up back at the police station."

Sandy chuckled as she backed out of the parking space. "Something tells me you don't usually spend your Friday nights like this."

Wes hooked his arm over the back of the seat and half turned toward her, trying to arrange his long legs more comfortably in the small space. She was an attractive young woman, he realized now that he had a chance to really look at her. Or perhaps not really attractive, but cute. She had a pretty face, round and snowy white, and the most striking, huge brown eyes he had ever seen. And a funny, quirky kind of grin that made him want to tease her, just so she would grin or laugh some more. She was totally unlike any woman he had ever known before, and he liked that.

"As a general rule," he answered her frankly, "no." Then he said, "I don't think I thanked you for coming down. I guess I pretty much spoiled your day...not to mention my own," he added as an afterthought.

Sandy shrugged. As far as she was concerned, her day couldn't have gotten much worse, and all in all, meeting him was the only bright spot in the whole of it. Besides, to be strictly accurate, it was she who had gotten him into trouble, not the other way around, but she decided it might not be wise to remind him of that if he had chosen to forget it. "It broke up the routine," she said.

Wes smiled dryly to himself. That it had done. He had left the house this afternoon looking for a diversion, but never in his wildest imagination had he envisioned anything like this. He would certainly be more careful what he wished for from now on.

After a moment of silence, in which Sandy carefully negotiated the wet streets and Wes had a chance to reflect once again upon what a truly close escape he had had, he reached nervously into his pocket and drew out his last cigarette. He started to light it, then hesitated. "Do you mind?"

Sandy glanced at him. Even wet, bourbon-stained and seen in the unflattering light of street lamps, he was gorgeous. "Sure, go ahead." Then, to make conversation, she ventured, "Are you from Philadelphia?"

The pungent scent of smoke mixed with bourbon was distinctively masculine. It filled the car and made Sandy feel suddenly as though she were in an alien environment, rather than comfortably behind the wheel of her own brother's familiarly ancient car. It made her a little nervous.

"I was born here, yes," answered Wes, still resting his arm casually on the back of the seat and looking at her. That made him seem very close. "I don't spend too much time here anymore."

Sandy nodded, and conversation faltered. That was when she realized why she suddenly felt uncomfortable. Sandy's experience with men was limited to brothers, coaches and other athletes. She didn't know how to flirt. She didn't know how make idle conversation. Those were all arts other girls learned at their mother's knee, but Sandy's life had been occupied with learning other things.

Your entire life, she realized slowly. *What a waste it's been.* How much time she had lost, and how much she had missed. She had never been dancing. She had never parked beneath the stars with a high-school sweetheart, wrestling with her conscience and her boyfriend's advances. She had never been to an all-night party or ever, in her whole life, had a real relationship with a man. And here she was, twenty-four years old, sitting in a car with the most perfectly gorgeous man God had ever created, and she didn't know what to do with him. She didn't even know what to say.

She glanced at her passenger, but he did not seem to mind the silence. He seemed, in fact, greatly preoccupied with thoughts of his own, which Sandy found neither surprising nor offensive. If nothing else, his brief presence in her life—or in her car, to be more accurate—had served as a graphic reminder of all she was missing, and for that she was grateful. It was the first step in beginning to reorganize her life.

The years she had lost in training and single-minded dedication were gone, and there was no way to reclaim them. But now she had a whole new life ahead of her, and nothing but time. She could do the things she had never had the energy or the attention to spare for before. The fun things, the aimless things, the exploratory things—the things every person should have a chance to discover along the road of growing up, but which she had denied herself. It was a wonderful thought, an exciting prospect, filled with possibilities. Freedom. Suddenly even the dismal rainy night looked better.

Wes realized when they were almost at the entrance of the mall that he had not been very entertaining company, and by that time it was too late to rectify the matter. Actually, he had been thinking about the bizarre twists of fate that had led him to the point of accepting a ride in a battered VW from a woman in a Santa Claus hat to a shopping mall, of all places. Wes had by no means led a dull life, but this night topped all recent adventures by half. He almost smiled when he thought how much his father would have enjoyed this story, and how much Wes would have enjoyed telling it to him. Then he wondered what the young lady—whose name he had yet to learn, he realized—would say if he asked her to dinner.

But he had pressed his luck far enough for one evening. The smartest thing he could do would be to get in his car and go home—slowly and carefully—where it was safe. And stay there.

"Where are you parked?"

"Hmm?" The sound of her voice jerked Wes out of his reflections. "Oh...over there. Near the pink Christmas tree." Not finding an ashtray, Wes rolled down his window to toss out the cigarette, releasing a flood of water onto his shoulder. Incredulity filled his eyes as he stared at the cold stream of water dripping down his shoulder and off his hand. This couldn't be happening. Everything always went his way.

Each aisle was marked with a different color tree, and Sandy found a parking place in the pink aisle without too much difficulty. Traffic had cleared up considerably for the dinner hour. "Okay, here we are." Sandy applied the parking brake and tossed her keys into her purse. They opened their doors at the same time.

"Thanks for the ride," Wes said, standing beside her car and trying not to shiver in his wet coat.

Sandy smiled at him, not too wistfully, she hoped. *Ships that pass in the night....* "Anytime," she said. There were probably plenty of men like him around, she assured herself, and now there was nothing keeping her from discovering them. This one really wasn't her type anyway. He was too well-dressed.

Wes stood there for a moment longer. The rain was really quite uncomfortable. "Are you going back to work?"

Sandy glanced toward the brightly decorated mall. Strings of lights, blinking Christmas trees, inviting storefronts, crowds of people... Hadn't she been responsible enough for one night? For one lifetime?

"No," she decided suddenly, her eyes coming to rest on the attractive script of a sign that announced "Turtles" in a prominent spot toward the front of the mall. "No, actually, I think I'm going to go get drunk." And, filled with the import of this decision, she gave him a cheery wave and rushed toward the shelter of the mall.

Wes watched her go, hands thrust into his pockets, shoulders hunched against the rain, eyes narrowed with debate. Then he tilted his head philosophically, dismissed his better judgment and shrugged off his misgivings. "Sounds good to me," he murmured, and followed her.

Chapter Four

Turtles was one of those trendy restaurant-bars that catered mostly to the after-work crowd and the occasional weary shopper. It served such items as quiche, nachos and steak sandwiches, along with a full array of specialty drinks. The atmosphere was dim and lush, with many potted plants and vinyl banquettes, a lot of conversation and upbeat popular music in the background.

Sandy had never been to a bar by herself before—she had not, in fact, ever been to a bar at all for the sole purpose of drinking—and the experience was both exciting and intimidating. The place was crowded at this hour, but she managed to get a small banquette at the back of the room, accepted the exotic drink menu with a smile and settled down to study the selections.

She didn't think about how furious Linda was going to be when she didn't return to work. She didn't think about the chaotic events of the past few hours, or the unpleasant task that still awaited her—breaking the news to her loyal family about her aborted career. In fact, the only thing she was thinking about was whether a Yellowbird Fizz was more potent than a Singapore Sling when a masculine voice said above her, "Drinking alone is a very bad habit."

A little thrill went through her even before she looked up, a warmth began in the tips of her chilled toes and spread upward. Lazy blue eyes smiled at her, and Wes said, "Do you mind if I join you?"

Sandy couldn't imagine why he would want to, but she had no intention of telling him to go away. But neither did she intend to let him know the extent of her surprise, or her pleasure, so she simply returned his smile politely, said, "Of course not," and turned back to her menu.

Wes was not accustomed to analyzing anything he did, and he was not about to begin now. He hung his coat beside Sandy's on the hook at the end of the booth. He had no idea why he had chosen to spend the evening in a shopping mall lounge with a funny girl in a Santa's hat, when he could have been at home being served lobster and chilled wine before his own fireplace. It was not that he wanted the company of a woman—if he had, it would never have occurred to him to seek out someone like her. Sexual companionship, or the lack of the same, was the farthest thing from his mind at this point of his life. Perhaps it was that he simply wanted companionship.

As he slid into the booth opposite her, Wes was quite certain he had made the right decision. He was not ready to go back to that house yet.

"What do you think?" Sandy said suddenly. "Yellowbird Fizz or Singapore Sling?"

Wes lifted an eyebrow that did not adequately disguise his distaste. "It depends," he said carefully, and took the menu she offered.

"Which is stronger? I don't know a lot about mixed drinks," she explained, which was an understatement. Except for the occasional glass of wine during the holidays, Sandy had been unwaveringly temperate her entire life. Anything else would have interfered with her training regimen.

Wes glanced briefly over the menu, which thoughtfully listed the ingredients of some of the more exotic drinks. "If it's strong you want," he decided, "the Purple Passion's your best bet."

"Sounds good to me," she agreed, satisfied, as the waitress paused beside their booth.

Wes was hungry, but a brief perusal of the menu assured him there were no offerings to his taste. He ordered a Cognac for himself, which would be hard to spoil even in a place like this, and a Purple Passion for the lady.

"We haven't been formally introduced," Sandy said in sudden realization when they were alone again. Now that they were in more or less neutral territory, she found that she was feeling much less awkward with him than she had before. Besides, *he* had followed *her*. That had to be a good sign. "I'm Sandy Garret."

Wes reached across the table to accept the hand she offered, amused by her sudden recollection of manners. She was like a child away from home for the first time, trying to remember all her mother's lectures on proper behavior. Hadn't her mother ever told her not to drink with strange men, he wondered.

"Adrian Wesley," he returned politely. "Wes." Her hand was small, still a little chilled, but very soft. He held it for perhaps a moment longer than he should have.

"Wesley," Sandy repeated. She liked the way his hand felt around hers. She had always thought one could tell a lot about a man from his handshake. Wes's hand was lean and surprisingly warm, strong despite its appearance of delicacy. And he did not clasp her hand in a traditional handshake, grasping from the palm; rather, he held her fingers, gently but firmly, in what struck Sandy as a courtly gesture full of old-world charm. She was sorry when the moment of contact was over. "Any relation to the mall?" she asked, simply for something to say.

Wes leaned back against the seat, linking his fingers together upon the tabletop. "I think I own it," he said casually.

Sandy tried not to look as impressed as she was. Of course. The preppy haircut, the imported coat, the stylish grace—everything about him exuded wealth with a capital *W*. But she did no more than tilt her head at him inquiringly and repeat, "You *think*?"

"My father had something to do with developing the mall," Wes admitted. "But I think he sold off his part of it some time ago. Dad never was one for staying involved in a project for very long."

"Ah," Sandy said, examining him now with new interest. "*That* Wesley."

Wes laughed, a little uncomfortably. "Is that bad? You're looking at me as though you've just discovered a new breed of animal, possibly one with two heads and three wings."

Sandy shrugged, not wishing to appear rude. "I just never met one of the idle rich before. I couldn't help wondering what it was like."

"Not so different from anything else, I suppose," replied Wes, having no idea whether that was true or not. He had never known anything else but being a Wesley.

"I suppose you have private jets and houses all over the world and friends with names like Biff and Muffy and Reggie," speculated Sandy.

Wes laughed again, startled and for some strange reason embarrassed. It was more than a little unsettling to be sitting in a booth in this very bourgeois place and listening to a young woman with incredibly studious brown eyes sum up his life—up to and including the names of his friends—in a handful of short words. "What makes you say that?"

"Your polished nails," she explained simply, and Wes glanced involuntarily at his fingernails, which were professionally manicured with one coat of clear polish and buffed to a high gloss. He could see nothing wrong with having a thing done right, and he dismissed the subject with a philosophic shrug.

"All right," he said easily. "Let me guess the story of your life. You have one house, no jets, and a busy little workshop filled with assistants where you spend all your time from September till December making quaint toys for expectant children."

Now it was Sandy's turn to be startled. "What makes you say that?"

Wes reached gracefully across the table and plucked off her Santa's cap. "This," he said, eyes twinkling.

Sandy laughed, and the laughter, and his brief nearness, tingled in her cheeks as she retrieved the hat from him. "I'd forgotten about it. I must have looked pretty stupid all this time."

"Adorable," Wes assured her, and though she knew it was nothing more than a practiced platitude, he said it so well that for a moment Sandy actually believed him.

Busily, she stuffed the cap into her purse. "That was kind of funny," she told him, "because that's really pretty close to my life—or at least my family's life. My dad makes Christmas toys," she explained, looking up at him again. "You saw them in the shop—the handmade wooden ones. And every year from September till December the only way members of the family get out of Christmas duty is if they have a communicable disease—or are lucky enough to be out of the country."

Wes thought that was charming, like something out of a work by Norman Rockwell, but from the tone of her voice Sandy did not agree. "What's wrong with that?" he inquired, genuinely puzzled.

Sandy gave him a look that generously forgave his ignorance. "After twenty-four years it gets pretty boring. I've got to tell you," she admitted frankly, "Christmas is not my favorite time of year. And this one—" she rolled her eyes slightly, recalling the events of the afternoon "—is getting off to a hell of a start."

Wes had never thought about Christmas, in terms of liking or disliking it, much at all. It was simply something that came, like April fifteenth, every year without fail. This one, however, he realized with the slow stirring of almost-forgotten pain, he would remember for a long, long time.

The drinks arrived then, before Sandy could notice the sudden sobriety that had come into his eyes, before the hollow depression could take full hold of him again. Wes quickly lifted his brandy snifter and smiled. *"Salud."*

Sandy looked dubiously at the foamy purple concoction that had been set in front of her before touching her glass to his. "Right."

She sipped cautiously from the straw, then grimaced her disappointment. "It tastes like grape Kool-Aid."

"It's not, I assure you." Wes watched her with mild amusement as she took another sip. "I'd take it a bit more slowly if I were you. Something tells me you're not exactly used to alcohol in large doses."

"No," admitted Sandy, and she lowered her eyes briefly to her glass, stirring the mixture with the straw. "I'm not used to anything in large doses—except work," she added with a totally unpreventable trace of bitterness in her tone.

"Making Christmas toys?"

Sandy laughed and took another sip of her drink. It wasn't all that bad, if one liked grape Kool-Aid. "No, skiing. And training. If you don't think that's work, you should try it sometime."

Wes grinned. "I'm afraid I wouldn't have the faintest idea what work is and is not," he admitted, totally without shame. "That's right—the police fellow mentioned something about your being a skier. Professional?"

She shook her head. "Not even amateur anymore." She was beginning to feel quite warm, relaxed and even a little tingly—and after only three sips. Perhaps that bartender did know his business after all. "I was a downhill skier, training for the Olympics. It's all I ever did, from the time I could walk...train for the Olympics."

"And?" he prompted, when she seemed to lose interest in the conversation and turned back to her drink.

"I made the team," she answered, as though it were of no consequence at all.

"I'm impressed," Wes said, and he was. He could not imagine the kind of discipline it took to achieve a goal like that. He could not imagine applying oneself for years to any one task. He had never known anyone who was capable of it.

Sandy smiled. "Don't be. I wasn't very good. But..." And her smile turned reflective. "It was something, being there. Getting that far."

"So what happened? Did you just get tired of the amateur circuit? Are you turning pro?"

Sandy could not help smiling at his naïveté. The very thought of anyone in her family just "getting tired" of anything was incredible. No, one had to have a better excuse for giving up than that where Sandy came from.

"An accident happened," she explained. "A freak thing. My boot release got jammed and I broke my leg in a couple of places and tore a few important ligaments." She shrugged when she saw Wes wince. "So after a year of therapy, we've finally come to the conclusion that a world class title is not in my future and—" she grinned, wonderfully and unexpectedly, and lifted her glass to him "—tonight, I'm celebrating my independence. What's it like to be rich?"

Wes almost choked on a sip of brandy and a gulp of laughter. Delicately, he touched his lips with the paper cocktail napkin, his eyes sparkling. What a unique, unpredictable and totally delightful woman she was. "First of all," he informed her, "it is not referred to as 'rich,' if it is mentioned at all. It's called being 'comfortably well-off.'"

"How vulgar of me," she agreed, and sipped liberally through the straw. Her eyes were very bright. "What's it like?"

He thought about it for a moment. "Nice. At least, I think so. I've never considered the matter much."

"You talk funny," she teased. "Like you're on a lectern all the time."

Wes's eyes danced. "They teach you to do that in prep school. It's a required course, along with lacrosse and How to Manage Servants, 101."

"Do you have a butler?" she inquired with interest.

"No. I have a cross between a male nurse and a street thug, whose schizophrenic tendencies include a very correct British accent—he was born in Kansas, by the way—and a fondness for patched blue jeans and moth-eaten sweatshirts—not to mention a habit of lapsing into gutter language that would make a sailor blanch when he's in a temper. I do have an upstairs maid in the house in Nice, though," he added helpfully, then paused. "At least I think so. I haven't been there in a while."

"Nice," she repeated dreamily. "Must be nice." She giggled at the unplanned witticism, and she was gratified to see Wes grin. What a wonderful face he had, especially when he grinned. "You're *not* perfect!" she exclaimed, delighted.

His brows flew up with a laugh of surprise. "What?"

"You have a crooked tooth! Right there, on the side." She reached forward as though to show him, and her fingertip had almost brushed his lips before she withdrew her hand, quickly, and explained, "Not that I don't like it. I think it's wonderful." Nervously, she took another sip of her drink.

"I knew all those years of fighting against braces would pay off," Wes murmured, watching her with relaxed amusement. He was very glad he had decided to follow her. He hadn't felt this comfortable with anyone since…well, he had to admit truthfully he had never felt this comfortable with anyone except his father. It was a strange feeling, being with her and relaxing with her and doing nothing but enjoying the moment, especially considering the bizarre circumstances that had precipitated their meeting. Especially considering the fact that the last thing he had expected to be doing today was enjoying anything.

"Anyway," she decided after a moment, "you're very lucky. To be able to go anywhere and have everything and do anything."

"As long as it's discreet and doesn't embarrass the family," he corrected with a wink, lifting his glass to his lips. He wondered how much of her charm was natural and how much was generated by the Purple Passion. At that moment it didn't matter much, because he had an instinctual feeling that the things he found most delightful about her would be present with or without the aid of alcohol. He had sensed that about her from the first moment they met, in the store—warmth, and openness, and other things he couldn't quite define. Things that simply made him feel good.

"Not that I'd want it, though," she announced, returning to her drink. "To be rich, that is. Too much responsibility."

"Oh, no? And what would you prefer?" Wes was surprised to find that he would really like to know. He generally did not take such an interest in people.

Her eyes grew thoughtful. "I'm not really sure." Then she smiled. "But now I've got plenty of time to find out." And that was a wonderful feeling. She could not describe how wonderful it was.

Generally speaking, Sandy was not a reticent person. Shyness had never been one of her afflictions, and it was common practice for her to make friends of perfect strangers with no more than a few minutes' conversation. If the Purple Passion was making her a little more garrulous than usual, it was a side effect she barely noticed. What she did notice was that the initial awkwardness she had felt with Wes had completely disappeared under the marvelously warming effects of the intoxicant, and she felt as at ease sitting here with him as she would have with one of her brothers. She also noticed that her fingertips were growing numb.

"I've never been drunk before," she commented, glancing down at her half-empty glass. And then she smiled, pleased with herself. "I think I like it. I'll bet you get to do it a lot...just go out and get blind staggering drunk for no reason at all."

Wes lifted his eyebrows in feigned insult. "Certainly not! I'm much too well-bred for that. The mark of a gentleman is to be able to hold one's liquor well," he said, imitating Mitch's very proper pseudo-British accent, and his eyes sparkled with gentle self-mockery as he lifted the glass to his lips.

Sandy laughed. He wasn't at all like she had first imagined him to be—although she wasn't entirely sure *what*, exactly, she had thought he would be like—and she found herself liking him more and more. Of course, she was still sober enough to realize that most of it was just chemistry. He was incredibly good-looking, suave, sophisticated and completely unlike any man she had ever known before. And there was something about him—an innate charm, a low-level sexuality that he exuded, probably unconsciously, with every gesture, every smile, every change of expression.... Something in Sandy recognized it and responded to it just as unconsciously. She was attracted to him, and it was for precisely that reason that she had been uncomfortable around him at first. She wasn't used to allowing herself to respond to men on a primitive level. She simply hadn't had time before.

Wes stretched his arm above his head, reaching for his coat, and extracted from the pocket a pack of cigarettes that he had bought on the way in. Sandy watched him through a warm and pleasantly detached fog, the length of his arm, the way the white sweater clung to his chest, the strength of his neck against the pale blue, perfectly starched collar of his shirt. His fingers were lithe and dexterous as he opened the package, extracted a cigarette and brought it to his lips. His lighter looked like platinum and had his initials embossed upon it. Every move was a study in grace and fluidity, as though he had spent hours with a dancing master learning nothing more than how to move his hands and his arms and how to tilt his head, just so, to capture the light to his best advantage. *Chemistry,* Sandy thought again, and smiled.

"Do you ski?" she asked suddenly, embarrassed to be caught staring when Wes finished lighting the cigarette and happened to glance at her.

Of course Wes did. He dropped the lighter back into his pocket, leaned back and relaxed in the easy flow of conversation on common ground. Of the American slopes, she was by far the more well versed, as she had been competing on a national level since her teenage years. But it was fashionable among Wes's set to seek out the least populated spots in Europe for winter sports, and he was able to tell her about some places she had heard of but never tried, many places she had not even heard of. Sandy was impressed to find that he had skied some of the more difficult slopes of Switzerland and Austria, and she was even a little envious by his casual references to long periods of time spent at places she would have given her firstborn child even to visit. Sandy realized then for the first time that she would really miss it—the sport, not the competition. She had loved skiing. What would she do with her winters without the snow in her hair, the numbing rush of cold wind in her face, the oxygen-starved exhilaration of flying down a mountain with only earth and sky for companionship?

Other things, she decided firmly, and finished off her drink. Lots of other things.

The conversation drifted, as it naturally would with Wes, away from the slopes and toward the resorts, and Sandy couldn't prevent a smug little smile of self-congratulation. She had suspected from the first that he would be a person more interested in après-ski than ski, and she was delighted with the accuracy of her observation. Besides, it was wonderful to hear him speak of all those quaint little snow-covered villages, the luxurious American lodges with their Jacuzzis and heart-shaped tubs and indoor tennis. It was like taking a mini-vacation in the heart of rain-locked Philadelphia, and it was exactly what she needed.

The waitress stopped by and Sandy immediately ordered another Purple Passion. Wes, who was still nursing his brandy, declined, but tried not to look too disapproving as he suggested tactfully, "Perhaps you should eat something. You don't want to become ill...."

Sandy laughed, indulgently, and reminded him, "The idea was to get drunk, remember?"

Wes lifted his glass to her, his lips tightening at one corner with a tolerant smile of restrained mirth. "And you're succeeding quite admirably."

"I'll be careful with the next one," she promised. "Just let me know when I start to get sloppy." She folded her hands under her chin, fixing her attention on him raptly. "Go on. Tell me about some more fabulous places."

Wes laughed a little, but was glad to oblige. It was not a usual thing to find someone so easily entertained—most of his friends, like himself, got bored quickly. And Wes did love to entertain. He told her amusing anecdotes about various escapades in various parts of the world, delighting in her laughter. He liked the way her eyes followed the movements of his hands as he illustrated a point or lit another cigarette or simply sipped his brandy, and her quickness to smile was a reward in itself. He liked her open, easily expressive face, and the way she sometimes tugged thoughtfully at one of the bouncy pixie curls that tumbled over her forehead. It was fun, sitting there with her and just talking, and it seemed, at that point in Wes's life, as though he had not had fun in a long, long time.

He told her about the Andes, and some friends of his who had set off on an expedition to explore them while Wes, whose enthusiasm for high adventure ended when the sacrifice of creature comforts was called for, had passed the time waiting for them in an ancient little village in the foothills, trying to cozy up to a French mademoiselle who was utterly unimpressed. He told her about an archaeological dig he had joined in Egypt, at which he had lasted almost three days, and left out the part about the beautiful young leader of the team, whose many charms were not worth the heat and the bottled water and the substandard cuisine. He made a minor reference to Tibet, where he had once been delayed almost a week en route to Nepal, and she demanded to know what it was like.

Wes thought a moment. "Cold and dusty, with a lot of little men in potato sacks wandering around chanting mantras."

She laughed, and it was a sweet, throaty sound that warmed Wes beyond what the brandy could ever do. "Tibet," she said dreamily, leaning her cheek on her palm as she brought the straw to her lips again. "I'd be happy just to see Nebraska."

Wes laughed. "That would be a first for me, too," he admitted.

"Egypt, the Andes, the Orient…." She sighed. "What an exciting life you've had."

Wes gave that some consideration, too, and his conclusion resulted in a wry half-chuckle of disbelieving amusement. "I used to think so, too, until tonight. The events of the afternoon make the rest of my life seem shamefully dull by comparison." And then he grew thoughtful again. "Actually," he said, and the ease with which he made this admission to a perfect stranger—much less to himself—surprised him, "I was bored a lot of the time. It's a cliché, I know, but after a while there's nothing new to do, and you get tired of looking for things." He shrugged. "Some of my friends keep pushing for the more and more outrageous—drugs, death-defying stunts, even crime. Anything for excitement. I never saw the point in self-destruction, so I stay bored most of the time."

Sandy nodded, appearing to understand. "Is that why you're here in Philadelphia instead of in one of those glamorous wintertime resorts? Did you get bored?"

Wes lowered his eyes, but not before she saw the unmistakable curtain of pain that fell there. "My father's funeral was yesterday," he said simply.

In that moment, Sandy was as sober as she had ever been. It was very clear then, the desolation and the misery that had been lurking just below the surface of this beautiful bon vivant all evening, something she had sensed subconsciously but had not been able to define. He was real to her in that moment, just as real as he had been when the police had escorted him out of the shop and she had seen the terror in his eyes...and just as vulnerable. Without thinking about it at all, she reached across the table and rested her hand lightly atop his. "I'm so sorry," she said softly.

Wes's smile was distant, sad; he made no effort at all to disguise the bleakness he felt inside. "Yes, so am I."

He turned his hand over beneath hers, and lightly captured her small fingers in his. What a strange feeling that was. He could not remember a time when another hand had reached out to him in comfort and sympathy. Perhaps simply because he had never had an opportunity to need it before. But it felt good, very right.

"Do you know," he said slowly, and half to himself, "it's an odd feeling. Dad has just…always been there. And suddenly he's not. It's like…" He tried to put it into words and when he glanced at her the understanding he saw in her eyes made it much easier. "It's as if a thick black line has been drawn down the middle of my life, separating what was from what is and…" He frowned, trying to get it right, and unconsciously his fingers tightened on hers. "I'm suspended above it all, not knowing which way to go. Nothing is the same anymore. Nothing makes sense."

Then he looked at her, and he saw, just as clearly as he had ever seen anything, that she knew what he meant. She knew exactly what he meant, and she understood. The sensation that slowly filled him in that moment was like nothing he had ever known before—deeper than relief, quieter than wonder, more complete than contentment. It was simply sharing, and it felt wonderful.

Sandy felt it, too, and she saw it in his eyes, as he must have seen it in hers. They had more in common than a love of the slopes and a bad day. They had more in common than she could explain, in her present slightly muddled state of mind, even to herself. She only knew that she was glad she had met him, and that he had chosen this particular moment to come into her life. "Do you know something, Adrian Wesley?" she said softly. "I really like you."

He really liked her, too. He would have said so, but at that moment another customer came in, bringing with him a gust of cold and damp, and suddenly the moment seemed to be broken.

She withdrew her hand, sat back and took another sip of her drink. "Do you know what else?" she announced flatly.

"Philadelphia in the winter is a lousy place to be when you're feeling low."

Perhaps it was that simple. Looking at her, Wes was almost certain it was. This town, this awful rain, that huge empty house... This was the last place he needed to be right now. "You're right," he agreed with decision. "We both need a vacation. Let's run away together."

She gave a startled laugh, but her eyes widened with delight. "Okay," she agreed readily.

"Someplace where there's snow," responded Wes, beginning to appreciate the idea. He lit another cigarette. "Aspen, Amsterdam, Lucerne, Canada..."

"Sorry," said Sandy with a shrug, but her eyes were twinkling. "I have to work tomorrow."

"You can get the weekend off," he said persuasively; and it came as absolutely no surprise to him to realize that he was serious. A weekend in a peaceful snowy place was precisely the antidote to the dreariness of the city, the only cure for this horrible, unfamiliar depression. He couldn't be gone long—he had promised the lawyers—and he didn't really want to go far anyway. Nor did he want to go alone. "We can go to the Poconos. Hampton Glen is less than two hours' drive from here."

Hampton Glen was a very exclusive resort Sandy had heard of only vaguely. The slopes were not considered very good, the prices were extravagant, and the clientele was far more interested in playing than in skiing. Consequently, Sandy had never been there.

"I know," Wes countered her next objection, "mediocre slopes—but we're not going there to ski."

"What *are* we going for?" Sandy asked, then wished she hadn't.

But Wes was far too caught up in the prospect of getting away, even for a weekend, to take advantage of such an obvious opening. "To relax. To see the snow."

Sandy looked at him for a moment, and her fuzzy, wonderfully disoriented mind could not think of a single reason to disagree. She laughed suddenly. "I must be really drunk. I think you're serious."

"I am," he assured her.

She sank back against the leather seat dizzily, looking at him in a very pleased and unfocused way. Why not? An adventure of her own. A weekend of snow. A weekend of completely irresponsible, reckless, unpremeditated fun. She had nothing else to do with her life but start living it. And what a perfect way to start. "I think I'm going to say yes," she declared, and almost laughed out loud with the delight of it. She really could have, at that moment, said yes. And the very prospect was intoxicating. What a wonderful, wonderful thing freedom was.

"Perfect," said Wes, and satisfaction beamed in his eyes as he stubbed out the cigarette.

"Of course," she warned, lifting a slightly swaying finger at him, "you realize I'm very drunk and you can't really believe anything I say. I'll probably change my mind by morning."

"I won't let you," Wes assured her. "We're leaving first thing in the morning." He pulled out his wallet and laid some bills on the table. The decision, once made, felt like the lifting of an enormous burden, and Wes felt better than he had in weeks, perhaps in months. "And for that reason I think we'd better leave now, or you'll be too hung over to travel in the morning."

"I think I already am," said Sandy, then giggled as she realized that that made absolutely no sense.

Before she knew it, she was on her feet and being bundled into her coat and out the door. She really was drunk, she realized dimly, but she didn't mind. It felt fabulous— daring and naughty and totally irresponsible. The cold, foggy air outside should have sobered her, but in fact it had exactly the opposite effect. Or perhaps she simply hadn't realized the full effects of the potent drink while she was sitting down inside a relatively stable environment. Strangely enough, the unfamiliar sense of intoxication had not affected her thought processes or her ability to hold a conversation, it was only her coordination that was impaired.

The wet asphalt was slippery and unsteady, and she was having a great deal of trouble maintaining her balance. Wes put his arm around her waist, and she reciprocated companionably. The world was a blur of red and green, silver and pink dancing Christmas trees, and dimly she heard Wes's laughter in her ear. He smelled like bourbon and brandy, cigarette smoke and evergreen, and she liked having him close, having his arm around her.

"This isn't my car," she was astute enough to notice as she climbed carefully into the passenger seat of a small, very smart-looking foreign car.

"Right you are," responded Wes, and closed the door. In a moment he slid behind the steering wheel, and she could see the amusement in his eyes. "I've had enough of the inside of police stations for one lifetime, thank you, and I've no intention of letting you get behind the wheel. Which way?"

Sandy snuggled as close to him as possible in the bucket seats, and then, without any inhibition whatsoever, she laid her head against his wool-covered shoulder. The look he gave her was filled with indulgence, and even a touch of tenderness, and he moved his arm to encircle her. That was much more comfortable, and very warm. Sandy gave him semicoherent directions to her apartment, closed her eyes as he started the car, and then promptly fell asleep.

The next thing she knew cold air was tickling her face, and Wes was very close. She smiled up at him dizzily, and saw one corner of his lips go down in a fight with amusement. He placed his hands under her arms to help her out of the

car and onto her feet. She swayed against him, but he didn't
seem to mind. He held her steady against him, their wool-
swathed bodies meeting at all points, and his face filled her
vision like something from a foggy dream. She felt warm
and comfortable and safe, standing there like that in his
arms.

"Is this it?" he asked.

She looked up at him dazedly. "Hmmm?"

His eyes were dancing. "Is this where you live?"

Sandy made a concentrated effort to get hold of herself.
She looked around carefully, frowning. "Hmm," she decided at last. And she pointed. "Second one on top."

Wes chuckled softly to himself as he slipped one arm securely around her waist and led her carefully over the short
patch of stubbled lawn and up the metal steps. He probably shouldn't have let her drink so much, but she hadn't
really even finished two drinks, and who had ever heard of
anyone getting drunk off the kind of mixed drinks they
served in lounges? Besides, Wes wasn't used to taking care
of anyone but himself. She would probably wake up in the
morning and think she had hallucinated this entire evening.
Wes found himself hoping she didn't. He hoped she didn't
forget him.

At the door he finally managed to persuade her to give her
keys to him, and he got the deadbolt unlocked even though
she kept trying to help. He reached inside and found the
light switch, and, with both hands on her shoulders, he
placed her firmly inside the threshold. "Go to bed," he instructed, speaking very clearly so she would be sure to understand. "I'll see you in the morning."

She looked up at him soberly. "You are really gorgeous,
do you know that?"

The dancing mirth that had been hiding in his eyes broke
through. "Am I?"

"Uh-huh." Her eyes were diamond-chip bright as they examined him, her cheeks rosy, her lips moist and slightly parted. "Would you like to kiss me good-night?" she invited politely.

Wes hesitated for only a moment. That, he knew, was precisely what he would like to do. His hands cupped her shoulders, and he leaned toward her. His lips had barely brushed hers when she somehow slipped away, dissolving into giggles and collapsing against his shoulder.

Startled, torn between amusement and disappointment, Wes caught her beneath the arms again before she slipped to the floor. "I'm sorry!" she gasped, grasping his forearms to steady herself. Her star-bright eyes were, for a moment, filled with contrition. "That was very rude. It's just that—I was thinking—I don't usually do this sort of thing!" And she burst into giggles again.

"Believe it or not," Wes murmured dryly, "neither do I." He guided her firmly over to a flower-print sofa and sat her down. With the greatest of self-control, that was all he did. "Good night, Sandy Garret," he said, and paused. Her sweet, childlike face was composed and expectant, her eyes clear and open. He touched the corner of her lips with a gloved finger, feather light, and he felt her soft catch of breath. He moved toward her, fractionally.

And then the inward debate of which he was hardly aware got the best of him. His lips turned downward with remembered amusement and he shook his head, dismissing the foolish notion. He straightened up. "Good night," he repeated, sternly, and left her.

Sandy, curling up on the couch and cuddling a pillow to her cheek, smiled dreamily to herself as she closed her eyes. "Good night," she murmured.

Chapter Five

At seven o'clock the next morning, Wes was propped up in bed, a silver breakfast tray with orange juice, fresh melon and eggs Benedict across his lap, the remote control to the television set in his hand. He ran the channels until he found a *Tom and Jerry* cartoon, then settled back to eat, his eyes fixed with an almost hypnotic fascination upon the screen before him.

Wes had two great addictions: books of any kind and television. His father had fostered the one and tried to suppress the other, with the result that, to this day, Wes could not walk into a bookstore without spending less than two hundred dollars, and he could not pass a television set without being drawn, as though through some mystical force, to the most mindlessly entertaining programs it had to offer.

The twenty-two-inch color set—the only one in the house—was a modern touch that jarred the perfect symmetry of the otherwise authentic eighteenth-century elegance of the room. The huge four-poster bed was draped in scalloped canopy and curtains of royal-blue-and-white damask, repeating the patterns on the heavy draperies that were drawn back from embrasured windows. The walls were covered in Williamsburg blue wainscoting and alternating panels of white and blue-on-white linen. A fire crackled in the marble fireplace, and the floor was covered in a deep blue and pale rose Oriental carpet. There was a chaise before the fireplace and a sitting group before the east window, and every piece of furniture was authentic to the period—except for the television set placed irreverently before the Queen Anne armoire.

Wes had always been an incredibly cheerful riser, and he awoke every morning at seven with a hearty appetite and an eagerness to begin the day—even if the day held no more in store for him than *Tom and Jerry* and old movies. For that reason Mitch had been concerned during the past week of the young man's residence to see the reluctance with which he had greeted the mornings, his tendency to want to stay in bed until noon and eat hardly anything at all. He had understood the reasons why, of course—he could not say he hadn't felt generally the same way since the death of his employer and oldest friend—but he had begun to worry that the condition for Wes might become permanent. Wes had been protected, sheltered and catered to since birth; a combination of fortunate circumstances and personal charisma had placed the world at his feet in an almost literal sense of the phrase. He was one of those rare people who led a truly charmed life, and he was completely unprepared to deal with adversity of any kind. The unexpected loss of the central figure in his life was a harsh awakening to the cruelty and inequity of a world to which Wes had never been initiated, and Mitch had worried that he might not be able to cope.

But this morning Mitch began to suspect that he had underestimated the young man, and he was relieved to discover that his fears were groundless. The resiliency of the young was an incredible thing, and Wes seemed to be well on his way to recovery.

Mitch scowled at his young employer now, crossed over to the television set and deliberately snapped it off. Wes sat up in midchuckle, exclaimed, "Hey!" and pushed the button on the remote control. Mitch blocked its reception. "If I may repeat myself..." he began, scowling formidably.

If there was one thing Mitch did not like, it was being called upon to repeat himself. Wes temporarily gave up his attempt to aim the remote control around the large bulk of the man in gray chinos and combat boots and sat back against the pillows, demanding, "All right, what?"

"As I tried to tell you on several earlier occasions," said Mitch deliberately, not budging an inch, "Mr. Wilcox called yesterday and asked that you return his call as soon as possible."

"What did he want?" Wes popped a slice of melon into his mouth and tried, with a subtle motion of his wrist, to angle the remote control around Mitch. It didn't work.

Mitch looked properly insulted. "I'm sure I don't know, sir. Not being privy to—"

"Give me a break, Mitch," Wes interrupted impatiently. "You know everything. What was it?"

Mitch considered for a moment telling Wes what he knew; if he chose to, he could make the young man listen to him. He even considered handling it himself. From the moment of Wes's birth, Mitch's single ambition had been to do the best for Alex Wesley's son; he had not always succeeded, but he had always tried. The boy had a long, hard road ahead of him, and Mitch would be doing him no favors by making the way easier. Growing up was never a pleasant process, but it was one that had to be undergone—alone.

"I believe his question had something to do with your personal finances," Mitch capitulated reluctantly. "It's a private matter, I'm sure...."

Wes shrugged, finishing off his orange juice. "I don't know anything about that. Tell him to call what's-his-name—my accountant. Is that all?"

"As a matter of fact, there are several other matters—"

"For crying out loud, Mitch, I don't want to hear any of this. Will you move?"

Mitch gave him a tight-lipped look and remained firmly planted between the remote control and the television set. "I believe Master Tom and Master Jerry will wait another few moments, sir," he returned implacably, and with an exasperated breath. Wes dropped the remote control onto the rumpled sheets beside him, folding his arms across his chest and painting upon his face an expression of polite interest.

"That's better," conceded Mitch with an almost imperceptible smirk. "What is your decision on the cards?"

Wes scowled, "What cards?"

"The Christmas cards. They've been printed and addressed already. Shall we send them or not?"

Christmas cards. His father must have ordered them, as he did every year, sometime in October, never guessing that by November his heart would have suddenly decided to stop beating. Wes felt his stomach tighten, and a gray fog seemed to seep into his chest. Hundreds of them, addressed to politicians, socialites, corporate leaders, friends around the world...the last greetings from Alex Wesley. Ghosts of Christmas Past.

Wes said quietly, "Whose name is on them?"

"The same as always," replied Mitch. If he saw, or felt, the shadow of pain that had fallen over Wes he gave no sign. "The Wesleys."

Only now there was only one Wesley.... With an inward curse, Wes steeled himself against the feathered wings of desolation that threatened to shade his day. He didn't want to deal with this. He shouldn't have to deal with this. "I don't care," he replied shortly, and turned his wrist in a gesture of dismissal. "Whatever you think—don't bother me with it. Is that all?"

Mitch looked at him for a moment. "Are you going to call Mr. Wilcox?"

"No." Wes picked up the remote control with one hand and a forkful of eggs with the other. "Move."

Mitch did not. "You," he said deliberately, "are a spoiled, self-centered, irresponsible brat. And quite incorrigible, I'm afraid."

Wes looked at him impatiently, but he felt like grinning. The fog inside his chest had begun to clear with the familiar disapproving words, and Mitch must have known that was exactly what he needed to lift his spirits from the plunge they had almost taken. As sour as he would have everyone believe him to be, Mitch had a heart of pure gold, and his perception was sometimes unnerving.

"I know that," Wes returned with a great show of forbearance. "Is *that* all?"

"That," replied Mitch politely, moving away from the television set, "is all."

Immediately *Tom and Jerry* flickered back on the screen, and Wes settled back contentedly to finish his breakfast. "By the way," he called, just as Mitch was making his customary silent exit from the room. He didn't take his eyes from the screen as he gestured to a pile of discarded clothing in the center of the room. "My coat needs to be cleaned. And I'm going away for the weekend. Pack for me, will you? No dinner clothes. And make a reservation at Hampton Glen."

Mitch lifted one discerning eyebrow. "For one?"

"Of course not," scoffed Wes, without looking around. Then, with unaccustomed thoughtfulness, he added, "And get a room overlooking the lake, not the slopes." He wasn't quite sure how Sandy would feel watching others do what she no longer could. "And don't bother with my ski clothes."

Mitch barely suppressed a sigh of relief. He should have known there was never any cause to worry. Wine, women and song...Adrian Wesley was going to be all right. And

Alex would have been pleased. "Indoor recreation, Master Adrian?" put forth Mitch slyly, very careful to keep that note of haughty disapproval in his tone.

Wes tried to smother a grin, keeping his voice severe. "Just do it, will you?"

"Yes, your lordship." Mitch gave a low, mocking bow as he picked up the pile of clothing from the floor. Wes groaned out loud. "Master Adrian" and "Sir" were bad enough, but he now appeared to be in for a season at an eighteenth-century court. He should have known when he was well off.

"Will you get out of here?" demanded Wes. "I'm leaving in an hour."

"At your lordship's command," replied Mitch, bowing out of the room, and Wes restrained the urge to throw a pillow at him.

Alone with *Tom and Jerry*, Wes finished his breakfast and anticipated the day ahead with a relish he hadn't felt in what seemed liked a lifetime. Of course, he knew that there was every possibility he might be going to the Poconos alone. Sandy might not even remember him—although Wes was of the opinion that alcoholic amnesia was a myth perpetuated by people who only *wished* they could forget what they had done under the influence—and he knew that even if she did remember, she might decide to renege on their impulsive plans. But for the first time in a week Wes was beginning to see his way out of the dark and endless tunnel in which he seemed to have been wandering, and he had every intention of continuing on the upward swing. If Sandy had forgotten him, he would make her remember. If she had changed her mind, he would make her change it back again. And if all else failed, he would go alone.

But whatever happened, he decided as he flung back the covers and headed for the shower, today was a new beginning. And he was going to make the most of it.

AT SEVEN O'CLOCK in the morning, Sandy was awakened by a shrieking in her ears that brought her bolt upright on the couch, where she had slept all night. Lightning stabbed in her head and she moaned out loud, grabbing her temples with both hands. The cold grayness of early morning swirled around her and she groaned again, sinking back down onto the cushion that bore the imprint of her head. But the shrieking wouldn't stop, and after a moment, Sandy fumbled for the telephone on the end table, not sitting up, and not opening her eyes.

At her mumbled, incoherent greeting, another shrieking began in her ears, and grimacing, Sandy held the receiver away from her face. It was the voice of her sister, Linda. "What in the world happened to you last night? You were supposed to come back to the store! I called your place and you weren't home—where did you go?"

Sandy cleared her throat, ran a thick tongue over the roof of her mouth, and managed the one syllable. "Out."

"*Out*? Out where? Sandy, this isn't like you. You know I depend on you—you're always so responsible. I was worried to death that something had happened to you—you've *never* just disappeared like that before. What in the world were you thinking of?"

What would Linda think, wondered Sandy fuzzily, and the thought came from absolute nowhere, if she were to disappear for a whole weekend? The prospect disturbed Sandy vaguely, but she simply couldn't deal with it this morning. "I'm sleeping, Linda," she grumbled hoarsely. "Goodbye."

"You sound awful. What—"

Sandy let the receiver clatter back onto its cradle. Purple Passion, she thought distantly, trying to huddle back into the blissful oblivion of sleep. Who would've thought? Foggily, she reached for the remnants of a shattered dream, something about snow and a Greek god with blue, blue eyes...Wesley. Adrian Wesley.

Slowly she turned over, opening her eyes a crack. She was cold, her muscles ached, her mouth felt like an unwashed sink and sleep was gone. And on top of all that, Adrian Wesley was no dream.

She had not closed her curtains last night, and one of the most miserable mornings she had ever seen was already drifting into her cluttered apartment from the two over-sized windows that looked out into the parking lot. The sky was a bland slate gray, and the naked branches of a skinny maple tree moved lazily back and forth with the wind. The sun had only been up for a few minutes, and the grainy light that filtered into the apartment seemed reluctant, and hardly worth the effort it made to get there. *Rain again,* thought Sandy with a muffled groan, and closed her eyes.

At least her headache wasn't as bad as she had thought it was. It must have been the abrupt awakening and that awful shrilling in her ears that had made her head threaten to explode. Sandy was not a morning person by any stretch of the imagination, and there was no ruder way to greet the day than with the ungodly shrill of a telephone in her ear. Linda should have known by now that to call Sandy before nine o'clock in the morning was to take her life into her hands. And Sandy was not about to call her sister back and apologize for hanging up on her.

All in all, Sandy thought, as she lay there with her eyes closed against the gloom and prepared herself to come slowly awake, the results of last night's indiscretion were not nearly as severe as she had expected. If she had managed to crawl into bed last night instead of sleeping on the couch, she would doubtless have felt much better, but a warm shower would work out the stiffness of her muscles and...

The phone rang again, and again lightning bolts shot through her head. Mumbling a curse her brother O.J. had taught her on his first leave from the navy, she snatched the phone off the hook. *"What?"*

The unmistakable rolling laughter of her brother Bill reached her ears. "Good morning to you, too, sweetheart. What's up?"

"I am, now," she replied ungraciously, propping herself into a semisitting position on the cushions, squinting at the murky room. "What do you want?"

"I just got a raving call from Linda, who wanted me to find out what was wrong with you. She said you walked out on her last night and sounded like death this morning. What's the matter? You sick?"

"Oh, for the love of...!" She broke off, exasperated, forced at last to open her eyes completely and face the unforgiving day. Trust Linda to make an international incident out of one impulsive move, and trust her family to come rallying to the fore at the first sign of anything unexpected in Sandy's behavior. "It's getting so that I can't even go to the bathroom without the whole family getting in on the act," she grumbled bitterly, then gave up the lecture she had planned. She really didn't have the energy to fight with Bill—or anyone—this morning. "As a matter of fact," she told him acerbically. "I went out last night and got drunk."

A silence, then an unexpected explosion of laughter. "Are you kidding me? Good for you, babe!"

This was not exactly the way Sandy had expected her small triumph of defiance to be received, and she didn't quite know how to respond.

"Not alone, I hope," Bill added good-naturedly, still chuckling, and the vision of an aristocratically featured, gently handsome face swam into Sandy's view. *Good heavens,* she thought in no small awe, *I really did it. I really sat down with an international jet-setter, got smashed out of my mind, and even agreed to go away for the weekend with him. Not bad for a first night out.*

And she responded, with perhaps just the faintest touch of wistfulness to her voice. "No, not alone."

"Oh-oh." Bill's perceptive tone indicated he had picked up on more than she had intended him to. "Little sister is growing up fast. Who is he? Anybody I know?"

Sandy was not used to keeping secrets from her brother, and the words "Adrian Wesley" were on her tongue almost before she thought about it. Fortunately, she caught herself in time. One word to Bill and she would be on the phone all morning, explaining to various members of her family how she had happened to meet Adrian Wesley of The Wesleys, what had happened between them, when she expected to see him again. She couldn't deal with that on top of a hovering hangover and another excruciating, rainy day. Besides, nothing had happened, she would never see him again and there was no point in bringing any of it up.

So she merely said, "No. Nobody you know." She realized that the enigmatic answer would arouse Bill's curiosity far more thoroughly than a straightforward "Adrian Wesley" would do, but she didn't know what she could do about it.

"Aha," Bill said, and then there was silence. Sandy could practically hear the whir of the wheels in his brain from here, and the image made her smile. As much as she loved all her brothers, she was still too much of a little sister to be able to resist teasing them whenever she got the chance. He said after a moment, "Do you want to have lunch?"

That was Bill's tactful way of asking if she needed to talk. It was apparent that all was not well with his favorite sister—first she walked off a job, then she did the absolutely unheard of and got drunk, and to top it all off there was a mysterious stranger in her life. Naturally, Bill was concerned. Naturally, he wanted to talk.

For a moment Sandy considered it. It might be easier to practice breaking the news of her failed career on Bill, who never pushed her in any direction she didn't want to go, who went out of his way to be sympathetic and understanding. But she really didn't think she was even up to Bill today. "No," she said, and the regret in her voice sounded almost genuine. "I'd better not. I still owe Linda three hours from yesterday, and I guess I'll go in early." The thought was almost overwhelmingly depressing.

Bill hesitated, but he knew when to give up. It was obvious he was not going to get an explanation for his sister's erratic behavior. "Okay, then," he agreed, when there was nothing left for him to do. "I'll see you at the folks' tomorrow."

"Right," Sandy said. Sunday dinner with all fifteen of them. What a cheery thought. She supposed she would have to tell them then, but at least she had bought a day. "Love to Cassie and the baby."

"Take care of yourself, babe," Bill said and meant it.

That's exactly what I'm trying to do, thought Sandy as she hung up the phone. *Take care of myself. For the first time in my life.*

But somehow the thought didn't seem quite as cheering as it had last night, and freedom was not as easily within her grasp. Maybe all it took was Purple Passions, she mused as she swung her feet reluctantly to the floor and planted them there heavily. And Adrian Wesley...

But today she would have to make do with a hot shower, she decided as she plodded wearily to the bathroom, along with a cup of coffee and maybe a couple of aspirin. Had she really agreed to go away with Adrian Wesley for the weekend?

By the time the stinging needles of a gloriously hot shower had brought her almost back to life, Sandy had decided that, indeed, she had agreed to go away with him. By the time she had tugged on a pair of faded jeans and an oversized fisherman's sweater, she had also decided it was a pity he hadn't had the car warmed up last night and ready to sweep her away to their mountain hideaway, because she probably would have gone. The very thought of spending a secluded weekend with that gorgeous hunk of man—or any man, for that matter—made her sigh out loud. She would never get a chance like that again.

As she watched the hot water drip over fresh grounds through her automatic coffee maker, she found the curiosity to wonder whether he could possibly have been serious. She decided, as she carried the cup back to her bedroom, that there was a fifty-fifty chance he was. Men like Adrian Wesley were probably accustomed to picking up strange women and flying them off via private jet to Aspen or Monaco or Cozumel or wherever their fancy struck. On the other hand, men like Adrian Wesley were probably equally as accustomed to making lighthearted passes at every woman who crossed their paths, thinking it was expected of them. By this morning, he had probably forgotten all about her and had set his sights on bigger game.

Then, as she was blow-drying her hair into a bouncy sheath of fresh-washed curls, she remembered his abortive attempt to kiss her, and she winced with embarrassment. She guessed *that* was a first for the well-bred Adrian Wesley who could hold his liquor so well. He was probably still chuckling to himself over the undignified behavior of the woman in the Santa Claus hat who was so drunk she couldn't even stand up long enough for him to kiss her. Then she shrugged philosophically to herself. So she had given him a story to tell; she would never be around when he told it. And she wouldn't begrudge him his laugh; it had probably made his day.

By the time she had swallowed two aspirin with half a cup of milk, she felt almost human again. And by the time she had poured a second cup of coffee she was almost beginning to believe she might even be able to face Linda and the rain and the nightmare of a retail store at Christmastime. And then the doorbell rang.

Adrian Wesley was lounging against her door frame in charcoal cords, suede boots and a blue parka that was absurdly close to the color of his eyes. The parka was open over a loose-weave sweater of black-and-gray tweed with a modified cowl neck, offset shoulders and false placket down the front; it was of such an unusual design Sandy knew instinctively it was one of a kind, and it was gorgeous. Scotland, she thought irrelevantly, or some little village in England...

Then Wes said cheerfully, "Good morning. Are you ready to go?"

Sandy stared at him, and with that dancing-master grace she so well remembered he straightened himself from the propped-up position and moved easily past her across the threshold. She realized then that, since she had been standing half-behind the door, peering at him like some tongue-tied child, he had no choice but to invite himself in if he wanted to look at her while he talked. And he stood before her now, smiling at her easily and confidently, looking as though he had every right in the world to believe she would welcome him.

Which of course he did, Sandy thought a little dizzily as she closed the door on the drafty hallway. Unless he was still teasing. How far did a man like Wesley go to get his laugh, anyway? Or maybe he was serious. Maybe he had really expected her to be packed and ready to leave with him this morning. Sandy felt her headache beginning again.

Wes tilted his head assessingly. "You don't look too bad," he decided after a moment. "Not as bad as I had expected, anyway. Your eyes are a little bloodshot. How do you feel?"

"I felt a lot better two minutes ago," Sandy mumbled without thinking, and Wes chuckled.

"I take it you're surprised to see me."

She glanced at him suspiciously, but in his eyes was nothing but a relaxed warmth, and it was difficult to accuse a face so young and unmarred of plotting her discomfiture. She agreed, still watching him somewhat warily, "You take it correctly."

He lifted an innocent eyebrow. "Did you really doubt that I was a man of my word? I told you I'd see you this morning."

Sandy looked at him skeptically. A man of his word, was he? She supposed now he intended to hold her to hers.

"Look," she blurted out, seeing no point in delaying further, "you didn't really mean what you said last night.... What I mean is, you didn't really believe me when I said... For goodness' sake," she expostulated, gesturing helplessly with her coffee cup and adding another splatter of stains to the already worn carpet. "I was drunk!"

Wes looked at her tolerantly, trying not to enjoy her embarrassment too much. Before he had even gotten in the car he had known the chances were more than even that he would be going to the Poconos by himself. He had come to Sandy's apartment first partly because the streak of mischief in him couldn't resist the opportunity to catch the look on her face when he did show up, and partly because, as corny as it sounded, he had never broken a promise to a woman in his life and he *had* told her he would come. On the drive over he had resigned himself to the fact that she would probably slam the door in his face and he would end up spending the weekend alone, and had even told himself it didn't matter. It was all a joke anyway, half-serious impulses born of too much to drink and no dinner that neither of them should take seriously in the morning. But suddenly, seeing her again, it did matter. Suddenly he realized he was just as serious now as he had been last night. He did not want to spend the weekend alone.

She looked even cuter this morning than she had last night—and cute was the word, tousled and huggable and altogether harmless. Her hair, fresh from the blow-dryer, was a shiny mop of soft black-brown curls, and exuded the warm, fresh fragrance of herbs. Her color was all pink-and-white, and her eyes, despite the slight redness and puffiness, were as large as he remembered them. The huge cable-knit sweater hid her curves, but met the tight thighs of her jeans quite enticingly. And all Wes was thinking about was how much he really wanted to be with her this weekend.

Searching about for a way to distract her from an outright refusal, his eyes fell upon the coffee cup in her hand. "Do you happen to have another one of those?" he asked pleasantly.

Sandy hesitated but she could find no good reason to refuse him a cup of coffee. He was already slipping off his jacket, his eyes wandering around the morning-dim room with interest, looking as though he had every intention of making himself at home. Sandy tried not to feel uncomfortable as her meager furnishings fell under the scrutiny of one of the richest men in a city known for its rich men, but she couldn't really help it—she felt uncomfortable. She went into the kitchen, where she wouldn't have to watch, cheering herself marginally with the fact that at least the place was clean. Sandy was a haphazard housekeeper, but her mother had made herself useful on a recent visit and there was no dirty laundry or unwashed dishes to embarrass her in front of aristocratic visitors. So let him look.

The living room, as it was somewhat optimistically called, was only large enough to hold a sofa, a coffee table and a small stand with a twelve-inch black-and-white television set. In a corner, next to the kitchen, was a small drop-leaf table and one chair. The kitchen itself was barely worth mentioning, and the bedroom, which opened onto the living room and was in full view at all times, was big enough for a double bed and a chest of drawers. Sandy's mother had added the homey touches—the warm yellow-and-red patchwork cushions on the beige floral sofa, the fire-toned afghan, the deep burgundy and pale blue hooked rugs that were scattered over the neutral carpet. Linda had added the style, contributing dried floral arrangements, on the coffee table and tiny drop-leaf whose summery tones picked up the sky blue of the rugs and the blossoming yellow of the cushions; she had also provided ceramic ashtrays and a cut-glass candy dish that Sandy kept filled with Hershey's Kisses. Midge had added the esoteric touch with a collection of candles and brass incense burners and one brightly colored feather fan that was supposed to have mystical powers. Rick, who insisted he was a better street cop than an artist despite Sandy's protests to the contrary, had supplied the four eye-catching paintings that drew the room together— one of a gaily painted clown in shades of yellow, blue and red, one of a whimsical mouse perched on a mushroom and a matching set of miniature landscapes, one winter and one fall. All in all it was an eclectic, warm and delightfully in- viting apartment that exuded a charm and personality that, even though it was none of Sandy's doing, somehow seemed to belong to her. And to Wes, who could have fit the entire apartment into one corner of his bedroom, the effect was more vivid than any designer's touch could have given it, and the small treasures that summed up parts of her seemed richer than the whole collection of antiques and rarities that were displayed in the mausoleum he called a home. Just looking at it, he wondered for the first time what it would have been like to have grown up differently. But of course he didn't wonder for long.

Sandy returned with his coffee, and he took it from her with a smile. The pottery mug had a bug-eyed frog glazed on it, and that made him smile again. "I don't have any cream or sugar," she informed him without apology, but

Wes was not daunted. He took a sip, didn't grimace and even told her it was good.

He had placed his jacket over the arm of the couch, but had not sat down while she was gone. The sweater was even more gorgeous than she had thought on first glance—it was oversized, of a bulky cut with many intricate folds and tucks, yet it seemed to hug his torso in all the right places. The sleeves were pushed up to just below his elbows, and Sandy noticed that he had very nice wrists—strong-boned yet delicate, like the rest of him. His forearms were long and graceful and lightly covered with gold hair, and the deep-cut shoulders and heavy neck of the sweater made him look broader and stronger through the chest and biceps than he probably was.

Sandy sank to the couch, and gestured that he do the same. There was no cause to be rude, after all. And she may as well get this over with. She could take a joke as well as anyone else, but it was getting late and she should be starting to work if she intended to be at the mall by the time it opened. "Anyway," she said easily, sipping her own coffee and continuing their previous conversation just as though it had never been interrupted, "I'm sure you didn't really expect me to go with you today...."

"Didn't I?" Wes said mildly, settling down beside her.

Of course there was no place else for him to sit but on the couch. It was just that Sandy hadn't expected him to sit so close. One long, corduroy-clad leg was practically brushing hers, and his arm did brush against hers as he sat back, the coffee mug cradled against his chest in both hands, and watched her with waiting blue eyes. He smelled of warmth and wool and evergreen, and his hair today was more silver than gold. Beautiful stuff. She wondered what it would feel like beneath the fingers, gathered by handfuls. She wondered if he would look half as good without that sweater as in it and had a dreadful suspicion he would look even better.

Something must have changed in her expression, a softening or a dreaminess, for Sandy's moods were always written in her eyes. He caught it, and a crease deepened at the edge of his mouth, the beginning of a knowing smile. Sandy jerked her eyes away. *Get hold of yourself, Sandy, my girl. Bodies like that are a dime a dozen.* But, she thought somewhat wistfully, she would have given her eyeteeth for that sweater. "I've got to go to work," she said abruptly, taking a last quick sip of her coffee before setting it on the table. She turned to him pleasantly. "So if you'll excuse me..."

He didn't budge. "You've already planned to take the weekend off," he reminded her. "And make it until Tuesday morning." A confidence had come upon him that was the result of sheer wanting. What Adrian wanted he most certainly got; it was an unquestioned fact of life. And he had absolutely no intention of leaving this room alone.

Sandy stared at him. "You are serious," she said slowly.

He smiled at her, reaching forward to place his coffee cup on the table beside hers. He had half guessed they would have to go through all this, and he tried not to be impatient. "Look," he said reasonably, "nothing has changed since last night. We both still need to get away." He gestured toward the window. "It's still raining. And—" now he fixed a questioning look on her "—you still like me, don't you?"

"I don't even know you!" Sandy protested.

Wes smiled confidently. "So much the better. Now what's the real problem?"

Sandy looked at him. Yes, what was the problem? So he was rich, beautiful, elegant, charming.... She shouldn't hold that against him. He was amusing, gentle, entertaining and, far beneath the surface, possessed of a sweet vulnerability that touched her. Oh, if she looked hard enough she would doubtlessly find plenty to dislike about him, but why bother? Why, for goodness' sake, look a gift horse in the mouth?

She realized then, to her absolute astonishment, that she was considering doing it. Seriously. Just packing up and going away for the weekend.

No, what was astonishing was that she was for even one minute hesitating. *Sandra Kathleen Meridan Garret, you must be out of your mind!* It exploded on her stunned conscience like an outraged voice of reason. *Here you are sitting not eight inches away from the most gorgeous hunk of man ever to cross your path, listening to him offer to sweep you away to a snow-covered paradise, and you're thinking of turning him down? You're crazy, that's all—completely, helplessly, certifiably insane!*

Nervously Sandy got up and walked over to the window. He was right; it was drizzling again. Okay, what was the problem? She pressed her hands together and tried to be reasonable. A weekend in the mountains. It sounded perfect. She owed it to herself; she deserved it. A weekend away with Adrian Wesley. It was exactly what she had been looking for. She would never get a chance like this again.

Wes, measuring his advantage, said softly behind her, "Don't you want to see the snow?"

It was her life, wasn't it? Wasn't it only yesterday that she had made her declaration of independence? For the first time in her life she was free of responsibility, her allegiance was only to herself, there was nothing to keep her from tasting all the pleasures life had to offer.

But still some small moral voice intruded and she felt compelled to argue. "No problem, really," she said, turning. "I mean, the whole thing sounds wonderful, a weekend in the mountains, but—"

"But you don't want to go with me," Wes said with thoughtful perception. He stood up and strolled around the sofa, nodding his understanding, and Sandy knew he did not understand at all.

"It has nothing to do with want," she tried to explain. If want was the only issue here she would be cuddled up next to him in that funny foreign car of his already, well on her way to a wild weekend of sin in the Poconos. "It's just that I hardly know you. I can't just let you pick me up and carry me off to a mountain hideaway."

"Oh," Wes said, suddenly seeming to make sense of it all. He tried to remember all he knew about middle-class values and the changing role of women in today's society, and came up with the conclusion. "You don't want to feel like a cheap pickup."

That was close enough, Sandy supposed. Closer still was the fact that if it felt right, it must be wrong, and everything about this proposed weekend felt very, very right. She nodded.

Wes thought about it for a moment, observing her from across the room. "That should be no problem," he decided, relaxing with the easy conclusion. "You can pay for your own part of the trip, if you like. Would that make you feel better?"

Sandy hesitated. Would that satisfy twenty-four years of strict moral upbringing? If she let him take her, it was going away for the weekend with a man. But if she paid for her own room and her own meals, it was just going away for the weekend. She grew cautiously excited as she thought it might really work. But she deliberately kept capitulation out of her voice as she said, "How much do you suppose a weekend at Hampton Glen would cost?"

"Not more than a couple of thousand," he assured her offhandedly, and her spirits fell.

"Well," she said, shrugging, and turned back to the window. "That's that, then."

Wes came over to her, gentle exasperation playing in his eyes. "Look, this is silly," he said. "If I asked you out to dinner, would you ask how much it costs? Would you insist upon paying for your own meal?"

Sandy looked up at him, resolve wavering by the minute. "No, of course not."

"Same thing." He dismissed the matter with an easy gesture of his strong-boned wrist. "Consider this a date, and I'm paying. I can afford it."

Sandy opened her mouth for a helpless protest, but just then the phone rang. Sandy moved gladly away from him.

"Hello, baby," came her mother's cheerful, Mrs. Santa Claus voice. "Tonight is cookie-baking night. We're starting right after supper, and you may as well plan to spend the night—"

Sandy stifled a groan and let her mother's voice fade out. Another annual event—the Garret bake-a-thon for the Westminister Methodist Children's Home. All the wives and daughters would gather in the kitchen while the sons and sons-in-law were relegated to the workshop downstairs and cookies and toys were turned out with gay assembly-line efficiency to the strains of "Deck the Halls" from the stereo and the background mayhem of eight nieces and nephews. Food coloring would stain the fingers, and nonpareils haunt the mind, for weeks. The clean-up job was enormous. Sandy would be sick for days from all the sample tasting she didn't seem to be able to resist. The day was looking bleaker and bleaker.

"Mom..." she heard her own voice interrupting before she even had a chance to think. "I'm not sure I can make it. I might be going away for the weekend."

In the wake of her mother's stunned silence she felt Wes's pleased smile and her own incredulous words echoing in her ears. But there was no way to take it back now.

Her mother said cautiously, "Oh? Where?"

Sandy deliberately did not look at Wes. "To the Poconos, I thought. I have a chance to go and—"

Immediately her mother was enthusiastic. "Of course you have to go. What a good idea! You can get some practice in. We should have thought about it before, you haven't been on the slopes all year. My, this *is* good news. When did the doctor tell you?"

Of course her mother would assume that Sandy was going to ski; of course she knew Sandy could not ski unless the doctor had given her the all-clear, and of course the doctor would not have done that unless he was pronouncing Sandy fit to return to competition.

Oh, God, Mom, Sandy thought miserably. *I'm sorry.* But she just couldn't go into it now. Not over the phone, and not now. "I saw the doctor yesterday," she hedged. "But I'm not really going to ski...." At least she made an attempt to tell the truth. Perhaps that would salve whatever was left of her conscience.

"Well, of course you'll take it easy. You're not going alone, I assume."

Her mother would naturally assume that one of her teammates or even her coach would be going with her. *Oh, what a tangled web we weave...* "I'm not even sure I'm going at all," Sandy began.

"Of course you'll go," her mother insisted. "You need to do this, and it's long overdue. You know what they say about getting right back on the horse."

Great, Mom, Sandy thought. *Just what every daughter needs. A mother who will talk her into keeping an illicit tryst with a man for the weekend.* But beyond all that, she knew something else, and it sobered her. Her mother was right. She did need to go this weekend, and for reasons with which Adrian Wesley had nothing at all to do.

"Well," Wes declared, and he was practically rubbing his hands with glee when she hung up the phone. "It's all settled, then. It shouldn't take you more than a few minutes to pack, and I'll go warm up the car—"

He had taken a step toward the door before Sandy found the presence of mind to interrupt, in a somewhat harried voice. "No! It's not all settled! I only told my mother that to get out of—well, it doesn't matter what I said, the point is…" Yes, what *was* the point? *You're being stupid, Sandy.…*

Wes should have been annoyed; he wasn't. True, the ladies he was used to never played these kinds of games and he wasn't accustomed to it, but strangely enough he didn't think Sandy was playing a game. He believed it was for her a real moral dilemma. He didn't understand the reason for it, but he tried to sympathize.

"Wait, let me guess," he offered lightly, and he was only half teasing. "You do want to go to the mountains—that much is clear. What you're having trouble with is going away with *me*. Now why can that be, I wonder." He pretended to muse, bringing one finger to the side of his face, hiding from her both the mischief in his eyes and the quirk of his mouth. "It can't be the way I look. I'm gorgeous— you told me so yourself only last night." Sandy felt a miserable flush creep out of the neck of her sweater, and he pretended not to notice. "I haven't been rude or done anything to offend you, you haven't known me long enough to see my mean streak, I'm clean and healthy and well groomed." He looked at her with mock perceptiveness. "It must be because I'm shallow, self-centered and ultimately boring."

Sandy fought with equal amounts of mirth and embarrassment. "It is not. That is, that has nothing to do with—"

And suddenly Wes understood. He cursed his own stupidity and was sorry he had teased her. He took a step toward her; he looked into those huge, doe-brown eyes and said soberly, as gently as he could, "Sandy, I'm not asking you to sleep with me, if that's what you're thinking. This weekend has nothing to do with sex, and I'm sorry if I made you think otherwise." And at that moment, he realized he meant it. All he knew was that he wanted to be with her, that if he wasn't with her the loneliness would be too much to bear, and sex had never once entered into the picture. "It's just two people who want to be in the same place at the same time, enjoying each other's company. I never meant you to think I was trying to put any heavy moves on you—I just like being with you. That's the truth."

Sandy turned away, hugging her arms over her chest, and she realized the moment she had done it that it was because she didn't want him to catch a glimpse of the disappointment that had suddenly coursed through her. Disappointment? It should have been relief. Now she didn't know what to think.

The ringing of the phone rescued her from having to think anything at all. It was Midge, the youngest, and she wanted to know if she could use Sandy's apartment that afternoon. What she really meant, of course, was that she and her latest boyfriend wanted to use Sandy's apartment, a fact Midge never tried to conceal but Sandy never wanted to know. Sandy felt she was being slightly immoral every time she agreed to Midge's request, but since she also couldn't help sympathizing with the problems of young love, she had decided to pretend Midge was doing nothing but watching television whenever she used Sandy's apartment in her absence.

There was a moment's hesitation, but Sandy knew she had made up her mind even before she said the words. "As a matter of fact, Midge, I was just on my way out the door. I'm going to the mountains for the weekend." Midge gave a squeal of delight and Sandy deliberately did not glance at Wes. "Do me a favor, will you, and call Linda? I'm supposed to work today. Tell her I won't be back until Tuesday.''

"You bet." Midge sounded exuberant. "And thanks a bunch. Let's get together next week."

Sandy hardly heard her. She could not restrain herself from looking at Wes one more minute. *I can't believe you're doing this,* she thought, and the stronger part of her mind retorted, *Who are you kidding? You knew you were going to do it the minute you opened the door and saw him standing there.* "I'd love it," she told Midge absently. "Thanks, kid."

"Sure thing." Midge was practically chortling with victory. "Have a good time."

Sandy hung up the phone and turned slowly to fully face Wes. He looked cautiously hopeful. "I'm probably going to regret this," she said.

Enormous relief washed over him. "Probably," he agreed cheerfully. "I am shallow, you know. Also spoiled, self-centered, irresponsible and quite incorrigible. I was told so only today."

But at that moment Sandy didn't believe she was going to regret it. Not for one moment. Elation surged through her, and excitement, and that wonderful feeling of knowing she was doing something for the first time in her life that was completely unacceptable, and that she was doing it for *herself*. "Give me five minutes to pack," she said, and wonder and anticipation tingled in her cheeks and brightened her eyes as she hurried toward the bedroom. "And whatever you do," she called over her shoulder, "don't answer the telephone!"

Wes settled down on the sofa, a smile of pure contentment spreading over his face, and he felt as though the biggest adventure of his life was just beginning.

Chapter Six

The suite looked like something out of *Bride* magazine. Two roomy bedrooms, both with king-sized beds and free-standing fireplaces, were connected by a spacious parlor, one entire wall of which was covered with a stone fireplace, the other wall made of glass and looking out onto a panoramic view of snow and lake and sky. Each of the bedrooms, as well as the parlor, had its own concealed television-stereo and fully stocked hospitality bar. There were two bathrooms, each with its own mirrored dressing room. One was beautifully appointed but rather small, with only a shower enclosure and what Sandy took to be a tanning area, but the other was magnificent. It was as big as her bedroom at home, tiled in black from floor to ceiling, with inch-thick white plush carpeting and an enormous sunken tub with Jacuzzi controls and piped-in music. There were even fresh candles, in black and white, lining the edge of the platform that surrounded the tub, and the soap was shaped like roses. Sandy couldn't wait to take a bath.

"It's beautiful!" Sandy exclaimed, returning to the center parlor. She twirled once around in the center of the slope-ceilinged, pine-paneled room, then went immediately to the window.

Wes suppressed a wry smile as he tipped the bellman and dismissed him. Mitch had told him before he left that the only rooms available with a view of the lake were suites; he hadn't bothered to tell him that he had chosen a two-bedroom suite. Score one for Mitch. And wouldn't the good man be surprised to know that his choice of sleeping arrangements suited Wes's own plans perfectly?

Sandy looked out over the terrace to the lake below, the mounds of evergreen-dotted mountains that seemed to sink right into it, the expanse of smooth, untracked snow below her, and her breath caught with the beauty of it. It was still too early in the season for the lake to freeze, and it was a portrait-perfect reflection of smooth white mountains and cloud-dotted blue sky. From the looks of those clouds there might be more snow tonight, and her skier's heart quickened at the thought of fresh powder, even before she realized the state of the slopes was no longer any concern of hers.

"A hot tub!" she exclaimed, and peered around the corner of the terrace doors to make out the shape of a tall wooden tub sitting against the snow-covered rail. "At least I think it is, isn't it?"

Wes went over to the breakfast table, where, as per his standing order, a cheese and fruit basket and a bottle of very fine Bordeaux awaited. The wine had been opened precisely one half hour before their arrival, and should have had plenty of time to breathe. He poured two glasses. "Sure," he replied, and tossed a grape into his mouth before picking up both glasses and coming over to her. "I'll turn on the heat and we can try it out later."

Sandy was dubious. "In the cold?"

"It's great," he assured her. "The cold air on your face, all that hot water surrounding your body." He couldn't help grinning at her expression. "What's the matter?" he teased. "Chicken?"

"It's not that," she admitted, glancing back a little uneasily toward the hot tub sitting in the snow, which, as a matter of fact, sounded like the most erotic experience she had ever imagined. "It's just that—don't you have to have a swimsuit?"

With great effort Wes kept a straight face. She was adorable. "Some people wear a suit," he agreed, handing her glass to her. "Some people go in naked."

She looked at him cautiously, accepting the glass. "Which do you do?"

He winked at her, his eyes twinkling madly, as he touched his glass to hers. "Guess."

Sandy swallowed back her irrational excitement and a sudden wonderful vision of his lean and perfectly formed body sliding nude into the water, and she even held his gaze long enough to take a sip of the wine. This was the best thing she had ever done. She was miles and miles away from anyone who knew her, alone for the weekend in this rustically elegant suite with nothing but snow and Adrian Wesley and a hot tub.... No one in her family knew where she was, and she didn't have to look at a Christmas shopper for three whole days. It was heaven, sheer heaven. If she lived to be a hundred she would never regret this weekend. It was the best gift she had ever given herself.

Smiling at him with the sudden brilliance of unadulterated joy, she set her glass down on the end table by the window and whirled toward the bedroom to which the bellman had taken her bags. The two bedrooms had been something of a disappointment when she had first seen them, but all in all she supposed it was best. It was enough just being here.

"Where are you going?" Wes called, surprised.

She turned at the entrance to the bedroom. "To unpack. I want to get started having fun!"

Wes laughed, shaking his head, happier than he had ever thought he would be that she had come with him. "We'll get a maid to unpack. Let's go down and get some lunch. Or would you rather call room service?''

Sandy opened her mouth to protest the absurdity of calling a maid to do what it would take her five minutes to do herself, but then thought better of it. What the hell, one weekend of luxury wouldn't spoil her for life, and she might as well live it up while she could. That was the whole point, wasn't it?

''Let's go down,'' she agreed happily. ''And let's take our outdoor gear so we can go walk in the snow afterward.''

The cathedral-ceilinged alpine restaurant was decorated with holly and red ribbons, but there was, thank God, no Christmas music. They were early for lunch, and the restaurant wasn't very crowded, which suited Sandy just fine. Every table overlooked the slopes, but for the moment Sandy was too excited to gaze out the floor-to-ceiling windows and watch the colorful mélange of weekend sportsmen make happy fools of themselves.

Wes glanced at her over his menu. ''What would you like?''

''To be beautiful,'' responded Sandy promptly. ''Also, a ten-speed bicycle, an automatic dishwasher and new curtains for my living room.''

Wes's eyes laughed. ''Anything else?''

''Yes. Everything on the menu. I didn't have any breakfast and I'm starved.''

The waiter stopped by to ask if they wanted cocktails, and Wes responded immediately, with a quick glance at her, ''No.'' He waited until the waiter was gone to apologize, with his most endearing grin. ''That was high-handed of me, I know. I thought one round of Purple Passion in twenty-four hours was all either of us could handle.'' And halfheartedly, ''I could call him back, if you really want a drink.''

Sandy's lips tightened against a reproving smile. When he grinned like that he could be as arrogant as he wanted and no one would care—and he damn well knew it, too. Strangely, Sandy did not find that offensive. She was having too much fun to find anything he did offensive. "Well," she admitted, "you happen to be right this time. But," she warned him, "if I *had* wanted a drink I *would* make you call the waiter back, so just ask next time."

"I stand corrected," murmured Wes, with the mischief still in his eyes. He folded the menu and lit a cigarette. The craving was beginning to taper off; today he was smoking only when he had nothing better to do, rather than searching for an excuse to light a cigarette. By the end of the weekend he probably would have forgotten to smoke entirely.

"Why a bicycle?" he asked in a moment, interrupting her absorption in the menu.

Sandy didn't look up. She couldn't decide between the scampi and chicken mushroom *élégante*. Everything on the menu was drenched in sinfully rich sauces and gobs of cholesterol. She was in heaven. "I always wanted one," she answered absently. "But my folks couldn't afford to buy ten-speeds for all of us, and they never showed any favoritism."

Wes nodded, watching her thoughtfully. "But why beautiful?"

Now she shrugged, almost deciding on the scampi. "I always wanted to be beautiful. Like Linda."

Vaguely Wes remembered the blond sister. He couldn't imagine why Sandy would want to change anything about herself. "You don't need beautiful," he told her frankly. "You've got something better. You're unique."

Sandy made a face, not at all certain that was a compliment. "That's what my father always says—all of us are unique. I'd rather be beautiful."

Wes wanted to pick up on that, but just then the waiter reappeared. Wes was delighted over Sandy's quandary with the menu—whatever this woman did, she apparently did it whole-heartedly. Such enthusiasm was rare in Wes's world. She finally narrowed it down between quiche, which she hadn't had in years, and the lobster thermidor, which she had never had, and when Wes lazily suggested she have both, her eyes lit up like candles and he had to laugh. Wes, who had had a big breakfast, ordered a chef's salad and a glass of white wine for both of them, and when they were alone again he said, "Tell me about your family. How many of you are there?"

Sandy settled back in her chair, wondering how he could possibly want to hear about such boring stuff. But there was nothing to do now but wait for the food, and in anticipation of the glorious feast coming, she would oblige him with anything. "There are eight of us. My mom and dad, three brothers, two sisters and me. Dad restores old houses when he's not making Christmas toys, and he's very good, too," she added with just the slightest touch of daughterly pride. "Bill's the oldest—he owns his own real estate and development company. It's not very big, but it will be someday. O.J.—his real name is Osmond Jerome, so you can see why he prefers O.J.—is next in line, and he's a lieutenant in the navy. Then there's Rick—you met him last night—he's a cop and an artist. Linda owns her own boutique, and the youngest is Midge, who buys her clothes at the army surplus store and goes to yoga classes and is majoring in communications. She'll probably have her own cable TV station by the time she's thirty—she's the smartest one of the bunch."

Wes gave her an appreciative glance as he stubbed his cigarette out in the ashtray. "A very impressive crew."

"Hmm." Sandy's eyes wandered, without volition, over his shoulder to the jigsaw paths carefree skiers were making down the slopes. *There but for the grace of God, go I,* she thought. "Success is a must in the Garret family," she said, and she thought her tone was totally noncommittal. "Second only to ambition."

But Wes picked up on a note of something—he thought it was resentment—and it interested him. "Is that bad?"

Sandy's eyes left the slopes and came back to him. She had forgotten how easy it was to talk to him. One corner of her mouth turned up in a quirk that was almost a smile, and she answered, "Only if you happen to have neither."

"Come on, Sandy," he said in mild objection, "you can't say that. It takes a lot of ambition to devote your whole life to amateur sports the way you did, and if the Olympic team isn't success, what is?"

What amazed Sandy was he seemed to be really interested. She shook her head slowly, trying to put it into words—as much as for herself as for Wes. "But I wasn't, you know," she said at last, half reflectively, "ambitious— or even very successful." She smiled a little in self-deprecation. "I was never any more than a mediocre skier. I knew that, my coach knew it, but my family wouldn't believe it. A Garret, you see, is always the best. It doesn't matter what you do with your life as long as you're the very best at what you do. And as long, of course, as you do *something* with your life." She shrugged, glancing down at her hands. "It was the way I was raised—I never thought to question it. Until after the accident, and I realized I hadn't ever really had the ambition—or the talent—to be a championship skier. I was the first Garret to ever fail at anything."

She was startled at how self-pitying that sounded when in all truth she didn't feel sorry for herself at all. She was, as a matter of fact, having the time of her life. She gave Wes a quick, light and apologetic smile, hoping he didn't think she was getting maudlin.

But Wes did not seem to mind. He seemed, in fact, genuinely involved in her story. "And do you still?" he wanted to know. There was gentleness in his voice. "Do you still feel like a failure?"

Sandy thought about it. "Actually," she decided with a lift of her shoulders, "I don't think I feel like a failure at all. I feel a little guilty, sometimes, for disappointing them, and sorry I couldn't be what I was supposed to be, but when it comes right down to it, it's still my life and I can't help it because I'm different from the rest of them." But even as she spoke her eyes wandered over his shoulder to the slopes, and the pang of regret that struck her was unexpected. She still hadn't dealt with the worst of it. She wondered what it would be like to live the rest of her life in the afterglow of someone else's dream.

But their lunch arrived then, and all sentimental thoughts were pushed from Sandy's head in the sheer sensual delight of it. There were enough calories, starches and cholesterol on the platters placed before her to give her coach a stroke from nothing more than horror, and Sandy dug in enthusiastically. She even managed, for the space of one meal, to put aside the guilt over wasting food that was the natural result of being raised in a large family, and she sampled both the quiche and the lobster liberally, knowing she couldn't possibly finish both of them and still have room for dessert.

Wes watched her with growing contentment and an unexpected creeping measure of affection. What a funny, complex, wonderfully challenging woman she was. Every thought she had was written in those enormous brown eyes the moment she thought it, but her emotions and moods were gone the very instant he tried to catch them. She was sweet; she was sad; she was brave and she was vulnerable; she was careless and she was strong. She made him feel tender one moment and exasperated the next. She amused him and touched him, and she made him feel close to her even though nothing in her experience related even re-motely to his. He understood her and she baffled him. He was very, very glad she was here.

For almost fifteen minutes she devoted herself entirely to the corporeal delights set before her, and then, pausing for a sip of wine, she inquired unexpectedly, "Why did you ask me to come with you, Adrian?"

"Wes," he corrected automatically.

She shrugged. "Whatever. Why?"

Mirth danced around the edges of his mouth as he lifted his own glass. "Because you cheer me up."

That was not precisely the answer she wanted to hear. Pausing a moment between courses, she touched her nap-kin to her lips, rested her elbow on the table, and propped up her chin with the back of her hand. "Do you have a lot of girlfriends, Adrian—Wes?"

He was too used to her frankness—in fact, to the frank-ness that seemed to come naturally to them—to give much undue thought to the question. "I have a lot of friends," he modified. "No—acquaintances. Some of them are women. Are you asking if I'm promiscuous?"

Her chuckle was a little startled, but she was glad it was out in the open. That was the general nature of what she had been wondering since she had first met him. "I guess so. Are you?"

The corner of his mouth deepened with that hint of a smile again; his eyes showed that he was outrageously de-lighted. "Not really."

She looked surprised. "Why not?"

He attempted to answer that question with all the seri-ousness with which it was asked. It wasn't easy. "First," he decided, "because I think I'm basically monogamous. Sec-ond, sex seems to lose its value when it's in easy supply." He lifted one graceful shoulder. "In short, I don't think I spend any more time chasing and seducing women than any other single man my age—probably a lot less than some. What about you?''

''I spend hardly any time at all chasing and seducing women,'' she responded pertly, and he laughed. Then she asked curiously, dipping her fork into the luscious thermidor sauce, ''Why didn't you ask one of your friends to come with you this weekend?''

Wes did not have to think about that for a moment. ''Because my friends are boring.'' And because, he realized slowly, they all seemed to belong to another era, suspended somehow in the shadows of that thick black line that had been drawn down the middle of his life. It was as though everything that had happened before that telephone call a week ago today was not quite real, not quite a part of him; his friends belonged to the good life and high times—they carried with them an aura of free and careless yesterdays— and Wes was not certain he could relate to that anymore.

Sandy noticed the faint hint of a shadow that had come over his eyes, but she did not think he would thank her for commenting on it. For all his easygoing charm, the pain that was inside him was never far from the surface, and Sandy was not surprised to realize that his quiet vulnerability was one of the reasons—perhaps the main reason—she felt so comfortable around him. She had always had a weakness for creatures in need—a sparrow with a broken wing, a sick puppy, a lost child, even a destitute Santa Claus—and when she looked at Wes she saw not only a gorgeous body, ineffable charm, wealth, style and patrician breeding. She saw a young man who had been terrified at the prospect of being arrested, who had reached out to her when he was uncertain, who was suffering, even now, quietly and unobtrusively. She was drawn to him. It was only natural.

She said now, taking one last bite of the quiche, ''You don't have to feel obligated to keep me entertained this weekend, you know. I mean, if you want to ski or pick up women or just be by yourself, I don't mind."

Wes wished he could be half as generous with her, but he had no intention of doing so. "If I had wanted to be by myself, I would have come alone," he answered. And then he grinned. "Besides, it would be rather difficult to pick up women with any efficacy when you and I happen to be sharing a suite."

Sandy couldn't argue with that, and though she looked hard for some sign of regret in his eyes for the rooming arrangements, she could find none. She found that inexplicably encouraging.

Sandy reluctantly refused the dessert she craved, knowing that if she ate another bite she would be incapable of doing anything but lying on her bed in a stupor the rest of the day. And she had far too much that she wanted to do.

Sandy would not have believed that any other grown-up person besides herself would enjoy an afternoon of doing nothing but walking in the snow, but Wes did. Brightly dressed skiers swooshed to the end of the run or trudged past them, laughing and carrying their skis, but he did not look at them with envy. There were toboggans, snowmobiles and an enclosed ice rink, but for the first few hours they did not look for outside entertainment. They walked; picked up handfuls of snow and scattered them through the air like gold dust; they laughed and they talked.

For Sandy, it was not an unusual experience to enjoy the company of a virtual stranger, to talk with him as though he were an old friend and to feel comfortable doing nothing at all but playing in the snow with him like a child. But for Wes, it was a rare and astonishing gift. It occurred to him once to wonder how he had gotten from the coast of Mexico as one among a crew of bored international playboys to an overrated commercial ski resort in the Poconos with a woman who had never even tasted lobster thermidor, and the concept boggled his mind. Then he tried to imagine where else he would rather be, and with whom, and he could not think of a single place or person. In a strange way, walking with her that afternoon in the snow, he almost thought he was happier than he had ever been in his life.

More than once, he caught her glancing with particular yearning toward the slopes, and occasionally she would be drawn to make some critical comment about this skier's style or that skier's form; then she would quickly look irritated with herself and change the subject. He wondered how it must be for her, to suddenly lose an entire life-style, to now only watch what she once had excelled at.

When he caught that musing, strongly wistful expression in her eyes for one last time, he felt compelled to say gently, "You really miss it, don't you?"

Sandy drew her eyes slowly away from the advanced run and back to him. *Miss it,* she thought somewhat bleakly. How could she not miss what had been so much the center of her life for as long as she could remember? But she was not ready to fully examine the complexities of the loss yet; she wasn't ready to face the final truth just now. Before the weekend was out she would have to, she knew. But not yet.

She smiled, suddenly and brilliantly. "Do you know how to drive one of those snowmobiles?" she demanded.

When she smiled her whole face lit up, and Wes's spirit surged to new life. When she smiled he felt like laughing. Her cheeks were wind-rouged and her lips cherry moist, her eyes as shiny and as clear as the snow surrounding them. A curl escaped from her bright yellow knit cap and was pulled by the wind toward her mouth. Indulgently, he smoothed the curl back with a gloved finger, smiling back at her, and suddenly he wanted more than anything else in the world to kiss that mouth.

That surprised Wes. He hadn't lied to her when he said that sex had nothing to do with this weekend, and desire had not been among the reasons he had asked her to come with him. Sex, like cigarettes, was something Wes could live without for long periods of time without ever missing it, and until this very moment, physical satisfaction had been the last thing on Wes's mind. But she looked so inexpressibly embraceable bundled up in her shiny red parka and bright yellow toboggan cap, her skin glowing and her lips parted, it gave him pleasure simply to imagine kissing her.

But then he wondered how she would react if he made a move on her after promising not to, and he didn't want to take any chances. So he responded instead, with mock hauteur, "Surely you jest! You happen to be talking to one of the top-rated snowmobile drivers in the northeastern United States." He grabbed her mittened hand, snow sparks playing in his eyes. "The only question is, are you ready for it?"

Sandy, at that moment, was ready for anything.

Wes drove the snowmobile with all the recklessness of his jet-setter background, tracing rapid cartwheels and figure eights in the snow, flying over moguls and dodging trees at breakneck speed, and Sandy loved every exhilarating minute. The wind in her face, the white landscape whizzing by, the sound of Wes's laughter and the sun sparkling like laser heat off the helmet of his hair.... It was better than skiing. Much better.

The clouds had grown thicker during the afternoon, the smell of snow was in the air, and dusk came early. The skiers began to trundle in from the slopes around five o'clock, and Wes turned in the snowmobile. They were both pleasantly exhausted and wonderfully exhilarated, and Wes slipped a companionable arm around her waist as they walked back toward the lodge. "What do you want to do now?" he asked.

Sandy didn't hesitate. "Take a bath," she declared, her eyes growing avid at the prospect. "Will you show me how to work the Jacuzzi controls?"

"We've still got the hot tub warming up," Wes reminded her, a glint of mischief playing in his eyes. "It should be just about perfect by now."

"I didn't bring my swimsuit," Sandy replied demurely, but her heart had speeded up just the slightest at his teasing, because for a moment she imagined she saw something far back in his eyes that could have been almost serious. What would he have done if she had said yes?

But whatever she saw in his eyes did not recur when they reached their suite and Wes filled the tub for her. He turned on the Jacuzzi controls and, in a streak of playfulness, dumped a handful of strawberry scented bubble beads into the foaming water. He left her alone without glancing back as a sea-tide of bubbles began to cascade to the top of the huge tub, and she thought she must have imagined that flicker of real desire she had seen before. What would a man like Adrian Wesley want with a woman like her, anyway? Men were friends or brothers to Sandy; they were never lovers.

But, Lord, what a waste, she thought with a soulful sigh as she sank neck-deep into the warm, swirling water. Alone for the weekend in this sensual paradise with a man who looked like something straight out of an erotic fantasy, and all he was interested in was being buddies.

Sex was something else Sandy had never had time—or the opportunity—for before. Throughout her teenage years, constant diligence to her sport had kept her out of the social scene, and throughout her young adulthood her world was so circumscribed unto itself that it rarely occurred to her to wonder what she was missing. By her twenty-first birthday it did dawn on her that no one should be a virgin at her age—somehow it even sounded aesthetically unappealing—but she wasn't often presented with an opportunity to do anything about it. She was training harder than ever before by then, her eyes fixed on an Olympic goal, and, as usual, pleasing herself was the last thing she thought about.

It was after the Games, in that downswing in which she realized that the only goal she had ever cared about—making the team—had been reached and there seemed no place left to go from here, that Sandy began seriously to assess the state of her womanhood. Training wasn't so rigorous that spring, and she began to see a young athlete—also a skier—with whom she had become friendly during the winter's competition. Matters progressed quite nicely, even to the point of Sandy's going on the pill, but before the one-month waiting period that the doctor had insisted upon for complete safety was over, the young man had grown bored and moved on. Sandy could not say she was heartbroken—she had never really liked him all that much—but she was disappointed. She continued taking the pill, however, telling herself that she liked the way it regulated her cycle. But she must have known even then that the time was not far away when she would be ready to change her life in a major way, and she intended to be prepared.

The time was now, and she was prepared, but she was beginning to think she might have made a tactical error in her choice of companions.

Oh, well, she tried to convince herself philosophically, she had made enough drastic moves for one weekend; she couldn't expect to make up for a lifetime of lost chances and missed pleasures in twenty-four hours or less. She had had her first experience with intoxication, she had gone away with a man for the weekend after having known him for less than twelve hours—never mind the arrangements were purely platonic. And here she was in this sinfully fabulous place, all expenses paid, overdosing on luxury in every way she had ever imagined and a few—like the hot tub—that had never even occurred to her before. Even self-indulgence had a limit, and she couldn't expect to have it all at once The world was filled with men, some of them probably even as good-looking as Adrian Wesley, and she had a lifetime to choose a lover.

Still, she couldn't help fantasizing, as she lifted a toeful of bubbles out of the tub and watched the glistening foam cascade down her leg, what would happen if she were to rise up out of the water and, wrapped only in a towel, walk into the parlor to find Wes. Or if she called to him right now, perhaps requesting a glass of wine. Or if she simply got up, wrapped herself loosely in the thick white terry robe that hung on the door, and walked into the parlor, and took his hand and, without a word, led him to the hot tub....

A dreamy smile softened her lips as she closed her eyes, sinking deeper into the water, feeling the massaging jets on her skin and imagining them to be Wes's fingers...an easy, harmless fantasy, because she knew she would no more parade around the suite wrapped only in a towel than she would turn cartwheels naked down the corridors of this hotel. And if he did stroll into this bathroom with a glass of wine she would probably dive for cover under the bubbles and not emerge until she had shrunk into a prune or until he left, whatever came first. She even locked the bathroom door when she was alone in her own apartment, for goodness' sake.

The glass of wine did sound heavenly, though. She wished she had had the foresight to bring one with her.

It was with great reluctance that she pulled herself out of the nirvana of gently pulsing jets and strawberry bubbles forty-five minutes later, and then only because she felt guilty about leaving Wes alone for so long. And because, she realized with a small measure of surprise, she missed the sound of his voice and the quick spark of laughter in his eyes and just watching the grace with which he moved. He *was* fun to be with, and she was growing attached to him already. And it was probably just as well that they weren't going to be lovers, because she hadn't the faintest idea how to begin seducing him, or what she would do if he tried to seduce her.

Besides, she decided happily as she pulled on the fluffy hotel robe and padded to her bedroom—carefully checking to make sure Wes was not in the hallway before she did so—she had everything she could possibly ask for, and more. She wasn't going to spoil the best time in her life by worrying about things she couldn't have—and probably didn't even want.

Chapter Seven

Sandy was not the type of woman who could go to Wes wrapped only in a towel, or call him into the bathroom while she was naked in the tub, but she hardly thought about it twice before pulling on the sexiest garment she owned—in fact, the only sexy garment she owned—a clingy, shiny soft hostess gown of burnished gold.

Linda, who was constantly trying to improve Sandy's wardrobe, had given the dress to her two Christmases ago. Sandy, who never entertained at home and whose idea of lounging clothes ran more toward footed pajamas and her brothers' discarded T-shirts than satiny lingerie, had never worn it. She wasn't even certain why she had packed it, except that she was saving it for a festive occasion, and this was about as festive an occasion as she was ever likely to have.

And she loved the sensuous feel of the material against her strawberry scented skin, the way the color brought out flecks of gold in her eyes and highlighted her skin with amber. The gown was full-cut, dropping from a high neckline to her ankles, with long, flowing sleeves and no trim whatsoever. The cut was not daring, and in fact in the box it had looked quite modest and even plain. But the slinky material somehow wrapped itself to her breasts like a second skin, outlining the full curves and even, if one looked hard enough—which Sandy did not—the shape of her nipples. The roomy garment gave the illusion of fullness as it drifted in tantalizing lines toward the floor, but in fact it molded itself to her shape, sketching her hips and the slight curve of her stomach and the length of her thighs. When she moved, every curve and dip was perfectly displayed through a gleaming shadow of gold. She felt wonderful in it—soft and feminine and gloriously self-indulgent, as only befitted a woman who, for this weekend at least, was living in the lap of luxury.

For a moment she even considered enhancing the effect with makeup and perfume, but she thought that might be going a bit too far. She so rarely wore makeup that what was in her cosmetic case was probably dried and caked by now, and besides, she would only have to wash it all off before she went to bed. And it wasn't as though she was really trying to impress anyone.

It was fortunate she wasn't trying to impress anyone, for when she went back out into the parlor Wes was lying on the sofa, several cushions propped up behind his head, and at first glance she thought he was asleep. *Miracle on Thirty-fourth Street* was flickering from the bookcase-enclosed television set, and a fire was lapping at the logs in the fireplace. Darkness had fallen outside with silvery luminescence, and the room was lit by yellow shadows and brights and darks from the television. Sandy went first to draw the curtains, then she moved quietly to turn off the television set so that Wes might nap undisturbed.

He made a sound and a movement of protest the minute her hand touched the control. Sandy turned, startled. "Sorry. I thought you were asleep."

He mumbled something incoherent and his heavily lidded eyes never moved from the screen. Sandy shrugged and left the set alone.

She settled down in a wing chair by the fireplace and for a time tried to watch the movie. But the classic Christmas tale was the last thing she wanted to see; it reminded her far too clearly of her least favorite season of the year and all that awaited her when she got back home. She turned and watched the romantic dance of the fireplace, but it was no fun sitting before a hearth fire alone. She turned on a small lamp for additional light, and Wes did not seem to object, or even notice. She wandered around the room for a while, trying to gauge how much longer the sappy movie could possibly last, and she was at a complete loss for distraction until she happened upon the room-service menu. She pounced upon it avidly.

She waited until a commerical, then asked eagerly, "Adrian—"

"Wes," he corrected automatically.

"Could we have room service tonight?"

He didn't break his fascinated absorption with a bathroom cleaner commercial. "Sure."

"Great!" She scanned the menu with greedy eyes. "What do you want?"

"Whatever." It was hardly a mumble.

"Oh, look—filet mignon. With béarnaise sauce and twice-baked potatoes—"

"Sure."

"Do you think..." She looked at him hesitantly. "Could we have champagne?"

The movie was coming back on. "Hmm."

But champagne at God-only-knew what prices was not a decision Sandy could make without his approval. She tried once more to get his attention. "Adrian—"

"Wes."

"Whatever. The champagne—what kind?"

"Hmmmhmmmhmmm." It was a fair imitation of "I don't know. You choose."

For the next fifteen minutes Sandy was kept marvelously busy making her selections. She phoned in the order and waited until the next commercial to inform him, "I ordered dessert for you. Black Forest torte. And shrimp cocktail to start."

He did not look around. "Sounds great."

Sandy found a crossword puzzle in the back of a magazine entitled Sights and Sounds of the Poconos, and it kept her busy until the food arrived. The waiter set the table before the window with white linen and candles in silver holders, unwrapped the shrimp cocktails, opened the champagne and asked if she preferred to leave the main courses and the rolls in the warming oven, and through the entire process Wes did not stir once. It was amazing. Either he was very tired, or he had led such a deprived childhood he had never seen the old movie that Sandy could have sworn every man, woman and child in America had seen at least half a dozen times. She signed the check, adding a generous tip, and had resigned herself to enjoying this sumptuous feast alone when the credits began to roll. Taking an enormous chance, she went quickly to the television set and flicked it off.

Wes sat up slowly, his eyes gradually focusing on his surroundings. His hair was rumpled, his eyes soft and sleepy-looking as he became slowly aware, and Sandy thought no one had ever looked more huggable. "Sandy," he said in some surprise. Then, noticing the table, "You ordered room service! Great idea. What are we having?"

Sandy stared at him.

He got to his feet with enthusiasm and went to inspect the warming cart. "Filet—marvellous. But champagne? No, we can't have that; it'll spoil the taste of your meat." He went to get the Bordeaux. "We'll save it for dessert."

Still Sandy only stared at him. "Adrian—"

"Wes."

"Where have you *been*?"

He turned, looking somewhat abashed. "I'm sorry—I should have warned you. Television puts me in a trance. You'll have to keep me away from it if you have any intention at all of carrying on a semicoherent conversation with me this weekend." He thought about this for a moment as he filled two glasses with the rich red liquid, and then qualified his statement. "Except for morning cartoons. I don't like to miss those."

He turned very politely to hand her glass to her. Sandy accepted it, still staring at him, and then she burst into astonished laughter. "Does mental illness run in your family?" she demanded.

He inclined his head to her regally, but the shared delight of her laughter was sparkling in his eyes. "We all have our little quirks, my dear."

He placed his hand lightly on her back and escorted her, still chuckling, to the candle-lit table. The remnants of television stupor had long since evaporated, and he couldn't help but notice how that incredibly sensuous dress clung to her hips and shaped her legs when she walked. He held her chair for her and the sweet scent of strawberries wafted over him as she was seated. He resisted an unexpected urge to touch the place where one shiny-silky curl nestled against her neck, to smooth it back or test its springiness. How long, he wondered, had she been in the room before he noticed, and how could he not have noticed?

On an impulse, he turned off the lamp before he sat down and the room was lit only by candlelight and the wavering glow of the fire. Her eyes looked like diamonds, and her skin took on a tinted alabaster hue that was arresting to the eye. Hadn't she told him only this afternoon that she wanted to be beautiful?

Wes lifted his glass to her, his eyes crinkling with a smile. "You missed a great movie," he told her, "but it was worth it. You look marvellous."

Sandy had never learned to accept a compliment gracefully, so she passed on the last comment and picked up on the first. *"Miracle on Thirty-fourth Street?"* She made a face. "No, thanks."

Wes chuckled as she picked up her shrimp fork and attacked the cocktail with enthusiasm, and he opened his napkin into his lap. "You really have it in for Christmas, don't you? What, exactly, is it that you have against the season of Peace on Earth, Goodwill Toward Men?"

"Do you mean the season in which crime doubles and suicide increases by twenty percent and all the fat bankers get fatter?" She shrugged. "Not a thing."

"Scrooge."

"I've been called worse."

"So tell me, little girl…" Wes assumed his best sage, psychoanalytical tone, leaning back with his finger laid thoughtfully against his cheek. "When did you first stop believing in Santa Claus?"

A half-amused, half-cynical smile played over Sandy's lips as she considered the question. There was another unbreakable rule in Sandy's family—no one was ever allowed to express to anyone even the remotest hint of an opinion that there might not be a Santa Claus. The penalty for such a transgression had never been spelled out, but imagining what it might be had kept six mischievous and daring children on the straight and narrow for all their childhood, adolescence and even adulthood. No one had ever told Sandy there was no Santa Claus.

But cynicism was something that must have been born into Sandy, for by the time she was six she had become convinced there was a conspiracy surrounding the entire Christmas scenario designed specifically to prevent Sandy's getting in on the joke. But her own suspicions could not stand up to her family's adamant convictions and persuasive logic regarding the little man in the red suit.

And then, on the summer of her seventh birthday, she came upon a method by which to prove or disprove her own theory—that Santa Claus was and always had been nothing more than a figment of her family's imagination. On a family vacation to Florida Sandy spotted in one of those tourist-trap souvenir shops what was to her young mind the most beautiful objet d'art ever created. It was a replica of a half-open oyster shell, painted to look like mother-of-pearl and studded with colorful glass gems and bits of rhinestone. Inside the shell, against a background of red velveteen, were two garishly glittering sea horses, one royal blue and one emerald green, poised as though in the midst of a dance. The whole sat on a base with the scrolled inscription "Florida" across the front. It was without a doubt the tackiest, most tastelessly designed artifact in the shop, and Sandy had never wanted anything as much in her life.

She begged her parents, to no avail; she even tried to cajole Bill, who would do almost anything for her, out of the five dollars Aunt Emily had sent him for his birthday. But there was a limit to even Bill's generosity, and Sandy left the state of Florida disconsolate and without her sea-horse souvenir.

But there was still Santa Claus.

Slowly Sandy began to devise the plan that would prove once and for all whether or not Santa Claus did exist. There was only one item on her Christmas list that year, which she addressed to "Santa Claus, North Pole," and placed in the mailbox on the corner by herself. She told no one else of her secret longing, and from Halloween to Christmas Eve she thought of nothing else. If there was a Santa Claus, he could fly to Florida and bring back the sea horses for her. If Santa was only a joke, she would get dolls and tea sets and a new

1. How do you rate _____

   (PLEASE PRINT BOOK TITLE)

   1.6 ☐ excellent   .4 ☐ good   .2 ☐ not so good
   .5 ☐ very good   .3 ☐ fair   .1 ☐ poor

2. Have you ever read a Harlequin book before?

   2.1 ☐ Yes   .2 ☐ no

3. If yes, have you purchased a new Harlequin:

   3.1 ☐ within the past 3 months   .3 ☐ more than 1 year ago
   .2 ☐ 3 months to 1 year ago

4. Please indicate how many romance paperbacks you read each month:

   4.1 ☐ 1 to 4   .2 ☐ 5 to 10   .3 ☐ 11 to 15   .4 ☐ more than 15

5. How would you compare this book to similar books that you usually read?

   5.1 ☐ far better than others   .4 ☐ not as good
   .2 ☐ better than others   .5 ☐ definitely not as good
   .3 ☐ about the same

6. If you have *not* read a Harlequin before, was it because:

   .6 ☐ not interested in romance   .10 ☐ too predictable
   .7 ☐ price   .11 ☐ unrealistic story/characters
   .8 ☐ not sexy enough   .12 ☐ too sexy
   .9 ☐ stories too simplistic   .13 ☐ not long enough

7. Would you recommend this book to a friend?

   14.1 ☐ definitely would   .3 ☐ probably would not
   .2 ☐ probably would   .4 ☐ definitely would not

   Why? _____

8. How likely are you to purchase another book in this series?

   15.1 ☐ definitely would   .3 ☐ probably would not
   .2 ☐ probably would   .4 ☐ definitely would not

9. Please indicate your sex and age group:

   16.1 ☐ female   17.1 ☐ under 15   .3 ☐ 25-34   .5 ☐ 50-64
   .2 ☐ male   .2 ☐ 15-24   .4 ☐ 35-49   .6 ☐ 65 or older

10. Have you any additional comments about this book?

    _____
    _____
    _____

Thank you for completing and returning this questionnaire.

 SA1

NAME _____

(Please Print)

ADDRESS _____

CITY _____

ZIP CODE _____

BUSINESS REPLY MAIL

FIRST CLASS   PERMIT NO. 70   TEMPE, AZ.

POSTAGE WILL BE PAID BY ADDRESSEE

NATIONAL READER SURVEYS

2504 West Southern Avenue
Tempe, AZ   85282

ski parka. She hoped with all her might that there was indeed a Santa Claus.

But there was no rhinestone-studded oyster shell with sea horses in it under the Christmas tree.

Sandy smiled a little, half in amused reminiscence, half in wry assessment of the suspicious little character she had been even at age seven. She had no intention of telling that story to Wes. She had never told anyone that story; it was entirely too sentimental.

So she merely replied, spearing a delicate shrimp, "When did you?"

His eyes twinkled. "Maybe I never did."

"Believe, or stop believing?"

He thought briefly. "Both, maybe. I can't remember anyone ever making a big deal about it. Christmas was always just Christmas, and it didn't matter whether the presents came from a fat man in red flannel or my dad...." And he grinned. "As long as there were plenty of presents."

Sandy laughed. "Same here." Then her face fell. "Which only reminds me I haven't even started my shopping yet, and I've got a list a mile long. Let's talk about something else."

Wes was happy to oblige. "You look very sexy tonight."

A startled pulse quickened in her throat, and when she looked at him his eyes were so soft and warm that her skin began to tingle. But she gave a light, rather nervous laugh, and she returned, "As opposed to looking like an overworked elf? Thanks!"

The warmth in his eyes only deepened, though now it was tinged with a sparkle of amusement. "Even overworked elves have a certain appeal when the—ah—circumstances are right."

She managed to keep her tone teasing even though that warm flush that was creeping over her body made her feel like melting—and all from only the sound of his voice, the look in his eyes. "The right circumstances being candle-light, firelight and wine?"

Wes's eyes moved sweepingly yet assessively over her face, the curve of her neck, and seemed to linger for a moment on the shape of her breasts before returning to her face. The glow that was in his eyes this time she did not recognize, but it made her heart do a funny little flutter. "That, too," he agreed—and Sandy did not know how to respond to that.

Wes had not intended to flirt with her, but he found he couldn't help it. And Sandy didn't seem to mind. He liked the surprise in her eyes when he said flattering things to her, and he wondered whether it was possible no man had ever told her she was a desirable woman before. The faint hint of a blush he thought he saw in her cheeks warmed him all over, and he wanted to see it again and again. And slowly, through the duration of the meal, Wes became aware of what Sandy had sensed upon their first meeting—a very definite spark of sexual chemistry.

But beyond that there was, as there had always been, the simple joy of being in her company. Everything she did was so natural and easy, completely without artifice; she made him laugh and she made him think and she captured his attention completely and continuously, which was not a usual thing for Wes to experience. Repeatedly his mind wandered back over the events of the past thirty-six hours, and the realization of how unexpectedly his life had turned amazed him. What had been the blackest moment of his life now seemed the clearest; what had started out to be a dreary exile in a place he didn't want to be with nothing but time on his hands and nothing but bleakness in his soul now seemed like the most fortunate thing that had ever happened to him. And for the first time in his life, the future seemed exciting.

Sandy devoured her meal with a vigor that would have made her Saxon forebears proud, but only as a prelude to the seven-layer torte and its accompaniment of champagne. This she savored slowly, with a transported look in her eyes, alternating the rich and gooey dessert with delicate sips of wine. Occasionally she would utter a deep and throaty moan or, with a guileless sensuality, run the tip of her tongue around her lips or lick a bit of whipped cream from her fork, and when she did that Wes could feel a thickening of his blood, a heaviness in his pulses, and the hint of erotic images that were beginning to form in the back of his mind were maddeningly tantalizing.

He couldn't finish his own dessert. He sat back and watched her, lighting a cigarette, trying to remember that he had invited her here for purely platonic purposes. "I know it's none of my business," he said after a moment, and the undertone of laughter in his voice was purely to disguise the huskiness that had crept into his vocal cords—and from nothing more than watching her. "But doesn't anyone ever feed you?"

Sandy slid the last forkful of whipped cream, chocolate and cherries into her mouth, then laid the fork upon her plate with a look of soulful regret. "Protein," she answered him with a sigh. "Only protein, for the past fifteen years of my life." And then she looked at him, her eyes widening with the realization. "Fifteen years. What a waste. But," she decided with a sudden brilliant flash of a smile, "no more!" She picked up her champagne glass and left the table, her arms stretched out grandly before her. "From now on, it's eat, drink and be merry." The satiny-shiny gold skirts billowed around her as she twirled once in the center of the room, catching the firelight, playing with the shape of her legs and snatching at her smooth white ankles before settling. "I've got fifteen years to make up for!"

She sank down before the fireplace, the folds of material puffing and shimmering romantically before settling themselves, once again, snug around her body. "But do you have to do it all in one weekend?" suggested Wes, rising. He

brought the champagne bottle from the ice bucket and refilled her glass, knowing he probably shouldn't. "You're not
going to get drunk again, are you?"

She smiled at him impishly as he settled his long body,
with all the grace of a floating feather, on the floor beside
her. "I might," she challenged him. "Would you get mad?"

"Dogs get mad. I would get—annoyed." But his eyes did
not look the least bit annoyed. His eyes looked delighted.

"Why?" She sipped the champagne, trying not to pay too
much unnecessary attention to the way his lean, corduroy-
covered thigh, so very close to hers, melded into his torso,
or the way his long fingers held his own glass with such
careless grace, his wrist bent loosely atop an upraised
knee...or the way the firelight danced in his hair like jewels
or the way his eyes smiled at her. It was his presence, she
realized dimly, that was the intoxicant, not the champagne.

"Oh, well," he tossed off with studied nonchalance, "it's
very bad taste, for one thing, public drunkenness—"

"Private drunkenness." She lifted her glass to him, and
he inclined an eyebrow in acknowledgment.

"And for another," he finished mildly, "it begins to make
one wonder why you feel it necessary to be intoxicated every
time you're alone with me."

"Sheer coincidence," she scoffed, but she had to quickly
and rather nervously look away because the way he said
that—so smoothly, so urbanely—made her wonder if he
were not suggesting she might have cause for artificial for-
tification if she remained alone with him too much longer.

But that was silly. She relaxed as she looked into the fire
and took another sip of her champagne. Adrian Wesley
wasn't interested in her. He was just being nice, doing all the
proper things that were required of him when a woman got
all dressed up and served him filet and champagne by candlelight—flirting, flattering, being just the least bit sugges-
tive. Making her feel wanted. She liked him for that. A lot.

She stretched around for the cushion of the wing chair, dragging it down onto the floor and lounging back against it. She also liked the fact that she *could* feel relaxed with Adrian; that she didn't have to spend too much time wondering what he was thinking. She said, propping her head up comfortably against the cushion and resting the champagne glass on her stomach, "All right—I won't get drunk. Not even a little tipsy. What do you want to do tonight? Watch television?"

He laughed, tossing his cigarette into the fireplace. "Not on your life. You might wander off and forget to feed me, and no one would find my body until the spring thaw."

"Play Monopoly?"

He stretched out beside her, propped up on one elbow. His face seemed very close to hers. "I'm a rotten Monopoly player," he confessed. "I spend all my money in the first round. Would you like to go dancing? There's live entertainment in the club."

Sandy felt so replete and relaxed that she really didn't want to stir from this room, and her reluctance showed in her eyes as she asked politely, "Would you?"

"No." He could go dancing anytime, with any woman. But it wasn't every night that he had a chance to just be alone and do nothing with a woman like Sandy.

Sandy thought he had sensed her reluctance and was just trying to be polite, so she suggested, a little halfheartedly, "We could always just go down and listen to the band, if you like."

"Or," he suggested, perfectly innocent, "we could try out that hot tub."

Sandy subdued the corners of a prim smile as she looked into her champagne glass. "I wonder," she mused, "if I called room service, whether they would send up a swimsuit."

Wes laughed. It was a soft sound, low and delicious and endless; it felt good inside him and it danced in his eyes. He couldn't resist reaching out one long hand to ruffle her feather-soft curls. "Sandy, I've had more fun with you than I have ever had with anyone in my life. Would you mind very much if I kissed you?"

Her breath caught as she turned her head to look at him, hardly believing she had heard correctly. In that instant, before the promise had even been registered, the actuality was upon her—his lips touched hers.

It was a delicate invasion of all her senses, soft and gentle and sweet, so sweet. His scent filled her like all things fresh and wonderful, a warmth began with his touch and spread throughout her, rising in her cheeks and tingling in her breasts, shooting like a low hum of electricity through her veins and even into her fingertips. His fingers spread along the plane of her face and then downward only a fraction, teasing the neckline of her dress. One of Sandy's hands clenched convulsively around the glass she was holding while the other, of its own volition, crept around his neck and gathered a handful of his hair, as thick and luxurious as gold between her fingers. Her heart sped and a glorious melting feeling overcame her. The crackle of the fire and the yellow-gold shadows behind her closed eyes faded away, and she was nothing more than a collection of sensory receptors and glorious feelings as Adrian Wesley kissed her.

When she opened her eyes he was smiling down at her, very close, very tenderly. She could have drowned in the warmth of his eyes. Her breathing was shallow and her heart was vainly trying to seek its normal rhythm, but nothing about her was normal. Every nerve fiber in her body still sang with newfound awareness, her blood was a heavy gush of warmth through her veins and in all the world there was nothing but the deep, deep blue of Adrian Wesley's eyes and the warmth of a smile that lingered there.

His fingers were still upon her face, playing with her hair near her temple, stroking the curve of her jaw near her ear. His lips curved in an indulgent, affectionate smile as he said softly, "Well? Did you mind?"

She was hardly aware that it was her own voice answering as she whispered, searching his face, "Not terribly much. Maybe—we could do it again, just to be sure."

In a single fluid motion he removed the glass from her hand and deposited it on the hearth. His face hovered over her and his smiling lips touched hers once, briefly, and again, soft delicate fingertips teasing the corners of her mouth, coaxing it to open.

And then, in a breathless liquid rush of shock, she felt the rich, warm invasion of his tongue. Sandy had thought she had reached her peak of sensual awareness with his first kiss, but in comparison to this sudden overwhelming rush of sensation what had gone before was child's play. His first kiss had been sweet, gentle, almost modest in its experimental, tenderly affectionate nature. This was a passion for which Sandy was prepared in neither mind nor body, and she wondered, in a brief rational moment before she lost herself completely to it, whether Wes himself had even expected it.

He tasted of wine and far beneath the surface a hint of cigarette smoke and chocolate. Sweet and sharp, strong and soft. Shyly, almost experimentally, she let her tongue discover the moist texture of his, and then she felt his breath and the tightening of his muscles and her arms wound around him helplessly, instinct taking over the deep thrusting mating of their tongues and their mouths. His hand slid down the length of her body, smoothly, gliding by excruciating inches, satin touch against satin fabric, tingling against her skin until it burned. His fingers rested against her hip and then curved beneath her, lifting her a little, turning her into him. She felt the strength of his thigh pressed against her and the beat of his heart heavy on her tender breast, and his fingers, hard and strong, tightening around the curve of her buttock. Power bloomed within her and left her weak, an aching rush of heat that swelled in her breasts and tightened between her legs, a dizzy mindless concentration upon nothing except the taste of him and the scent of him and the sensation of him as they were joined together, one part of his body filling hers and giving her such pleasure....

His hand moved around and rested upon her abdomen, long fingers gently massaging the small curve of her stomach, accentuating the ache that was building there. His lips left hers briefly and she could feel his breath, hot and stinging, as his tongue swept around the shape of her mouth, as he dropped a light kiss upon her cheek and the corner of her nose and then her lips again. And then the hot, damp and slightly coarse texture of the lower part of his face as he nuzzled her neck; the wonderful scent of evergreen that drifted from his hair, and the weight of his head, firm but not heavy, upon her chest.

Wes had to stop. It was moving too fast; faster than anything had ever moved him before, and he had had no intention of beginning it in the first place. His head was roaring and his pulses were hammering; the tight, aching urgency of his desire was enormous and all-encompassing. He wanted to lose himself in her, to feel her engulfing him and surrounding him, to hear her small cries of pleasure and see the look of rapture fill her star-bright eyes and transport her, and him, into mindless ecstasy.... He wanted her, every part of her, with a swift and sudden intensity that was unlike anything he had ever known before.

But he didn't want her to think he was using her, quickly and mindlessly, for physical satisfaction and nothing else. Sandy was much too important to him for that. He wanted her to know that it was her, all of her, to whom he wanted to make love, and that he wanted to *make love*, not simply to possess.

And that was an uncommon feeling for Wes. He had enjoyed many women, he had given them pleasure and he had taken pleasure from them, and when it was over both their lives were a little richer for it. But—and it was difficult to explain, even to himself—he had never *known* any of those women. He had never been close to them in anything other than the physical sense. Sex was simply something men and women did together; it sometimes seemed like the only thing men and women did together. It was accepted, it was unquestioned, it just happened. But he felt close to Sandy; he had known her as a person before he knew her as a woman, and sex with her would be more than simply a way to pass an evening. It would be special, very special, and he wanted to savor every minute of it.

Sandy's fingers threaded slowly through his hair and she was trembling, all over, mostly from the incredibly powerful pulse of her heart. Her breaths were short and shallow and she felt feverish, alive, pulsing with sensation. She could feel the ache for him, in her breasts, deep within the core of her abdomen, spreading with a tight flare of need to specific, aching points below, and it was a confusing discomfort for which she knew no cure except to bring him closer, to press herself into him and to take his mouth again.

But Sandy was not quite bold enough to do that, and in half fear that whatever she might do to assuage her need would only increase it, she lay quiescent against him, her fingers stroking his hair, trying very hard to breathe normally and to regain control of her runaway heart.

Wes slipped one arm beneath her, drawing her head onto his shoulder; the other hand came up to encircle her waist and shift her weight as he curved one leg around her ankles, drawing her close to him, nestled into him at all points. It was wonderfully cozy, delightfully snug, and Sandy gloried in it, relaxing in the sensation of being completely wrapped in him. For a long time they remained that way, until the steady rise of his chest did not seem quite so labored anymore, and the pace of his heart beneath Sandy's open hand was slowed and quieted; until the heat that seared her own body receded into a warm glow and she felt as though she had never known a time when she had not been like this, safe and secure in Adrian Wesley's arms.

And then his head dipped, and she could feel the gentle brush of his lips atop her hair. There was a smile in his voice as he said softly, "Do you know, Sandy Garret, you couldn't have picked a better time to come into my life."

The sound that came from deep in her throat was like a chuckle, only richer, and more pleasure-filled and deep with contentment. She felt wonderful with him. She had never imagined it could be this good with a man. "Just in time to save you from a life of crime, hmm?"

His smile drifted into something more thoughtful. "I was more frightened than I've ever been in my life," he confessed, and though he would not, in other circumstances, have ever been able to imagine himself saying something like that out loud, or even thinking it, with her the truth seemed only natural. "And when I saw you come in the door at that police station, it was like—" he released a soft breath, trying to find the words "—waking up from a bad nightmare. Knowing everything was going to be all right. It was the best thing I had ever felt in my life. Relief." It was a lot like he felt now, holding her. As though everything was going to be all right. It was the best thing he had ever felt in his life.

Sandy reached up and found his hand, which was encircling her shoulder. She linked her fingers through his, and his immediate tightening reciprocation was wonderfully warm. "Adrian," she said thoughtfully, and Wes did not correct her this time. Somehow even the hated name sounded beautiful when she spoke it. "Why didn't you tell them who you were, when they arrested you?"

He sounded puzzled. "I told them my name."

"No, I mean who you *were*. Adrian Wesley of the Philadelphia Wesleys. They surely would have gotten the whole thing straightened out sooner if they had known who they were dealing with."

There was a brief, uncertain pause. Then Wes responded with all the innocent conceit of a man whose letter of credit is welcomed in twenty-seven countries and whose monogrammed luggage is recognized by every concierge of any repute in hotels around the world, "I assumed they did know. It never occurred to me that they wouldn't."

Sandy laughed, the softness of it shaking against his hand, the loveliness of it filling his senses. She twisted her head to look up at him, her eyes dancing with the reflection of the fire and a thousand inner lights. "You are impossible, do you know that? A great big, overgrown child."

"Oh, yes?" His fingers, still entwined with hers, lifted to trace a tantalizing pattern along the line of her jaw. "If I'm so impossible, why did you bother to rescue me? And why did you agree to go away with me for the weekend?"

"Easy." Sandy snuggled back into the curve of his shoulder, relaxed and content. "Because you're gorgeous. I told you that already."

"Is that all?" he teased. "Are you sure it wasn't my incisive wit or my radiant personality or my astonishing intellect?"

Sandy glanced at him skeptically. "Summa cum laude, I presume."

He looked offended. "But of course." And then he relented, confessing, "Well, I could have been, if I had ever mastered the theory of rational numbers."

She chuckled, and he loved it.

"I'm not, you know," he said after a moment.

Wes's hand had left her waist and had come to rest in a more comfortable position, just beneath the curve of her breast. Sandy's attention was so concentrated upon the position of his hand, and the possibilities it evoked, that she almost missed what he was saying. "Not what?"

"Gorgeous. Look at me." He moved his hand to grasp her chin lightly between thumb and forefinger, turning her eyes to his face. His smile was indulgent, a little amused. "My nose is too long. My face is too thin and my ears are all wrong. I'm much too thin, and too tall for my weight. You only see gorgeous because you want to see it."

Chemistry, thought Sandy hazily, but she hardly thought anything at all because she had become lost in the slow, lazy deepening of his eyes as he looked at her, the barely discernible throb of passion that was building again and drawing her in. "There's nothing wrong with your ears," she whispered, and lifted her hand, beneath his hair, to trace the shape of his ear, lifting her face to him as he moved closer.

He kissed her, gently, tenderly, taking her lips between his and clasping them, releasing them, then again, a light and restrained foreplay to what was to come. And then, very carefully, he slipped both arms around her, gathered her close. His breath swept across her face and warmed her neck. "Sandy," he whispered. "I want to make love to you. Let's go in the other room."

Sandy registered nothing more than the sudden lurching of her heart, a catch of breath, a heat that swept through her and could have been a preface to excitement, anticipation, or even fear. But Wes, tuned to her every mood so carefully, sensed something more—enough to make him draw away a little and look into her eyes, searching for an answer and finding only another question there.

Immediately contrition filled him, and it was almost enough to make him abandon his persuasion. His hand moved to the side of her face, comforting and tender, one long forefinger gently stroking the corner of her eye as though with it he could smooth away the doubt, and even the hint of fear, that was so eloquent in those large brown eyes. He said softly, "Sandy, I'm sorry. I know I told you that this was not why I asked you here, and it wasn't. I don't want you to think—"

"It's not that," she said quickly, breathlessly. "I want you, too, Adrian, you must know that and I was hoping..." Then she had to lower her eyes, suddenly shy. The next was almost a whisper. "It's just that I—well, I've never been with a man before."

Everything within Wes went very still. He had no cause to disbelieve her, but he wanted to disbelieve her. And in the next moment he realized how irrational that was and he felt like a cad. He should have known. Something about her guilelessness, her total lack of artifice, her quick and unquestioning acceptance of life and of him, little hints of shyness, a shade of uncertainty, the surprise when he first kissed her, those huge eyes, innocent and trusting despite her claims to cynicism.... Everything about her should have told him. Now, he didn't know what to do.

Sandy sensed his withdrawal, and everything within her tightened in mental reprobation. *Stupid,* she cursed herself. *Stupid, stupid... What a thing to say to a man. Take me, I'm yours...but be careful because I'm a virgin.* Just what a freewheeling bon vivant like Adrian Wesley needed to hear. *Great going, Sandy. Keep it up and you'll be the oldest living virgin in history.* She felt like a fool.

Adrian saw the creeping color in her cheeks that had nothing to do with arousal, and he knew the confession had embarrassed her. His hesitation had probably hurt her. He did not want to hurt her, but Adrian had never been in a situation like this and it required some thought.

Sandy glanced up at him, forcing a stiff little smile. "Well, you've got to give me credit. I do know how to break a mood." But what was she supposed to do, she thought in some irritation. He would have found out sooner or later. She started to disengage herself from his light embrace, just wanting to be away from him and alone with her own misery. "Now, if you'll excuse me..."

Wes did not believe he had ever handled a moment so badly in his entire life. All he could seem to do was stare at her, watching her go from embarrassed to wretched to angry, doing nothing to make it easier for her, not even knowing what he wanted to do. It wasn't until she started to get to her feet that he collected himself enough to say, "Sandy, wait—"

He was holding her arms lightly, and she caught his wrists, trying to push him away. Surprisingly, he didn't let her go. She looked up at him, dark eyes wide with a conflict of hurt and embarrassment, anger with herself, nervousness and, trying to disguise it all, a measure of brave nonchalance. "Look, I understand." She tried to keep her voice normal, but the tightness came through. "You're used to women with more experience. No problem. Let's just forget it, okay?"

"No, let's not." The words surprised him, but that was the only natural thing to say. He had no intention of forgetting it—or her. All he wanted to do was get that awful look of self-conscious apology out of her eyes, for knowing he had put it there made it even worse. He managed a smile, touched her chin in a light, teasing gesture. "You startled me, that's all. Don't look so serious. It's not a social disease, you know."

It was the right thing to say, or at least close. It drew a tight, nervous little laugh from her, even though she lowered her eyes, and her arms felt a little stiff beneath his hands.

Wes released a breath, of relief or else an expression of unknown deeper emotion, and in an easy motion, he turned her around within his embrace, drawing her between his knees with her back pressed against his chest, his arms loosely encircling her waist, his head resting lightly atop her hair. He could not let her go away now, feeling hurt and rejected, especially since the last thing he intended to do was reject her. But neither was he going to sweep her into bed. For the time being, he thought it best if he just held her. He said, after a moment, "I think we need to talk about this."

Cautiously, Sandy relaxed against him. Talk. What an incredible man he was. Who else would have shown such gentleness, such care, such thoughtful consideration for a woman who, only moments ago, was a heartbeat away from his bed and who, with a few clumsy words, had shattered the moment irreparably? She was glad, in a way she had never thought she would be glad, that it was Adrian Wesley who had wanted to make love to her.

But having made the statement, he did not seem exactly certain how to continue the conversation. After a moment, Sandy cleared her throat, brought her hands to rest lightly upon his wrists, and ventured, half glancing at him, "If it's that you think I might get pregnant, I won't. I wouldn't have tricked you like that. I would have told you."

That possibility hadn't crossed Wes's mind, which only proved how completely ill-equipped he was to deal with a woman like Sandy and her very special needs. But something else she said struck a chord. It was the word "tricked."

Wes had not lived twenty-seven years without becoming aware of the nature of his persuasive charms. He was experienced, he was skillful; he knew how to sway the female heart and the female body to whatever his desires dictated. It was a power he had never questioned before, nor even thought much about at all, but now it seemed like a burdensome thing. He was not consciously aware of using any of those subtle tricks on Sandy, but perhaps subconsciously he had. From the first moment she had been special to him, not to be used and discarded or enjoyed and forgotten, and now she was even more so. He didn't want to ensnare her with wily games and subtle charm. She was too important to him for that.

"Sandy," he said, choosing his words carefully, "you should think about what you're doing. This is a big step."

She uttered a small, tight sound of derision, which was probably overlaid with nervousness, and she seemed to stiffen in his arms. He knew just how to touch her, just what to whisper, to make her relax again, but he didn't. He simply held her, and let her feel what she would feel honestly. "That's an outdated attitude, Wesley. You sound like my mother."

He smiled, slowly, against her hair. "Please. I'd rather not hear about your mother under the circumstances. I feel guilty enough as it is."

She turned then, and looked in some surprise into his face. "Guilty? Why?"

The corners of Wes's smile tightened, and the gesture was a mixture of helplessness, exasperation, and not a small measure of frustration. "Ah, Sandy, I don't know." His hand came up, his fingers threading tenderly through the rich luxury of her firelit curls. "Because you are so lovely and so vulnerable and when I look at you I want you so badly that it hurts. Because I know that you want me, too, but I'm not sure why." His hand moved down, stroking her face; his eyes were full and dark and as vast as the sky. "The first time should be very, very special for you," he said softly. "It shouldn't be taken lightly or gone into carelessly, and you should be very sure this is what you want—on all levels, not just the physical one." Because, he knew slowly, to become the lover of this unique and very precious woman—her first lover—would be an enormous responsibility. And because he wasn't sure he was capable of accepting it. "Because," he finished simply, "I'm afraid that you might regret it later, or that you might hate me in the morning, and I don't think I could bear that."

Sandy turned in his arms, resting her head once more against his shoulder, letting the soberness of his words sink in. What an exceptional man he was. And how very right. How could she be sure what she wanted when it had all come upon her so quickly, this whirlwind of luxury and freedom, this hunger for life and everything it had to offer. If she went to bed with Wes now, under the powerful spell of passion he evoked so expertly and which was all so new and confusing to her, she might regret it in the morning. She hardly knew him, after all. She hardly knew herself.

She had a lot of decisions to make, and an entire past to face, before she could know with any degree of accuracy what she really wanted. Wes had a right to have her come to him with certainty and honesty, with nothing held back and nothing unresolved.

She smiled a little, somewhat sadly. "It's not as simple as wanting and taking when there are real people involved, is it?"

"No." Wes had never realized that before. "I suppose it's not."

His arms tightened around her in a brief, reassuring squeeze, and he brushed her hair lightly with a kiss. "It's just that you've made a lot of impulsive decisions the past few days, I think. I don't want this to be one of them."

Sandy supposed he deserved that, at least. She nodded.

"And now…" With a great strength of will, he got to his feet, bringing her with him. "I have a suggestion. There are two beds; I propose we each make use of them tonight and pretend to behave like the well-brought-up adults we are. Tomorrow we'll try out one of those toboggans or even go skating; the weekend has only begun, and I don't want to spoil it with a lot of sober reflection on the first night.''

Sandy smiled at him, warmth and affection washing over her for the man she hardly knew and did not understand, but whom she was liking more and more. She caught his hands; she leaned forward and kissed him lightly upon the lips. "You're a nice man, Adrian," she said. A faint dimple appeared near her mouth as she stepped away from him, reluctantly releasing his hands. "And a lot smarter, I think, than you give yourself credit for.''

But Wes, as he watched her go alone to her own bedroom, did not feel like a nice man, or very smart, either. He felt, in fact, like the biggest fool who had ever lived. With a wry and regretful twist of his lips, he turned to go into his own bedroom, where he watched television until he fell asleep.

Chapter Eight

"Are you sure you want to do this?"

Wes's voice sounded worried and his face was plainly doubtful as he lifted his hand to push back the heavy gold hair that the wind persisted in parting toward his eyes. Sandy wished absently that she had known his stylist while she was still skiing the circuit—a cut that could endure such buffeting and still remain unruffled was the envy of every athlete in the world.

Sandy replied, a little tersely, "I'm sure," and they moved forward in the lift line a step.

Fresh snow had fallen last night—not much, but enough to make every skier in the resort anxious to be the first one down the slopes. The day was crisp and not too bright, with a thin shadow of cloud cutting the brilliance off the fresh powder. The wind wasn't too bad. Conditions were as near to perfect as they were likely to get this weekend, and Sandy saw no reason to postpone the inevitable.

There were only two more people in line ahead of them. The next chair would be theirs. Wes glanced at her uncomfortably, trying one more time. "Sandy, I really don't think this is wise. There's no reason to—"

"Look," she said shortly, "you don't have to go with me if you don't want to. I'd rather you didn't anyway. You already talked me out of the advanced slope—not that there's anything advanced about it. If this little baby hill makes you nervous, then stay down here and watch. I'm only going to make one run anyway.''

Wes's lips tightened, and he said nothing.

He's angry, Sandy thought, and she was sorry she had been short with him. But she couldn't spare too much concern for what Wes was or was not feeling; she had to concentrate all her attention on what lay ahead—what might possibly be the most important challenge of her life. And then she almost smiled, because she never would have imagined a time when the intermediate slope at Hampton Glen would represent any sort of challenge.

Wes thought he knew why she was doing this—or at least he knew it as well as she did—which, he suspected, was not very well at all. But he couldn't understand it, nor could he admire it. Nothing in his background prepared him to relate to people who took insane risks for nebulous principles.

She limped in the mornings—not much, it was hardly noticeable at all unless one was looking for it, but Wes had noticed that morning. He had awakened early with his usual cheerful enthusiasm, decided to surprise Sandy with breakfast in bed and was just dialing room service when he heard her in the parlor. When he came out she was sitting by the window, a very thoughtful expression on her face, and then she turned and announced that she wanted to ski that morning.

That was when Wes experienced a totally alien emotion—concern. The concern grew deeper when she went to get dressed and he noticed the slight stiffness in her right leg. That was when he tried to talk her out of the plan, using every charm and persuasion technique at his disposal. But her stubbornness could outlast even Wes's considerable experience in cajolery, and directly after breakfast she had him in the pro shop, choosing equipment.

The limp had disappeared by then, but Wes's anxiety had not. That was when he did something else completely alien—he took a firm and unshakeable stand on something that was none of his concern. He told her that there was no way she was skiing the advanced slope, and the look of unaccustomed will in his eyes must have surprised even Sandy, for after a moment she capitulated, however reluctantly.

The chair arrived, and they mounted with the ease and grace of two seasoned skiers, poles lifted, skis tipped. There was no turning back now, and the knot of worry in Wes's chest tightened. He didn't know what he would do if she injured herself. And he couldn't help worrying whether that look of grim resolve that had been in her eyes all morning had something to do with what had happened between the two of them last night.

At the top of the run, Sandy paused. Brightly colored skiers whooshed past and glided below like pretty dolls on a blank canvas. It was early and the run had not been too badly massacred by other skis. It should be a piece of cake. But Sandy stood there, her cheeks chapped by cold and wind, her adrenaline pumping as surely as it ever had before a championship race, her eyes absorbing every dip and curve and rise and mogul. Sandy hadn't been on the slopes for almost a year, and she was scared.

"You go first," she told Wes. Quite suddenly she knew that she did not want him watching if she made a stupid mistake, if she panicked or if she just couldn't do it....

But Wes shook his head. His eyes, snow-light, were hard and determined. "We can stand here and argue about it all day," he warned her, when he saw impatience cross her face. "Or you can do it and get it over with."

Sandy turned back to the decline with a breath that was both irritated and resolved. She didn't want to argue. This was between her and the mountain; it had nothing to do with Wes.

With one last, half-prayerful breath, she pushed off.

She made it halfway down the run. Her knee simply couldn't support her on the turn, and she fell.

Wes watched the fall with his heart in his throat. He was not far behind her and he reached her in a matter of seconds, but it seemed like a lifetime of flying snow and slow-motion scenery and dodging the lighthearted recreationists who had no idea that his whole world, at that moment, was teetering on the edge of collapse. He was frightened. White-faced, weak-kneed frightened in a way that made his fear on the night of his arrest seem like nothing more than a touch of nervousness. Wes had seen ski accidents before, some of them quite bad; he had even been involved in one or two, but nothing he had ever seen or felt affected him like this. Never before had it been Sandy.

She was sitting up, her face buried in her knees, and dimly he realized a stab of relief. He turned to a stop beside her; he knelt on the snow, grabbing her shoulder roughly. "Are you hurt?"

She shook her head negatively, but did not look up. Residual fear washed through him like a shudder, and all he wanted to do was take her in his arms and hold her, very tightly, to keep her safe. He didn't want anything ever to hurt her. He never wanted her to be in danger again.

And then he was angry, because she had taken such a foolish chance, and confused, because he didn't understand the courage it required to take it, and then a great rush of tenderness came over him because he suddenly realized that, for Sandy, there was nothing else she could have done.

He moved her quickly out of the path of other skiers, and then went to gather her skis, which had released properly with her fall.

When he knelt beside her again she looked up at him, and her face was wet with tears.

"Oh, Sandy," he whispered, and the sight of those beautiful eyes filled with tears went through him like a knife; her unhappiness crept into him and left him desolate. "Oh, love." He placed his arms around her, drew her gently, very gently, into the circle of his caring. And he held her as though he would never let her go. "Please don't be sad."

Sandy wound her fingers into the slick soft material of his parka, never having known there could be such wonderful comfort as a man's strong shoulder, a man's warm arms sheltering her, sharing with her. She didn't want to cause him distress. He had no part in this, he shouldn't have to share the burden. Yet it seemed, unpreventably, he was doing so.

"It's not...sad." She gulped, but she didn't seem to be able to stop the free flow of tears, a cleansing, purifying dam of denied regrets and hidden fears that had been buried for too long. Much too long.

Last night Wes had told her she had made too many impulsive decisions; she had been made to realize that she could not look forward until she had looked back, one last time. She had known from the beginning that her life would never be hers to do with as she pleased until she faced the life that had been taken away from her. She had felt her skis gliding over the snow, felt the tug of the wind and the brilliance of the sun, known the exhilaration and the fear, the anticipation and the dread; she had tasted victory and she had known defeat...one last time. She knew she would miss it; the tears were in part for that. She recognized the anger, because something she once had loved would never be hers to enjoy again. There were tears of defeat, for knowing a lifetime's goal of championship would never be reached, and for all the wasted years. But mostly the tears were of relief. She had faced it all now, there were no unexplored regions or hidden guilts or secret regrets to haunt her at unexpected moments for the rest of her life. It was really over, and she had faced it in the best way she knew how. The tears were mostly a sign of renewal.

Wes held her, rocking her gently, understanding the best that he could, until after a very long time the worst of it was over. She looked up at him, smiling tentatively and a little weakly, and he smoothed back her hair and kissed her softly on the lips. And with their arms around each other's waist, they made their way slowly back to the lodge.

"It was silly, I guess," Sandy said thoughtfully. "I told myself I had adjusted to it, and that I was even glad it was over. But all those years—my entire life was invested in this one thing and suddenly it's gone, and I knew I'd never be completely resigned to it until I had been on the slopes again, and really faced what I had lost." She glanced at Wes, a little shyly. "That was one of the main reasons I agreed to come with you this weekend."

"And?" Wes prompted softly.

They were sitting before the fireplace in the parlor of their suite an hour later, sipping hot spiced cider and watching the flames. Wes had drawn up a hassock for her leg, which still ached, although she insisted it was not much worse than it usually was after exercise. He had wanted to have the house physician look at it, but there she held firm. She let him instead drape a blanket over her shoulders, because she was still a bit chilled from the fall, and she had to smile at his solicitude. She would have thought Adrian Wesley was more accustomed to being pampered than to pampering, but then, he was always surprising her.

She answered his question, after a moment, with all the soberness it deserved. "I'll always miss it," she said simply. "It'll always be a part of me, and maybe the rest of my life will be nothing more than a reflection of the time that was before." And she smiled. "But it was a good time, with a lot of good memories. I hated the discipline and the dedication and all the time it took from me, and I knew all along I was never anything more than a mediocre competitor. But it's a part of me, you know? I don't regret that, and now I can make the best of the rest of my life without looking back.''

Wes nodded, understanding at last. He wished he had the courage to face his own loss with such equanimity, but then he realized that, strangely, just knowing her was making it easier. He said, ''You could always coach.''

She shook her head, smiling a little, sipping from her mug. ''I don't want to. The fun was in the sport, and I don't want to spend the rest of my life replaying a dream.'' She looked at him. ''Does that make any sense at all?''

He nodded, his eyes upon his own mug. ''When my dad died,'' he said slowly, ''it was like—I don't know, the sunset on a whole era of my life.'' And he glanced at her, a little uncertainly, finding nothing but encouragement and interest in her eyes. He continued, a small reminiscent smile touching his lips. ''He was more than a father, you know— he was kind of a symbol of all that the Wesleys have stood for for generations.'' The flicker of a teasing grin lit his eyes as he glanced at her. ''Staunch Republicanism, Harvard alumni, breeding and class with capital letters and, of course, a refined enjoyment of all the Better Things of Life.'' He spoke those words with a kind of mock dignity that made Sandy see them in capital letters. She smiled, and so did he.

Wes glanced briefly into his mug again. ''He was such a dynamic man, so larger-than-life. He, and what he represented, was all I've ever known. And now he's gone, and it's like—the aurora borealis. Memories of a light that's not there anymore. A time that can't be brought back, but the afterglow will haunt you the rest of your life.''

Sandy looked at Wes, dimly aware of a feeling as though she were being slowly filled inside with something that was nothing more than the wonder of him. "Adrian Wesley," she said softly, "you are the strangest man. You try so hard to be the shallow, self-serving, fun-loving, international playboy type, but there's so much more to you than that. Why do you keep it hidden?"

He lifted his mug to her, his quick, light smile not disguising for a moment the warmth in his eyes, or the seriousness of his tone. "Because nobody would understand it except you."

Sandy felt something within her reach to him then, something that seemed to come from some hitherto unrecognized core of her; a warmth and a need that had been building from the moment he had looked at her from the arms of a policeman with desperation and pleading in his eyes, something that had drawn her into his embrace last night and led her to share the most important crisis of her life with him this morning. It seemed only natural that it should culminate now in a quiet look, a single strong yet subtle emotional touch. Understanding. That was all it was. And that was all either of them needed.

But the contact was entirely too poignant, too rich and too filled with meaning for Sandy, unaccustomed to such emotions, to maintain for long. She gave him a brief, somewhat nervous smile, and she placed her mug on the hearth. She got up and walked to the window, favoring her leg only slightly. "Oh, look!" she exclaimed softly. "It's snowing again!"

Wes got up and stood behind her, watching the fat, lazy flakes drift toward the ground, creating small ripples on the lace-embroidered lake, clinging to bushes, reflecting the glow in Sandy's eyes. A quiet wonder stole over him, a heavy feeling of simple contentment, and he wanted to hold her. He did.

Sandy felt his arms go around her from behind, and she leaned into the gentleness of his embrace, letting his presence, and the rightness of it, flow through her like a final, wonderful benediction to the day. There was tenderness to his touch, a bond of companionship, a simple need. Yet there was more.

Last night in the haze of passion and her own headstrong impetuosity, she had thought she had known what she wanted. But now she was certain. To touch another, as she was touching Wes, not only with her body, but with her mind and even her heart. To reach an intimacy that was possible only when two people shared the kind of natural understanding she and Wes had shared almost from the first moment they had met. It might not last, it most certainly would not endure the pressures and the conflicts of the real world, but in this snow-shrouded moment when there was something special to be shared between two people she could think of no reason to deny what must be right. What had begun in her life almost a year ago had reached a point of fulfillment, and she wanted to share that fulfillment with Wes.

She turned slowly in his arms; she reached her hands up and cupped his face lightly. Everything was written in her eyes then, for she couldn't have hidden it if she had wanted to. And then she kissed him.

How quickly was this thing called passion reborn, from the low-burning ember of tender affection to the quick-melting heat of a thousand unspoken and hardly recognized desires. With the meeting of lips, the caress of a hand, the strong warm contact of bodies drawn together through need and joy, the dizzying euphoria of last night built again within her, racing in her pulse, throbbing in her skin, robbing her breath and taking all reason far away into the nether regions of sensory delight and deep, unquestioning emotional demand.

Wes's hands were unsteady as they ran the length of her back—slowly, as though attempting to explore and memorize every curve; gently, as though afraid too much urgency would frighten her away. She could feel the hard muscles of his arms as she let her own hands drift down the shape of them, straining as though with the need to crush her. She lifted her arms again and wound them around his neck, and his body came fully against her as she felt his indrawn breath. His kiss was drawing from her as greedily as she was from him. She was consumed by him, all of him, yet she wanted more. She wanted his hands upon her naked skin and she wanted to feel the smooth clean texture of his own flesh beneath her fingers. She wanted to lie with him, to wrap herself around him and fill herself with him, to lose herself in closeness and need.

His lips touched her neck; his breath was hot and moist and uneven. His arms tightened around her, and she could feel the fine, high-wire quiver of his muscles. Her own muscles felt like rubber, as though if he released her she would dissolve into a helpless uncoordinated bundle at his feet. He kissed her cheek, and she clung to him; he lifted his hand and touched the corner of her eye, very lightly. She looked hazily into a smile that was sleepy and pleasure-dazed, heavy eyes lit by a spark so deep that it took her breath away.

"Does this mean," he inquired somewhat huskily, his fingers busily and delicately arranging a collection of tousled curls behind her ear, his eyes moving over her face, drinking in every inch of it with avidity and delight, "that you've thought about it?"

Sandy's fingers moved as of their own volition to his face, tracing the shape of his brow, touching his hair. Her heart wouldn't stop pounding. "As I recall," she whispered, her own eyes filled with a hesitant question, "it was you who turned me down last night."

Wes looked at her, soberly, yearningly, carefully searching her face and not knowing what he wanted to find there.

He knew, as clearly as he had ever known anything, that he wanted no other man to be her lover. He wanted to take care of her, to nourish and protect her, to bond himself to her in a way that could last forever. He wanted the awesome responsibility that would come with that bonding, he welcomed it. But he did not want his desires to confuse hers. He wanted her to come to him with all her heart and all her soul, welcoming and open. He wanted her to be sure.

Oh, God, he thought deeply, *let it be right. Don't let me push her. Don't let me convince her of something she doesn't really want. Don't let me hurt this rare and fragile creature....*

And to Sandy he said, softly, aching to hear an answer but not certain what he wanted it to be, "Are you sure, love? Are you very sure you want it to be me, and now?"

Sandy placed her hands against his chest, letting him read it all in her eyes. She had never been more sure of anything in her life. "Teach me, Adrian. Teach me how beautiful it can be."

Wes lowered his lips to her hair for one long, intoxicating breath of wonder. Then he bent and lifted her into his arms.

Wes laid Sandy gently upon the snow-brightened, daylight-radiant bed, pausing to lightly kiss the top of her tousled head. He removed her shoes, and then his own, and he smiled down at her. "Would you like me to close the draperies?"

Sandy shook her head. She wanted to see him, to remember him and everything about this day in unshadowed clarity.

Wes lay down beside her, gathering her close, warming her with his body, sheltering her, telling her, more clearly than words could do, that he understood her fragility and would treasure it. He lifted his hand, resting it just beneath her left breast, testing the loud and steady beating there. He smiled at her, nuzzling her cheek. "Frightened?"

She looked at him, hesitantly, and tried to return his smile. "A little, maybe." Her throat felt scratchy, and she cleared it. Her fingers tangled in his hair. "Nervous."

His smile deepened, lighting his eyes, building a gentle fire far back within their depths that sent its warmth all the way to Sandy's chest. "No need to be. It's the most natural thing in the world, two people loving each other. This—" and in an easy, fluid motion, he sat up on his knees, catching the hem of her sweater and tugging it upward, over her head "—is the hardest part." His eyes, playful and sun-dazzled, danced down at her. "People have the damnedest conventions about getting out of their clothes."

Sandy laughed, partially in astonishment, partially in relief for the quick evaporation of awkwardness. And then Wes's eyes swept downward, over her bare torso and the shape of her breasts. His fingers, warm and nimble, found the front clasp of her bra and released it with a touch that was so light she hardly felt it. Her breath caught as his hooded eyes dropped and he separated the two parts, slipping the straps down over her arms. Then, very slowly his face came down to kiss her naked breasts.

His breath, warm and moist, tingled through her with a shiver that went straight to the center of her spine. His hands cupped, his long, experienced fingers delicately traced a pattern around her suddenly distended nipples, and then his tongue replaced his fingers, so light, so silky and coarse and expertly tantalizing that she gasped out loud. She closed her eyes against the spiraling pleasure, her hands going automatically to cup his head, to test the cascading texture of his hair, to hold him there within the circle of this mindless pleasure.

But then his lips left her breasts, moving downward, and her moan of protest was quickly replaced with a small sound of unexpected pleasure as she felt his kisses upon her rib cage and that delicate area below her sternum, and lower still until he met the barrier of her jeans. Suspended in anticipation, she felt his fingers loosen the clasp of her jeans, then lower the zipper, and the sensation of his deep, drawing kisses upon the bare skin he exposed generated a tightening deep within the core of her abdomen, a slow, swelling heat that centered itself between her thighs.

Then he sat up, fastening his fingers beneath the material. He gently tugged jeans and panties downward until she lay completely naked beneath his soul-absorbing gaze, until her heart was pounding in crazy, two-step time and a flush began to thread its way through every fiber of her skin, and still he looked at her.

Sandy was not ashamed of her body. It was strong and well kept, lean and muscled through years of conscientious dedication. But never had a man looked upon her with such rapturous absorption before. Never had she lain so vulnerable and exposed before any person before. The way he looked at her made her want to reach her arms around him and draw him down, burying his face against her, sheltering her body with his own.

And then Wes whispered, "Lovely lady. Beautiful woman." He drew his hands lightly up the outside of her legs, caressing them. He discovered the series of scars that ran along her knee, and he bent and placed a lingering, ultimately tender kiss there. Then his hand trailed to her abdomen, where it rested, lightly and protectively, as he brought his head up to kiss her lips.

He smiled and stood up, and Sandy watched as he pulled his sweater over his head and tossed it aside; she averted her eyes as his hands went to his belt. The undressing was done quickly, carelessly, without the care or reverence with which he had uncovered Sandy's body. His clothes were discarded, and in only a moment she felt the dip of his weight beside her again, and it was only natural to turn into the welcoming warmth of his arms.

He touched her lips lightly, the warmth of his smile lightening the deep blue of passion-hazed eyes. "Now it's your turn, love. See if I'm as gorgeous as you thought I was. Look at me. Touch me."

Whatever shyness she experienced was only a surface thing as she let her hands glide like silk over the smooth planes of his chest. She wanted to touch him, she wanted to know him. Her hands drifted over him, relaxing in the deep look of contentment that spread across his face, discovering the firmness of his chest, the lean knot of biceps, the sweep of his waist, the flatness of his abdomen...but no lower.

His laugh was a little shaky as he caught her hand. "It's all right. You can touch me there, too." Very gently, watching for any sign of resistance, he drew her hand back down, between his legs.

She saw his eyes close as he felt her touch, and he seemed to be holding his breath. Tentatively, her own breath tightening in her chest, she let her fingers close around him. He felt huge to her, the strangeness of this act of intimacy between two human beings almost overwhelming. She started to withdraw, hesitantly.

"Not so strange, Sandy," he breathed, reading her thoughts. He captured her other hand and brought it against his chest, above his heart, and she felt the strong, hot rapidity of its beating beneath her fingers. "That's what you do to me. All that, and so much more. Just as it should be." And he turned her in his arms, and he kissed her. Her vision was filled with his sleepy-bright, love-widened eyes.

She pressed against him, she felt the heat and the hardness of him against her bare stomach and it was an exhilarating feeling, still a little frightening but mindlessly powerful. His hands upon her body stroked her and soothed her, enflaming her skin in deep electrifying caresses, the demanding love play of his tongue against hers left her breathless and heated and restless, the puzzling tightening of discomfort low within her only growing more intense.

Wes's skill as a lover was not the result of practiced expertise; it was simply that, as in all areas of his life, his own happiness was almost entirely dependent upon the happiness of others. It was his instinct to give, and never had he wanted to give more to anyone than he wanted to give to Sandy.

It would be hard for her the first time; Wes knew that with regret and sadness. Her untutored body had much to learn before it could accept the fullest pleasures of a man. That she must experience pain before she could know the fulfillment was something Wes recognized but could not entirely accept, and it frightened him a little. He had never before thought of sex as anything but lighthearted fun; there should be nothing unnerving or distressing about it. The newness of this experience shook him, touched him profoundly, for nothing of any meaning was achieved easily. And with Sandy, everything had meaning for the first time in his life.

The enormity of the responsibility of being her initiator weighed heavy on Wes, yet he welcomed it. He wanted so badly for everything to be perfect for her. He wanted to make it easy for her, this suddenly complicated act of love. He wanted to treasure her, and care for her, and promise her vistas of unblemished joy. The very thought of hurting Sandy was repugnant to him, though he knew it would be done. But first he wanted only to give her pleasure.

His hand moved around, stroking her hip, the curve of her thigh, moving closer to the part of her that cried out desperately for his touch. A shudder went through her as she felt his hand against her, gently caressing, inciting the heat into a flame. Her thighs parted and all of her seemed to go

limp, mind and body dissolving into the sensation, every fiber of her concentrated into the dizzying, world-
encompassing pleasure, and building in anticipation for she
knew not what. She moaned, arching a little against him,
and then she gasped, her unsuspecting flesh clenching instinctively against the gentle insertion of one long finger.

"Ssh, love." His kisses soothed her brow, whispering over
her face. "Relax. It's only me, loving you...." He lowered
his mouth to her breasts, and she could no longer resist the
spiraling urgency that was building within her, the pleasure
that he was drawing from her. Her muscles loosened and
sank into it, were absorbed with it, and she lost herself in the
hitherto unsuspected delights of her body, which only he
knew how to evoke. The skillful manipulations of his fingers were mind-stripping, maddening, twisting the ache
within her into a sharpness she did not know how to ease.
It was frightening and it was powerful, and she moaned
against it and she writhed against it helplessly. But it built
until she was to the point of sobbing for what she did not
understand. She cried out, "Adrian, don't—" But then,
unexpectedly, the tension within her blossomed and exploded and carried her away into a senseless, shuddering
rapture, clouds upon snowy clouds of billowing pleasure
that left her drifting and dazed until she opened her eyes and
the adored face of the man who was her first lover floated
into view.

Wes held her, he caressed her, he soothed her, he gently
and expertly brought her back to a new awareness of what
had only been partially fulfilled before. She knew a need for
him she could not define, an ache to have him closer, to
blend with him and be filled with him. She tasted the salt
upon his shoulder and the coarse texture of his neck; she
explored his tight muscles and his smooth planes; she resisted not at all as one of his firm legs nudged hers apart.

He poised above her, his face damp and sweet and flushed with tenderness and passion, his eyes deep as the sea and alight with a need that sparked within her and leapt to a quick, sharp tendril of indefinable desire. He brought his hands to rest on either side of her face, stroking her hair, and he said, very softly, through uneven breaths, "Do you want me now? Do you want me inside you?"

She could feel him pressing against her, a gentle intruder that frightened even as it compelled, and through a blur of need and swirling dark desires unlike anything she had ever experienced before, she whispered, "Yes."

The slow sharp burn of flesh as he pushed into her surprised a gasp from Sandy, and he stopped, dropping a kiss onto her forehead, soothing her with gentle stroking motions upon the side of her face. "I'm sorry, love," he whispered. "I'm sorry it has to hurt." She could feel the trembling of his hands and the tautness of his muscles, and she relaxed, cautiously. It was only Adrian, whom she had chosen. "Put your arms around me," he commanded gently. "Hold me."

She did, closing her eyes against the slippery soft texture of his skin, the strength of his back, drawing him cautiously closer as the strange fullness inside her deepened and expanded, pushing aside the pain in the wonder of it. He came to rest deep within her, as completely a part of her as it was possible for any human being to be, and she looked up into a face so tender, so awash with passion and affection, and she thought in cautious wonder, *This is what they mean by love.*

"Oh, Sandy," he breathed, and the look upon his face was slumberous and transported. She was filled with light and need only from looking at him. "I wish...I could tell you...how this feels...."

But then the rigid control he had maintained for so long could not be maintained another second longer, and he began to move within her, covering her mouth with his deep, drawing kiss, drowning within her, losing himself gladly to her, for it seemed he had waited his entire life only to belong to his woman, to give himself to her and to make her a part of him, completely, without reservation, forever.

For Sandy it was not hard to find that point of desire, to let it concentrate itself into the rhythmic sliding pressure of Wes's body inside hers, to be transported outside herself and into a place where nothing existed except Wes and she and a realm of possibilities never dreamed of before. She let the need blossom, she let it consume her, she let Wes guide her and enflame her, and she clung helplessly to the fulfillment he seemed to promise until it peaked and exploded and left her drained and senseless, floating somewhere beyond her own reason or knowledge with only Wes as her anchor.

His movement, and his slow reluctant sliding from her, were her first promptings back to consciousness. She registered his absence with a moan of protest, but before it was even completed he had drawn her against him, his arms encircling her, one leg thrown loosely over hers, her head resting comfortably against his shoulder. She opened her eyes and looked rather giddily into his tender smile, his soft-focus eyes, and a huge surge of warmth and happiness swept through her; she wanted to throw her arms around him and hug him hard. But she simply did not have the energy.

"Oh, Adrian," she said, sighing, and snuggled closer.

The corners of his lips turned upward in a teasing, indulgent smile. "Does that mean you don't feel too devastated?"

She glanced up at him. "How do I look?"

His fingers gently smoothed away a tendril of hair that had become caught in the dampness of her face. His eyes were sleepy and hooded and filled with lazy love sparks. "Exhausted," he replied after a moment. "A little feverish. Very rumpled. Beautiful." He lowered a light kiss upon her nose.

"So do you," she whispered, and then rested herself contentedly against his shoulder again. The room was awash with late-afternoon light, and a light curtain of snow still drifted past the window. That surprised her. It seemed a lifetime ago that she had stood at the window and watched the first flakes fall. It *had* been a lifetime ago. She had been a different person then. Now she was renewed, refreshed, changed completely, standing at the very threshold of a life that swept before her in an endless collage of panoramic colors. *It must be love,* she thought. *Nothing else could feel this wonderful.*

Wes inquired solicitously, "Are you very sore?"

She glanced up at him coquettishly. "Are you?"

He chuckled, his whole body shaking with his laughter, his eyes dancing with the delight of her, sending a new and languorous thrill of warmth through her that felt better than anything she had ever known—or almost anything. "You are a wonderful, wonderful girl—correction." He sobered a little, bringing one of her fingers to his lips and kissing it gently. "Woman." Then his eyes crinkled again with a teasing, utterly relaxed contentment, and he said, "As a matter of fact, I am. I feel like I've just run a particularly satisfying marathon and every muscle in my body has reached its limit. In a minute," he promised, reaching down to draw the tangled covers over their perspiration-chilled bodies, "we'll go take a bath and soothe away our various aches and pains...." His eyes teased her again as he drew her back into the circle of his arms, warm and secure and naked against him beneath the blankets. "And later we might even finally make it to that hot tub. But right now..." The softness of his sigh feathered across her hair as he settled back against the pillows, holding her. "This is the best part. The afterglow."

His voice grew sleepy and low, his hands lazily stroking, and Sandy thought he might be right: this was the best time, lying in his arms, continuing the bond they had shared, basking in the radiance they had created together. "The time," he said, "when we just hold each other, and feel for each other, and talk to each other and think about each other...." *Yes,* Sandy thought, *the best part.* And she closed her eyes, content with the sound of his voice, the security of his embrace, the lingering warmth of their coming together, which was like a glow that would never fade, that would light her life forever.

So much like love, she thought, letting her hands drift lightly and caressingly over the strong, lean lines of his body, this man who a week ago was a stranger to her but who had now changed her life irretrievably. She knew it was only a feeling—it was nothing real and nothing permanent—but it felt so good. Of course he was a stranger to her, of course there was no possibility of anything permanent between them, and in a few days they would part company, in all likelihood never to see their paths cross again. Sandy may have been inexperienced, but she was not ignorant; she knew that the emotions following sex—especially a first sexual experience—were deep and compelling, but they had more to do with chemistry than with commitment. Soon the glow would fade and there would be nothing to bind them together. But it felt so very, very wonderful while it lasted.

It was a long time later, when she was almost asleep, that his hand, which had been quiet against her brow, moved once more lightly to smooth back her hair. "Sandy," he said softly. "It was like the first time for me, too."

What a beautiful thing to say, Sandy thought drowsily, snuggling closer to him. *And how very, very lucky I am to know you....*

Of course she knew it wasn't really love. But it was nice to believe, for just a moment longer, that it might be.

Chapter Nine

Sandy awoke the next morning looking into her sleeping lover's face, and for a time all she could do was marvel over the fact. In all her distant daydreams, when she thought of what it would be like to make love with a man, she had never imagined it could be like this—so warm, so tender, so loving. And she had never even begun to imagine the best part—waking up the next morning and looking at him.

Adrian Wesley. How beautiful he was. Even in her most daring fantasies she had never imagined that she, plain old Sandy Garret, would end up with a man like him. Fashion-model gorgeous, wealthy, sophisticated—he was every woman's dream, but he was here, with her. It just didn't make sense.

Sandy turned over carefully, staring at the ceiling, a thoughtful frown vaguely shadowing her features. No, it didn't make sense. *Lord, Sandy, you sure know how to pick them. I mean when you decide to change your life-style, you don't fool around....* Hundreds of perfectly nice, hardworking, family-loving men in the world—well, maybe not hundreds, but dozens at least—and she had chosen to give her virginity to a careless international playboy who would have forgotten her before the week was out. Every value she had ever known rebelled at that, and the warm glow of contentment with which she had awakened was suddenly shadowed by a dull emptiness.

But wait. She took a breath; firmly she subdued the depression that was threatening to rise. This was what she wanted. A carefree weekend, no strings attached, the experiment of being a woman without the complications involved. Certainly the last thing she wanted was another person in her life, the entanglement of a heartsick love affair. She hadn't meant to get *involved*, for heaven's sake. No, what she and Wes had, temporary and pleasant, was exactly what she wanted...wasn't it?

She had been so sure last night, but now she was only confused. Obviously, there was a lot more to sex than what they showed in the movies, and Sandy had never expected to feel so...so changed. She had not expected to be thinking so much about the time she and Wes would say goodbye.

There were a lot of things, Sandy realized with a sigh, her mother had never told her. Why did this have to be one of them?

"Regrets?" Wes said softly in her ear.

Sandy turned her head, surprised, to meet Wes's alert, brilliant blue eyes. How sweet his face was, so tender and concerned.... Sandy had to reach out and touch it, to smile and smooth away the faint lines of anxiety she saw forming there. What a special man he was. How could she ever regret what they had shared together?

"No," she said softly, and moved warmly, gratefully into his arms. Even if it ended today, she would never, ever be sorry she had known him. Determinedly, Sandy closed her eyes against the future and let his kisses and his soft caresses sweep her away into the present. Nothing that could happen tomorrow would spoil what they had today.

MOST OF THE TIME remaining to them was spent in the room, in bed or out, laughing and touching and learning together of love and loving, and, to Sandy's very great distress, the end was growing closer with each passing moment. It would be hard to part with him. It shouldn't be, she hadn't planned it to be, but it would be, nonetheless. Perhaps she had made her first mistake by knowing him too well.

When finally they talked themselves into dressing and going down for dinner, Sandy tried to make things a little easier on herself by injecting a touch of reality into the paradise they shared. Indulging herself with a feather-light, sinfully rich Amaretto soufflé, Sandy looked up over the low-globed candle and inquired casually, "What do you think you'll do with the rest of the winter, Adrian?"

Wes found the question difficult to relate to. In the past few days with Sandy, time seemed to have stopped, and the future was no more than a nebulous dream at best. It was hard to imagine life outside this place; impossible to imagine that anything at all existed without her.

He grinned lightly and suggested, "Spend it here?"

Her heart did a peculiar little flip-flop, and then she had to remind herself not to take him too seriously. He was a practiced flirt, remember? He had to be, to lead the life he did. He was only saying what he thought she wanted to hear.

"Really," she insisted, but kept her tone nonchalant. She made a great business of scooping up the last of the Amaretto sauce with her spoon so she would not have to meet his eyes. "You must have some plans. I know you don't want to spend the winter in Philadelphia."

He thought about it for a moment. "I don't know. Tahoe is nice." He wondered if Sandy would like it there. Or maybe something more exotic. "Or Egypt," he suggested, the hint of a playful grin beginning to dance in his eyes.

"There's a pyramid there I've been meaning to visit. Do you like pyramids, Sandy?"

"Well," Sandy murmured modestly, "I know so few of them on a first-name basis."

They laughed and they teased each other, and never once did Sandy let it be known by her face or her manner what she was thinking. Pyramids. Egypt, Tahoe, the moon... This weekend in an obscure little mountain resort with a funny young woman who worked in a mall and wore a Santa's cap was just a sideshow in the great carnival of life for Adrian Wesley. He liked her, certainly, he was having fun with her, no doubt, just as she was with him; it was even within the realm of possibility that he might want to continue their frolic after the weekend was over. But one day he would grow bored, just as all men like him eventually must, and soon he would be in Tahoe or Egypt or Greece or Lord only knew where with another woman on his arm—and Sandy would be only one more face rapidly fading from memory. There was nothing sad about it, nothing to be angry over, nothing to resent. That was simply the way it was.

Sandy had learned, through Wes's very excellent tutelage, the wonder and the magic two people could make through intimacy and love. Only experience could teach her the remainder of the lesson—sometimes hurt, sometimes loss. Like all human beings, Sandy was frightened of what she did not know, and she had set up her own instinctive defenses to guard against it.

She made no demands on Wes; she expected none from him. This had been fun, of course—more than fun. It had been one of the singularly most important experiences in her life. But she certainly wasn't looking for a commitment. She was just beginning to live, she had no intention of being weighed down by the emotional and physical baggage of another person's needs and wants. She simply didn't have time to fall in love, and fortunately, she had chosen as her lover the one man who truly understood the nature of fun and games.

She told herself all that, and she smiled and joked and she enjoyed Wes while she could. And all the while she refused to think what it would be like when the time came to say goodbye....

IT WAS TUESDAY MORNING. The bags were packed and by the door, waiting for the bellman. Sandy stood at the window, gazing for one last time out at the snow-sparked loveliness that surrounded her, but already a part of her mind was plodding ahead, back to Philadelphia and reality.

Tuesday. She couldn't believe she had been Absent Without Leave for four whole days. It was unheard-of. Linda would never forgive her for deserting the store at the busiest time of the year. Her family would be buzzing with concerned speculation. Had Sandy lost her mind? Was she having a nervous breakdown? The next thing they knew she would be dropping out and joining a cult.... The questions would never stop.

Sandy's lips curved with a small mirthless smile as she imagined what they all must be thinking. She had a lot waiting for her back home. The idyll was over, and it was time, as her mother would say, to pay the piper.

She felt Wes's arms encircle her from behind, and her hands came up automatically to cover his wrists. "God," she said softly, "I'm going to miss this place." And, in an instant echo that reverberated with a pang she had not expected, she thought, *And I'm going to miss you*. So much more than she had ever expected to, or had any right to.

She could feel his smile against the back of her neck as he brushed a kiss there. "You needn't sound as though its the end of the world, you know. I'm willing to wager there is life outside of Hampton Glen—and maybe even snow."

And that, of course, was the problem. Life was waiting for her, and in many ways it was a newer and more exciting life than she had ever known before. But it was *real* life, and it was no part of what she and Adrian Wesley had shared here in their snowy paradise.

Sandy's emotions were mixed. In the days she had spent secluded with Wes she had come to a new knowledge of herself as a person and as a woman; she felt stronger than she ever had before, and she was eager to go out and explore the new life that awaited her. She was also a little frightened—that was only natural. But mostly there was an incredible sadness for all she would leave behind in this place.

In the past two days Wes had taught her more about life and loving and sharing than all the rest of her twenty-four years combined had done. He had shown her passion in all its varying degrees, he had taught her trust in a way that can only be learned between a man and a woman in their deepest moments of intimacy and vulnerability. He had shown her tenderness and patience; he had given her quiet times and the excitement of discovery. He had taught her more than the simple secrets of physical intimacy. He had taught her about making love.

But Sandy had never been a romantic, and she was not about to start becoming one now. She knew that the heart-wrenching attachment she felt for him, the soaring happiness she felt whenever he was near and the bleak loneliness that assailed her whenever she realized they must soon part, the deep and abiding tenderness she felt for him, the moments of intense adoration and soul-absorbing contentment—these were only side effects of their physical relationship, a temporary but perfectly understandable emotional reaction to the man who had been her first lover. Chemistry. It would fade as soon as they returned to the real world and picked up their separate lives. Knowing that did not make the letting go any easier.

"Adrian," Sandy said thoughtfully, leaning back against his shoulder, "if you could do anything you wanted to with the rest of your life, what would it be?"

Even as she asked it, Sandy knew it was a silly question. Adrian Wesley was one of the few people in the world who *could* do anything he wanted to with his life. Still, he gave it due consideration, as he did everything Sandy said. "I don't know. The rest of my life is a long time. But if I had to choose only one thing…" He grinned, and she could feel the endearing curve of his smile against her hair. "I've always wanted to play lord of the manor, noblesse oblige and all of that. I think I'd like to give a huge party and have the whole world come."

Sandy couldn't help smiling. Being Adrian Wesley, what else would he have said?

And then he asked, "What about you?"

They both knew that the question for Sandy was not a hypothetical one. The weekend had been a turning point in more ways than one for her, and Sandy had used the time to consider her options and begin to make some decisions. The details of her future plans were not entirely clear yet, but one thing she knew for certain—the rest of her life would be as far removed from the first part as it could possibly be. "Nothing useful," she declared, and she meant that. She had devoted fifteen years to structure, discipline and goal-oriented achievement. The rest of her life she wanted to devote solely to pleasing herself. "Travel, I think, like one of those old-time drifters. Staying in one place just long enough to earn the money to move on." That sounded like exactly what she wanted. And what was to stop her from doing it?

She turned to him eagerly, her eyes lighting with the possibilities that were flickering through her head. "There's so much, Adrian, that I've never seen or done. If it didn't have snow and mountains, I wasn't interested. But now—there's a whole world out there I haven't explored!''

His eyes teased her lovingly. ''Is that what you want to be when you grow up? An adventuress?''

''Yes,'' she agreed immediately. She liked the sound of that word. ''An adventuress.''

Wes laughed softly, drawing her against him, loving her. What a miracle she was. And what incredible fortune had brought her into his life. ''Ah, Sandy,'' he said, sighing into her neck. ''Do you believe in fate?''

She laughed a little, taking a small step back to look at him. ''Are you kidding? I don't even believe in Santa Claus.''

''Well, I do.'' His eyes were bright and eager and filled with joy, and just looking at them made Sandy feel like flying. He cupped her face with both hands, those lightning-bright eyes searching hers with all the delight and anticipation of one who is about to receive the perfect gift. ''Sandy,'' he insisted earnestly, joyfully, ''I can show you the world! Paris, Rome, Venice—Monaco, Biarritz, Tokyo, Hong Kong, Naples, Madrid…everything you've always wanted to see and more. Even Tibet,'' he added, the spark in his eyes deepening.

She laughed, a little nervously, completely caught off guard. ''But all I wanted to see was Nebraska!''

His hands slipped down to her shoulders, squeezing gently, his face alive with the possibilities. ''Then that's where we'll start. Whatever you want to do, wherever you want to go, we can do it all, Sandy!'' That was what he meant by fate, for every moment spent with her was more magical than the one before, and life, which had once seemed so uncertain, now spread before him in vistas of shimmering opportunity. It was because now there were two of them, and he would never see himself in the singular again. Because she had come into his life and enhanced it and doubled it and every day with her was a living miracle.

Because he loved her, and he would never be apart from her again.

Sandy stepped away, a little disturbed. She half thought he was serious. No, she *knew* he was serious, and the fact was only a graphic reminder of the differences between them. For Wes the fantasy never died, but Sandy had twenty-four years of strict values and work-oriented ethics to fall back upon, and for her it was not that easy. She didn't even want it to be that easy.

She said, as lightly as she could, "Adrian, come on! A weekend in the mountains is one thing—but a trip around the world?" She tried to laugh, but her fingers were holding on to her elbows, hard, and she could not look at him. Already she could feel it slipping away, this wondrous time of fairy-tale perfection they had shared, shadowed too soon by the specter of reality that hovered just around the corner. "Get serious!"

"I am serious." Wes was too filled with the possibility of their future to sense her hesitant withdrawal. All morning it had bothered him, vaguely, what would happen when they returned to Philadelphia. He did not want the weekend to end. He did not want to let her out of his sight even for the time she would spend working. They had found each other, and he could see no reason why they should part even for the briefest of times. He was entirely too happy, too filled with the joy of his plans, to admit even the tiniest edge of uneasiness into this perception of the future. And then she turned.

Distress and uneasiness were written clearly on her face. Wes could not imagine what could have put that look there, and he came back to earth with a jolt. He lifted a concerned hand to embrace her, but she did not come to it as she usually did. She just stood there, hugging her arms, and she said, sorrowfully, "That won't work, Adrian. You know it won't."

Wes knew nothing of the kind. "Why not?" he replied, puzzled. "You have things you want to do, I can help you do them in style. We can do them together."

She sighed helplessly. If only he knew how tempted she was. But the streak of practicality ran deep in Sandy, and she knew her limits. It was nice to dream about, but she was not cut out to be a jet-setter. She could never adjust to his freewheeling life-style, and if the truth be told she didn't really want to. She wanted to learn about life, real life, and experience it to the fullest, in her own way. She had had her fantasy—now there were so much more important things to do.

"Because it's Disneyland, Adrian," she answered, as gently as she could. "A nice place to visit, but I don't want to live there. I want—" she gestured helplessly "—real people, real places, real challenges. I've been sheltered and secluded from real life since I was nine years old and first started training seriously, can you understand that? I don't want to trade one kind of isolation for another. I want to live *everything*."

Wes was not entirely sure he understood, but he tried. All he really understood was that something seemed to be going very wrong. He answered, carefully, "All right. Forget Paris and Rome and Tibet." He smiled a little, with an effort, desperately searching her face for what he was half afraid was coming. "We'll see America from the back of a van if that's what you want."

A little pang caught in her chest, and she thought, *He means it. He wants me to stay with him.* For a moment that was all she thought about, staying with him, and her heart soared and her head reeled with the possibility.

But it was Wes who didn't know when to let go of a fantasy, not Sandy. And it was hurting her, spelling it out to him, facing the truth herself, denying herself what she wanted so badly—just to be with him for a little while longer, to delight in his company, to be swept away by his smile, to love him.

But it wasn't really love. She had to keep reminding herself of that. "Adrian," she said patiently, trying not to sound as upset as she was beginning to feel, "think about that for a minute. Think about the differences between us. This—" she gestured to include the room, the view, the remnants of a luxurious breakfast on silver serving platters "—the whole weekend was perfect, it was wonderful, it was beyond belief—but it wasn't me. It's not what I want *forever*. I'm used to simpler things. And you—how long would you last in a rattletrap van on the back roads of some little nowhere town eating hot dogs and chili and sleeping in one-star motels with nineteenth-century plumbing?"

"I could get used to it," he put forth cheerfully. "It would be fun."

She looked at him soberly. "Would it? Could you really live without your vintage wines and your gourmet meals and your designer originals? Could you learn to carry your own bags and make your own bed and figure your own income tax? Could you do your shopping at Sears and drive a Ford? Could you ever—" she took a breath "—live like any other ordinary guy off the street?"

He thought about it for a moment, hardly believing she was serious. And then that playful quirk of a grin turned up a corner of his mouth and he admitted, reaching for her, "Only in my worst nightmares. Now, what has that—"

But she stepped away, throwing up her hands in helpless exasperation. "Adrian, don't you see?" The touch of sadness in her eyes was the only thing that alerted him to the fact that she was, indeed, serious, and he felt a cold premonition tingle through him. Sandy tried to gentle her voice, dreading to say this, dreading to hear it. "You're Peter Pan and I'm Pinocchio. You'll never grow up, and I just want to be a real person.''

He knew what she was trying to say, but he couldn't believe it, couldn't accept it. There was more than that between them. What they had found in each other...it was magic, it was fate and it was meant to be forever. But was it possible he was the only one who could see that?

He said, very quietly, watching her, "What are you trying to say, Sandy?''

Oh, God, she had never expected it to be this hard. She had never expected it to be like this at all. She had expected they would say a cheerful goodbye, thanks for the memories, and then go their separate ways. That was the way it was *supposed* to be. Sandy, sensible and for the most part levelheaded, had known that from the beginning.

There would have been sadness at their parting, that was only natural. They had shared a wonderful time and they would both be sorry it was over. Perhaps Adrian, honorable man that he was, would have even made some vague plans to see her again, but they both would have known nothing would come of it. He would go back to his family mansion and she would go back to her tiny apartment and the Christmas rush at the mall. She would be lonely for a while and he would think of her fondly, but pretty soon she would be wrapped up in the challenges of her own life and he would get a phone call and be off to Yucatán or the Amazon and they would never think of each other again.

But she had never expected it to hurt so much. She had never expected to become so attached to him in such a short time.

"Adrian," she said painfully, her eyes pleading with him to accept and to understand what she was trying to say, to not make it any harder for her. "What you've given me this weekend—I'll treasure forever. You'll always be an important part of my life because of it, you know that. But it's over now, and we've got to get on with our lives.''

"Over," he repeated, staring at her, not really comprehending the meaning of the word. "Just like that."

No, not just like that, she wanted to cry. *I don't ever want it to be over. I don't ever want to leave you....* But she knew that was only hormones and deceptive emotions talking. Chemistry. Of course it was over. What else could it be?

He persisted, his face very still, "Do you mean that we are to leave this place and never see each other again? Just like that?''

Sandy knew that was exactly what she meant and exactly what she did not want. The sooner he was out of her life the sooner she could start relegating him to nothing more than a pleasant memory. She did not want another person in her life, not now, when everything was starting anew for her and she was just learning to live for the first time. She didn't want the complicated emotional attachment that could come if she continued to see Wes, to be charmed by him, seduced by him, drawn into his beauty and his compassion and the wonderful, wonderful things his body could do to hers, to continue that mystical bond of friendship they had shared this weekend and to start to believe it could last forever—because it couldn't. Sooner or later their difference would separate them, and Sandy did not know whether she could bear that. Because Wes did not belong in the real world, he *couldn't* last forever, and what she was feeling now was only make-believe. If this went on much longer it would only hurt so much more later, and Sandy had no intention of being hurt.

"I think it's best," she said with difficulty. She tried to smile, to make him smile. "I really don't need another person on my Christmas list.''

The way he looked at her made her feel as though she had just stepped full-grown out of a spaceship, complete with horns and tentacles and green skin. It twisted something deep inside her, and then it made her angry because he had no right to be surprised, or hurt. She had not expected this of him.

Wes said, very quietly, "I love you, Sandy. I want to spend the rest of my life with you."

The room was suddenly still. The entire world was still. And Sandy was caught between one breath and the next, her whole life suspended in the echo of those words, *I love you*. Part of her soared with dizzy joy and she thought, *Yes!* Another part, the strongest part, shrank back in shock and disbelief and could not accept it. She knew nothing of men and their ways; she knew even less of Wes. Was this what he felt was the proper thing to say on the occasion? Was this his way of telling her he wanted the fun to last a little longer, or that he was genuinely fond of her and didn't want to lose her friendship?

Sandy couldn't handle this. This was not at all the way it was supposed to go.

Without even being aware of it, she was shaking her head adamantly, even a little desperately. "You can't love me," she said, "you don't even know me! We're strangers to each other—we only met four days ago. And don't you see that, except for a crazy twist of circumstances, we never would have met at all—we never should have met. We have nothing in common, we live in different worlds." Horrible clichés and trite at best, but that was the best Sandy could do. She swallowed hard, hating the look of ice that was coming over his vulnerable blue eyes, hating herself for putting it there, not knowing what else to do. "We were lucky, Adrian, to have had this weekend—but it was only a weekend. No strings attached, no commitments implied. I thought you realized that. I thought you of all people would realize that!"

And now the ice block in his eyes was complete. He hardly seemed to see her through it. His face had a stiff, pinched look, and he said, without any expression at all, "In other words, you used me."

A stab of pain flared in her heart and seemed to tear right down through her solar plexus. She opened her mouth for an immediate denial, but what could she say? Wasn't that, in effect, precisely what she had done?

Wes turned and walked toward the fireplace, everything within him straining to draw inward and seal off the pain. He couldn't believe it. He couldn't believe it was all over. For the first time in his life he had found something real and genuine, something worth holding on to—and she wanted to rip it away.

He rested his elbow on the mantel, his back to her, his fist cupped loosely against his chin, trying to think. But was it real? Maybe she was right. What did he know about love? He had never loved a woman before, never wanted to be with her always, to care for her and take care of her and keep her happy, to give all of himself to her for all time.

But he did know Sandy. He knew her stubbornness, her determined shortsightedness, her unshakable convictions. And he knew her needs—for freedom, for self-reliance and self-discovery. He knew that he could not give her what she would not accept.

And he knew he could not let her go. Not this easily. He couldn't just walk away and never see her again.

He turned, forcing a smile that was remote and false, but it was the best he could do. His heart was pounding. "Well, all right," he decided, sounding very casual. "I suppose I don't mind being used. You have, in fact, my permission to use me as often as you like." As long as he did not have to say goodbye to her. As long as it wasn't over.

Her heart was breaking. She could feel it, like something turning and twisting inside her. She didn't know she could be so cruel. She didn't know how she could do this to herself. But she knew it would hurt so much more later. She wanted to keep this memory intact, perfect and untarnished, the golden beginning of her new life. She didn't want to face the disillusionment of seeing what they had shared dissolve into dust the moment they tried to make it last in the real world. Why couldn't he understand that? Why was he making it so hard?

But she knew why. Because Wes was a dreamer. It was part of what she loved about him. But she had no room for it in her life.

She couldn't look at him any longer. She was suddenly very tired, and she had to drop her eyes. "It won't work, Adrian," she said softly. "I'm sorry."

It must be love, Wes thought dully. *Nothing else could hurt this much.*

"Your final word?" he said, heavily, and she nodded.

For the first time in his life, Adrian Wesley didn't know what to do. He could not make her love him. He could not make her stay. He could not make her anything but what she was.

"It's best this way, Adrian," Sandy said, and her voice sounded hoarse. Her eyes were filled with pleading, but she did not know what she was pleading for. It *was* best.

Then why did it feel so wrong?

Wes gave her another one of those distant, achingly remote smiles, and then he extended his hand to her. He didn't know what else to do. "I suppose we'd better be going, then."

After a moment Sandy swallowed hard and nodded. She had never felt so miserable, so alone and bereft, in her life, and if he had asked just one more time she would have thrown herself into his arms and gone to Tibet or Timbuktu or anywhere in the world with him....

But he didn't ask, and all the way home she kept telling herself it was for the best. But she knew it would be a long, long time before she believed it.

Chapter Ten

Sandy told her parents about the results of her final examination and the verdict on her skiing career. In the midst of all the bleakness that surrounded her following her last goodbye to Wes, this seemed like a small chore indeed.

Of course they were hurt, sorry and more disappointed than they tried to show, but they had known all along that this was a possibility. After a year of therapy and cautious hope, the shock value of their worst expectations was mitigated a great deal. Still, they wanted to be optimistic. "It's probably for the best, sweetie," her father declared bracingly. "The sport's getting too dangerous for my liking anyway. And you'll be a great coach. Kids will come from all over the country—"

Sandy interrupted, "I don't want to coach."

At the shock and the patent disbelief in her father's eyes, Sandy's mother came to the rescue, looking loving and concerned and only a little stunned. "She may be right, dear. Maybe it's best if she got out of sports entirely. So many painful memories, you know." She beamed her encouragement at Sandy. "Why, you're young yet, baby! Plenty of time to start a wonderful new career for yourself. You could go back to school—"

Sandy shook her head patiently. "I don't want a career. I don't want to go back to school. I've spent my whole life doing what everyone else expected of me, now I want to do something for myself.'' Through the hurt and denial in their eyes, Sandy explained to her protective, concerned, success-oriented family that all she wanted to do with her life was to move from one place to another, take whatever jobs she could, meet different people, see different things.

Her father, with horror in his eyes, exclaimed, ''But that's crazy, girl! How do you expect to support yourself? You can't just go gallivanting around the country doing nothing!''

Sandy, the strictures that had bound her all her life causing her patience to grow thin, explained that in the past year alone she had worked as a bookkeeper, a secretary, a receptionist, a clerk and a shop assistant—there were plenty of jobs she could do. ''But that's not *working*!'' her father insisted. ''That's just staying alive!''

Her parents simply couldn't understand that Sandy's success was not in the winning, it was in the doing. And she did not try to convince them otherwise. They would simply have to learn to understand that she was a big girl now.

Finally her mother, trying to push the worried look out of her eyes, suggested tactfully, ''Sandy's just had a big shock, dear; of course she's uncertain. She's not going to rush into anything. She'll feel better after she's thought about it a while.''

Sandy smiled but did not try to correct her. She had never been more certain that this was what she wanted to do. Maybe it would only last a year or two, maybe it would be for the rest of her life, but right now, at this moment, no one was going to take away from her what she had worked so hard to earn—her own freedom of choice.

Rick had already told her she could keep his car for as long as it lasted. Come the first of the year, she would return Bill's apartment key to him. She had already called an aunt in Ohio who would be more than glad to have Sandy stay with her for a while. She had three hundred dollars saved, and that would get her to Ohio. From there Nebraska, maybe. Or Colorado or California. The whole world was waiting.

But meantime, there was Christmas to get through, and those dreams of endless highways and undiscovered towns seemed very far away. She wondered if the empty feeling that had settled in her stomach the day she had stood on the sidewalk and watched Wes drive out of her life would ever disappear.

But this was real life, in the here and now. Sandy worked, she shopped, she went to her niece's school pageant and her nephew's Christmas recital. She gritted her teeth against the tinkle of Christmas bells and painted a pleasant smile on her face for the throngs at the mall, and gradually the afterglow of romance faded away into the demands of everyday living, the dreariness of another Christmas season. And sometimes, for as long as an hour at a time, she did not think of Adrian Wesley at all....

WES WATCHED *Holiday Inn*, *Charlie Brown's Christmas*, *The Littlest Christmas Tree*, *How the Grinch Stole Christmas*, *Bob Hope's Christmas Special*, *It's a Wonderful Life*...and on and on, day and night, rarely moving from his room, never stirring to go out of the house, and the television set was never turned off.

His friends began to call, first with awkward condolences, then with invitations to one party or another, this event or that event. Wes discovered he wasn't interested. He had grown bored with his friends. He even realized that, all in all, he had never liked them much to begin with. Eventually he stopped taking their calls.

Once it snowed, and it had been all Wes could do to keep his hand away from the telephone, to keep from calling

Sandy. She didn't want to be bothered by him. He wouldn't bother her.

His accountant called several times on matters relating to taxes, and for the first time in his life Wes swore at another person in anger, telling the mild little man to do his goddamned job and stop bothering Wes with trivialities.

And he didn't stop thinking about Sandy once.

Wes was stretched out on the Louis XIV chaise in his room, his arms behind his head, his eyes glued vacantly to the video music channel, when Mitch stopped before him and, without a word, dumped an armload of freshly laundered shirts on his face.

"Will you for God's sake do something with yourself? The atmosphere in this damned house is so low my cakes won't rise!"

Wes sat up, disentangling himself irritably from the shirts, scowling at Mitch. "What's gotten into you?" he demanded.

Mitch met his glare ounce for ounce and eventually overpowered it. He was not in his Proper British Butler mode today. "Look at you!" he sneered, gesturing shortly. "I thought you were worthless before, but this beats it all. What're you planning to do—grow to that fancy couch?" Irritably, he snatched away the shirts that Wes was wrinkling hopelessly as he tried to disentangle himself. He fixed a formidable look upon his young charge. "Why don't you get up off your butt and go find her, damn it! Or didn't you even bother to find out the last name of this gorgeous creature you're going to love for life?"

Wes lay back down, ignoring the lure of the television set for the more interesting attractions of the ceiling. He hadn't really been aware of anything that had flickered across the screen in the past couple of days, anyway. "I know her name," he said dully.

"Well?" Mitch stood above him with all the compassion of a Sherman tank.

Wes stretched his arm over to the end table and gathered his cigarettes and lighter. "She doesn't want me." The words were said flatly, without emotion, and he did not look up as he lit a cigarette.

There was a moment of astonished silence, and then Mitch burst into outrageous laughter. Wes's eyes flew to him, momentarily shocked out of his lethargy. "Bless God," Mitch exclaimed, practically roaring with amusement. "If I could find her I'd kiss her feet! Turned you down, did she? It's about time somebody taught you you're not the be-all and end-all of God's sweet creation! By damn, that's rich!"

Wes moved his eyes back to the television set, drawing on the cigarette. "I'm glad you're entertained" was all he said.

Mitch looked at him peculiarly for one long moment, then went to hang up the shirts.

He still loved her. Every morning Wes awoke surprised by the knowledge, every night he went to sleep with it still haunting him. It was the real thing. It wouldn't go away. For a while Sandy had almost had him convinced. He, who knew nothing about loving, could not know with such absolute certainty that this was his one and only love. Perhaps in a moment of vulnerability, still mourning the death of his father, she had caught him off guard with her sweetness and her charm. Perhaps he was merely infatuated. Perhaps it would go away.

But all those possibilities were considered and dismissed within a matter of moments. The love he felt for her had been building from the moment he met her, had culminated the morning he watched her face a mountain and conquer her own fear, and it would not go away. Not ever.

But there was nothing he could do but do as she asked. He wanted the best for her, and if the best meant a life without him...

Mitch finished with the closet and began stalking about the room, gathering up discarded clothing, empty coffee cups, half-nibbled plates of food, overfilled ashtrays. "The girl doesn't know how lucky she is by half," he muttered. "She got out before she had to live with you. Look at this damn place. You're a pig."

Wes did not even look up, and finally Mitch stopped in front of the television screen, demanding his attention. "You've got to make her want you," he announced with conviction.

Wes almost smiled as he tapped his ashes into an ashtray. "Oh, yes?"

"Damn it, boy," Mitch said with a glower, "you're a Wesley! No Wesley ever played martyr for any man, woman or child in history! Are you going to spend the rest of your life vegetating in this room feeling sorry for yourself? Get out and do something!"

Now Wes did smile, and he extinguished the cigarette lazily. "Funny thing, Mitch," he said. "You never taught me what to do when the answer was no."

Mitch was silent for a time, and his eyes were sober. "There are a lot of things I didn't teach you," he said at last. "Mostly because it wouldn't have done any good. Some things a man just has to learn for himself."

Rejection, Wes had already realized, was one of them. But maybe learning to persevere in the face of rejection was another.

"Well, you can do what you want," Mitch said gruffly, turning toward the door with an armload of dirty clothes and dishes. "But when I get downstairs I'm pulling the circuit breaker on this room and you're going to be left up here with nothing to do but watch traffic."

Wes took out another cigarette, tapping it thoughtfully against his palm, not lighting it. What a fool he was. Sandy was young, inexperienced, facing a multitude of crises in her life and dazzled by everything that had happened to her in such a short time. Then he came along and, with all the arrogance of *droit du seigneur*, began rearranging her life for her, throwing wild propositions at her, overwhelming her with demands. What was she supposed to do, how was she supposed to react? How could she possibly, in such a short time, have known what she wanted? Even Wes, with all his experience, had been thrown by the suddenness and the intensity of his feelings for her. Even he had doubted the validity of them. But he was her first lover, and naturally she would be overwhelmed by everything. Naturally she would be hesitant about trusting her feelings.

A week had passed. Maybe she saw things differently now.

And the possibility was just as strong, of course, that she did not.

But it wouldn't hurt to see her one more time. There would be something in her eyes, and he would know the moment he saw her. But he wouldn't crowd her. He wouldn't rush her. That had been his mistake before. This time he would give her plenty of time, but he would be there, available, just in case.

He still didn't like the idea of setting himself up for more rejection. He wasn't sure how he would handle it if he saw her and there was nothing but anger or irritation in her eyes. He was beginning to think it might be best to leave well enough alone. But now that the idea had been raised, he couldn't get it out of his mind, and he didn't like the idea of going through the rest of his life wondering whether or not she had changed her mind.

He would go to the mall, he decided. That wasn't too much of a risk for his battered ego to take. He could see her, in a public place, and he would know immediately whether she welcomed him or rejected him, without all that awkward conversation that could result if they were alone. Yes, he could do that. He could go to the mall and just stop casually by her shop.

He hoped she was working today. Because if she was not there, Wes knew he would never have the courage to seek her out again.

THE SMALL LIVING ROOM was strewn from one end to the other with a litter of gaily colored wrapping paper, ribbons and boxes. In the midst of it all sat Sandy, unwrapping foil-covered Hershey's Kisses from the candy dish at her elbow, muttering Scroogelike curses between bites of chocolate and searching for her scissors. Her brother Bill lounged comfortably on the sofa, sipping a glass of Lake Country red and watching his sister with tolerant amusement.

"Eureka!" exclaimed Sandy, holding up the scissors with a look of grim triumph, then savagely sliced through a length of ribbon. "Why do presents have to be wrapped anyway?" she grumbled. "Three seconds after Mom says, 'Let's open the presents,' all this hard work is going to end up in the fire anyway."

"Ah, but they look so pretty sitting under the tree for two weeks," replied Bill. Then, just as casually, "So what's with you, babe? More than just this sudden decision to turn into a hobo and go traipsing around the country in search of truth, or whatever you're in search of. Something's bothering you. Give."

Sandy hesitated, then laid the scissors down in favor of another piece of chocolate. After a moment she looked up at him. "I had a lover, Bill," she said simply.

For a moment a tangle of emotions flickered in his eyes, the appropriate reactions of a man who has just discovered his innocent little sister is no longer innocent or little. And then, at last, he smiled. "That's great, Sandy," he said genuinely. "It's about time you grew up and realized what life is all about. So why haven't we met him? Who is he?" Sandy lowered her eyes, and Bill's tone gentled as he slowly understood. "And why do you look so sad?"

Sandy reached for a Fisher-Price toy and set it in the middle of a square of wrapping paper that would no doubt be too short. "His name is Adrian Wesley," she replied slowly, "and he said he loved me. He wanted me to go around the world with him."

Bill stared at her. "A nut, right?"

Sandy tried to laugh, shaking her head. A little nervously, she reached for another Kiss. "No, he meant it. He's rich. And very nice. Probably...the nicest person I ever met in my whole life." She did not realize her voice was softening with emotion until the last was barely audible. "I liked him a lot."

Bill looked at her, and he was silent for a longer time than it actually took for him to understand the situation. He knew his sister too well to miss even the smallest nuance of expression or movement or tone, and he knew what she was feeling now. He almost, in fact, could have told her the entire story, but he wanted to give her a chance to put it into words. So he repeated, "And why is it you look so sad?"

Sandy gave up her struggle with trying to fit the oversized box into an undersized sheet of paper, and she looked up at him helplessly. "We only knew each other four days, Bill!"

Bill lifted one shoulder, hiding a smile by sipping from his glass. "So you didn't have to go around the world with him. But you didn't have to make yourself miserable, either. What did you do, tell him to get lost?"

Sandy lowered her eyes unhappily, taking up another roll of paper. "I thought it would be fun and games. I thought he understood that. I never expected to get so involved. And

I really hurt him." But worse, as she had come to realize over the past week, she had hurt herself. She had never known anything could hurt so much as the loneliness she felt with the absence of Wes.

Bill asked simply, going straight to the heart of the matter, "Do you love him?"

She looked up at him with wide, pain-filled brown eyes, almost as though seeking exoneration. "How can I?" she insisted. "Four days—nobody can fall in love in four days! Not if it's the real thing."

Bill had to smile. "I fell in love with Cassie after talking to her for less than an hour. We made love eighteen hours after we'd first met; I asked her to marry me three days later. And what about Rick and Judy? They met, married and had their honeymoon all within a two-week vacation period. Of course, Linda has always been the conservative one. It took her three months to decide to marry Paul. Let's face it, kid, love at first sight seems to run in this family."

Sandy had to smile in agreement, a little wryly, a little sadly. "Except for Midge," she pointed out.

Bill grinned. "She's young yet. She'll find hers."

Sandy looked at him frankly. "So how many women were there before Cassie?"

"Why do I get the feeling that if I answer that I'm going to hear a lecture about the double standard?"

"But don't you see?" Sandy tried to make him understand. "I don't have that kind of experience to fall back on! How can I know whether it's the real thing or not?"

Bill looked at her thoughtfully. "I think we all only know what we want to know. I think maybe you don't want to even admit the possibility that this could be the real thing because you don't want it to be. Because it just might screw up your plans for your free and independent life on the road. But let me tell you something, little sister," he advised soberly, "you'd better be damn sure it's *not* the real thing before you go tossing it away, because there are no guarantees it will ever come again.''

Sandy concentrated fiercely on her struggle with the recalcitrant wrapping paper, avoiding his eyes. His words hit entirely too close to home. She didn't want to think about them. "You still didn't answer my question," she grumbled.

Bill's eyes twinkled. "About the women in my life? No way. But about how you can tell if it's real..." He shrugged. "Maybe we have to go back to what Mom always says about Christmas—it's the measure of the love, not the measure of the gift. Maybe it has to do with when you stop thinking about what you can do for yourself and start thinking about what you can do for the other person."

And that, Sandy thought with a strange mixture of pathos and relief, must be that. Maybe it was selfish, maybe it was cruel, but she did not have room in her life to think of anyone else but herself. She couldn't afford to love Adrian Wesley. It was as simple as that.

But it didn't feel that simple. Not at all.

WES WAS ABOUT THREE BLOCKS AWAY from the freeway entrance and still debating whether he had the courage to go at all when he spotted a bizarre scene. It was Santa Claus, on his hands and knees, peering into a sidewalk grate. And, as incredible as it seemed, Wes couldn't help thinking the ancient and battered figure looked familiar. He was approaching a traffic light and he slowed down a little, unable to resist a closer look. He was right. It was the same crazy old man from the night in Sandy's store.

Wes pulled the sleek little Austin over to the curb and got out. "Having trouble, old-timer?"

The old man looked up at him, a ridiculous sight in his stained suit and ragged beard, but the faded eyes seemed to register recognition. "Well, young man, just in the nick of time! I seem to have dropped a quarter. I wouldn't worry with it, you know, but those reindeer of mine are still missing and I need it for bus fare.''

Wes could barely keep the laughter out of his face as he stepped up on the curb and examined the situation. The old man had half-pulled the grate up and was vainly trying to find the lost quarter amid a pile of old leaves and trash that was a good foot below his reach.

''Let me try,'' Wes suggested, getting on his knees beside him. ''My arm is longer than yours.''

Santa beamed at him. ''Well, isn't that charitable of you? Please, be my guest.''

Of course, even Wes's long arm could not reach the bottom of the grate, and it would have been impossible to find anything in the litter of trash that had accumulated. But Wes reached down, conscious of the amused stares of passersby and trying not to stain his freshly cleaned coat, and in a moment he presented Santa with the quarter he had sneaked from his own pocket when the old man wasn't looking.

Santa pocketed it, pleased. ''Well, lucky for me you happened along. Thank you.''

''What are you doing on this side of town?'' Wes asked, warming his hands in his pockets. It was cold and windy, and he wondered how the man's frail and aged physique could stand the rigors of a Philadelphia winter in nothing more than a flannel suit. ''I thought you worked the suburbs.''

Santa gave an airy wave. ''Wherever I'm needed, my boy. Wherever I'm needed.''

Wes smiled, shivering and anxious to get out of the cold. ''Listen, it will be an hour before the bus comes.'' Wes had no idea how often public transportation ran. ''No sense in your standing out here freezing. Let me give you a ride. Save the bus fare.'' Anything, Wes thought, to postpone making a fool of himself with Sandy. It probably wasn't a good idea to go out there today anyway. If she had wanted to see him again, he wasn't all that hard to find.

"Well, I don't mind if I do," replied Santa, pleased. "You're a nice young man, aren't you? You never did tell me what you wanted for Christmas."

Wes's smile was bittersweet, the bleakness that passed over his eyes impossible to disguise. "Nothing you can give me, old-timer," he replied, and opened the car door for him.

Santa's eyes twinkled as he got in. "Oh, I wouldn't be too sure of that."

Alternating rising and dropping temperatures had turned the snow that had blanketed the streets two days ago into muddy piles of frozen slush on the sidewalks and parking lots, catching the garish reflection of blinking neon lights from storefronts with a kind of decadent gaiety. Wes thought he had never seen the city look so ugly, and he understood why Sandy hated Christmastime. He wondered if he would ever look at another string of lights or a holiday wreath without thinking of her.

Maybe he wouldn't go to the mall. Hadn't he had enough disappointment, enough pain, in the past few weeks? Why set himself up for more?

He did not realize that Santa's directions had taken him out of the city and into an older, though well-kept, suburban area until the old man instructed him to let him off at the next corner. Wes looked around and saw a small shopping center, a few fast-food restaurants, an apartment complex or two. He thought the neighborhood was safe enough, but he wished the old man would let him take him to a mission or a community home or wherever it was people like this sought shelter from the cold.

"Are you sure you're going to be all right?" Wes leaned over the seat to inquire as Santa got out.

"Merry Christmas, young man," replied Santa cheerily. "And thanks for the ride."

Wes watched him saunter across the street toward the shopping center, and he was struck by a vague sense of familiarity. He looked around at the signposts, and suddenly he knew where he was.

He was right in front of Sandy's apartment.

Wes did not waste another moment with agonizing decisions. He parked the car, got out and locked the door, and he was smiling to himself as he went up the steps.

Fate?

"WHY DON'T YOU HELP?" demanded Sandy grumpily as she taped together yet another less-than-perfect wrapping job.

"What, and deprive you of all the fun?" retorted Bill. "Besides, I've already offered my fingers for three bows. What do you want from me?"

"Another bow."

Obligingly Bill put down his wineglass and extended one finger from each hand for her to wrap ribbon around, and then the doorbell rang. With a martyred sigh, Sandy struggled to her feet, kicking aside the wrapping paper that tangled itself around her ankles, muttering curses and promising dire consequences if it was another charity solicitor at her door, and then Wes's smile swept over her and took her heart away.

She looked at him, his smile so gentle, his eyes a little uncertain, the face that was too thin and the nose that was too long and the ears that were all wrong, and she had never expected it to be this powerful. She looked at him and she was awash with memories and need—the way the smooth planes of his face felt beneath her fingers, the way his eyes crinkled when he laughed, his funny half-grin, the softness of his touch, the strength of his chest. She looked at him and there was wonder and surprise that made her heart start to pound, but there was also a gentle contentment in his familiarity, and it filled her chest like the sight of her oldest and dearest friend. She looked at him and she could not believe she had kept herself away from him for so long. She looked at him and she saw a part of herself, and it felt like the most natural thing in the world to simply float into his arms, to melt into his kiss, to hold him and hold him, for she was so very, very glad to see him.

And with all of this, with happiness soaring through her pulses and wonder cascading in dizzy circles through her head, with every muscle in her body going lax and every nerve ending opening to him, still she managed to say, in an almost normal tone, "Adrian. What a surprise." She stepped back from the door a little. "Won't you—won't you come in?"

Wes looked at her, and he knew. Everything within him sang with the joy of it and it was all he could do to keep from grabbing her face with both hands and kissing her hard, then drawing her against him and kissing her slowly, lovingly, all over. She was glad to see him. He had done the right thing. And then he saw the man in her living room.

Bill got to his feet easily. He needed no introduction, for the look the two young people at the door had shared told him all he needed to know. "You must be Adrian Wesley," he said, smiling. He did not attempt to traverse the wrapping-paper-strewn floor, but gestured welcomingly with his wineglass. "We've just been talking about you. I'm Bill, Sandy's brother. Come on in and have something to drink— but be careful where you step. God only knows what booby traps she has under all that paper."

Her brother. And they had been talking about him. Wes's spirits soared. He carefully traversed the papered floor to shake Bill's hand, immediately liking the big, curly-haired man. "I'm Wes," he said. "It's good to meet you."

Sandy trailed behind him a little uncertainly, apologizing. "I was just wrapping Christmas presents, for the kids, you know.... The place is really a mess...."

"I'll help," volunteered Wes, turning from Bill back to Sandy. His eyes glowed with immediate enthusiasm for the prospect, and they reminded Sandy of the way they had shone that morning he had asked her to see the world with him. He was already taking off his coat. "I've never wrapped presents before, but I'm a quick study. Just show me what you want me to do."

If Bill found anything peculiar in that statement, he hid it by asking quickly, "What would you like—wine or beer? You do have some beer, don't you, hon?"

Sandy tore herself away from the magic light of Wes's eyes and answered her brother distractedly, "Um, yes, I—"

"Wine will be fine," Wes told him, and Bill disappeared into the kitchen.

"Three ninety-five a bottle," Sandy warned him, and Wes laughed. Everything within her melted at the sound of his laughter. He could not know how badly she wanted to sink into him, to wrap her arms around him and to laugh with him, from nothing but the sheer happiness of seeing him again.

Oh, no, she thought. *This won't work at all.* He had only been here a few minutes and already he had her head scrambled and her pulses on fire. Why had he come? Why was he doing this to her?

She cleared out a path of wrapping paper and sat back down on the floor, reaching first for a handful of candy, then for the scissors. She didn't know what else to do but keep busy and act casual and pretend that her whole world hadn't been rearranged the moment she opened that door. Wes turned to hang his coat on the hook by the door, then returned to sit beside her. Too close.

She could smell his fresh, clean fragrance and she could almost feel his warmth. And unexpectedly she was reminded of the texture of his bare skin beneath her fingers, and the sweet drawing rhythms of his body inside hers, and it made her stomach tighten and a warm flush creep up her neck. Nervously, she began to peel back the foil on a piece of candy. Then, quickly, she remembered to act casual. She offered one to him. "Would you like a Kiss?"

"Very much," he said softly. He was watching her with those deep, gentle, soul-absorbing eyes and everything within her was drawn to him, opening to him. *Oh, no, Adrian Wesley,* she thought dimly, *you can't do this to me. You can't come back into my life just when I'm almost sure I could get over you.* But it was too late. She had always known if she ever saw him again it would be too late.

She thrust the piece of candy at him and he smiled. She moved her eyes away quickly, popping her own candy into her mouth. It tasted heavy and too sweet, and she was having enough difficulty swallowing as it was. She began, busily, to measure another piece of paper.

"Sandy…" She felt the feather-light brush of his fingers on the back of her neck and she jumped, her eyes immediately going to his. The wanting and the fear he saw in those huge brown eyes almost broke Wes's heart. "I didn't come to ruin your life," he said gently, and with a final caress, he took his hand away. "I'll go if you tell me to. But I hope you don't tell me to."

She couldn't seem to tear her eyes away, and she couldn't keep the truth out of them. She didn't want him to go. But if he stayed… "Why," she managed a little hoarsely, "did you come?"

He smiled. What infinite tenderness was in his smile. It was richer than any caress. It touched her very soul. "Just to tell you," he answered simply, "that I still love you. And I still want you with me."

Oh, Adrian, she thought helplessly, looking into the kindness and the gentleness and the tender adoration in his eyes. *I can't love you. I still want you, but I can't love you. Please don't let me love you....*

And Wes, understanding, lightly smoothed a curl behind her ear and added, just as casually as Sandy wished she could feel, "And to ask you if you would have dinner with me tonight." Because it suddenly occurred to Wes that he had never courted her. He had met her, loved her, taken her away. A woman like Sandy deserved to be courted, and he wanted to do it in all the grand style available to him.

Sandy had cause for the first time to bless her family and their insane Christmas traditions. An evening alone with him and she would be lost forever. "I can't," she said, and turned busily back to her wrapping paper. "I have a party to go to. I mean, it's not exactly a party, but I have to go. It's just that my family always makes a big deal out of trimming the tree—"

"Great idea." Bill, with timing too perfect to be true, came through the kitchen with Wes's wine. "The folks would love to have Wes come. The more the merrier."

Wes didn't give Sandy a chance to reconsider. He accepted his wine from Bill with a grin and said, "Thanks. I'd like that, a lot." Then, with a rush of enthusiasm, he turned back to Sandy. "Come on, Sandy, show me what to do and we'll have this finished in no time."

Sandy looked in exasperation from her brother to Wes, and then she picked up a roll of ribbon and thrust it at Wes. "Make bows," she commanded, because exasperation wasn't really what she was feeling at all. She was feeling happier than she ever had in her life.

Chapter Eleven

Sandy's parents spared no expense on Christmas decorations. The modest-sized house in the unassuming suburban neighborhood was a showplace of its kind, and every year a steady stream of cars would cruise in front of it, oohing and aahing over the extravagance.

The roof was carpeted in rows of multicolored lights, and on top of it perched a back-lit Santa complete with sleigh and all eight reindeer. Every window was lit with blue candles and outlined with red and green lights. Similarly, the shrubbery along the walk and in front of the house was draped with colored lights, and a soft blue spotlight shone upon the crèche on the lawn. The door was wrapped in ribbon topped by a huge candy-cane wreath, and the entire front porch was lit by a red spotlight. It was a riot of color and celebration, and Wes's eyes widened as he stepped out of Bill's car, trying to take it all in.

"Good Lord," he said softly, and brother and sister chuckled.

"My parents have cornered the market on tacky," Sandy said, half in apology, half in amusement. Adrian Wesley had no idea what he was letting himself in for tonight, and it was probably for the best that Bill had railroaded him into coming. Now he would see what Sandy had meant when she said they came from different worlds.

But Wes only looked at her in astonishment. "Are you kidding? It's magnificent! I haven't seen anything like this since I was a kid. You're one lucky lady, Sandy," he told her sincerely, "to have Christmas like this every year."

Sandy simply stared at him, and Bill looked rather smug as he led the way up the walk.

From that point things only got more confusing. The house was filled with overexcited children and too-tolerant grown-ups. Six-year-old Bess was trying to pick out "Silent Night" on the piano while a Christmas album blasted "Silver Bells" from the stereo. Sandy's father was arguing with Rick about how much of the huge fir tree should be trimmed off to accommodate the star. Sandy's mother had just gotten word that O.J. would be home on Christmas Eve, having once again arranged leave to fly from whatever part of the world he was in to be with his family for Christmas, and she was jubilant. Midge's latest boyfriend was sporting a punk haircut and a muscle shirt. Linda was serving her famous eggnog, and her husband, Paul, was insisting it needed more brandy. It was a zoo—but Wes was delighting in every minute of it.

Of course, everyone loved Wes—that came as no surprise to Sandy. Midge, sidling up to her with an envious look in her eyes, declared that he was a "hunk" and how had Sandy ever managed to snare him? The kids, who had never met a stranger, crawled all over him, pestering him to play cards or video games or give them a piggyback ride, and to Sandy's absolute astonishment he enthusiastically joined in with it all. Rick enlisted Wes's aid in the argument about the tree, and Linda insisted he pronounce judgment on the eggnog. Sandy's mother plied Wes with cheese puffs and homemade cookies, and before Sandy knew it, her father had dragged him off to see his workshop.

While the men were busy in the workshop or setting up the tree, the women gathered in the kitchen to prepare the buffet supper. Of course they were all burning with curiosity about Sandy's new boyfriend, and none of them were shy about asking questions. Sandy handled them as gracefully as she could, but if she could have found Bill she thought she would have strangled him.

Judy, who was not easily impressed, could not get over the fact that Adrian Wesley of *the* Wesleys was such a nice person. Cassie remembered reading about his father's death in the paper, and remarked what a sad Christmas it would have been for the young man if—and she smiled benevolently at Sandy—the season of miracles had not brought Sandy into his life. Midge kept sighing over what a hunk he was, and everyone agreed he must make no other plans than to spend Christmas with them. Sandy's mother, who had married her father six days after meeting him, gave her daughter a brief squeeze and declared, "I knew we were all worrying for nothing. Here you've met this nice young man and you're going to settle down and give us a whole houseful of new grandchildren." And Linda, with uncharacteristic charity, told Sandy, "I know it was hard for you—giving up skiing. But don't you see, hon, it's the best thing that could have happened? Now, you've met Wes and there's nothing in the world to stop you from being happy."

Do I look happy? thought Sandy somewhat frantically. *My whole life is being plotted out for me here in the kitchen and I'm supposed to be happy? This is not at all the way it was supposed to go....*

But when Wes came up from the workshop a long time later, laughing and talking with her father, Sandy's heart gave such a lurch that she knew why everyone assumed that Wes was the best thing that had ever happened to her. *Because he is,* Sandy thought with a sudden intense insight, which she could not deny no matter how hard she tried. *He's the best thing that ever happened to me.* And when she saw him, her face lit up and her eyes felt starry because that was what he did to her. And then she did not wonder anymore why her family had accepted him so easily, why he fit in with them so naturally. It was because he was a part of her.

Wes was still talking with her father and Bill, but his eyes were already searching the room for Sandy. When he found her and their eyes met it was as though he had read her thoughts from across the room. There was a moment of instant contact, of sharing and contented acceptance, of glorious welcome, that shot through Sandy like a lightning bolt and only confused her more. Before she could break the contact Sandy's father had noticed her, and he declared, clapping Wes boisterously on the back, "Your young man is mighty good with his hands, daughter, mighty good! I only had to show him once and he was working that jigsaw like a pro! Took my own boys twice as long to learn. What a Santa's helper he's going to make next year, eh?"

Sandy looked in helpless embarrassment from her well-meaning but far too presumptuous father to Wes, who was now standing beside her. But Wes's eyes were twinkling. "Did you hear that? I'm good with my hands. I never knew that before."

Sandy, caught by the carefree delight in his eyes, thought helplessly, *I know.* And right then all she wanted in the world was to feel those hands upon her.

But her mother was calling everyone to the table to fill their plates, and there was nothing more chaotic than a buffet at the Garret house—unless it was a sit-down dinner at the Garret house. The only time Sandy was even close enough to Wes to talk to him was when someone commented on the potato salad Sandy had brought, and Wes looked at her with amazed appreciation. "Do you cook, too?"

Sandy grimaced. "The last time I cooked, three people got food poisoning. That's why I do my shopping at the deli."

Wes winked at her. "Well, I cook. Gourmet, as a matter of fact. See what a perfect team we would make?"

As she was forming a picture in her head of Wes in apron and chef's hat presiding over a kitchen, he was pulled away by one of the children, who had saved a special seat for him by the fireplace. True, Sandy realized slowly, she knew very little about this man with whom she was trying so desperately not to fall in love. But what a wonderful experience it could be to learn....

Eating was something that was accomplished sitting or standing, while ornaments were pulled out of boxes and children jumped up and down with excitement and everyone decided that yes, this was definitely the largest tree they had ever had. The room was filled with the scent of evergreen and cranberry garlands, spices from the kitchen and hickory wood. Eventually Linda went to the piano and started playing "Deck the Halls," which was the children's signal to dive into the ornament boxes with gusto. Soon everyone was singing along, pulling out colorful strands of tinsel and yards of lights, exclaiming over this ornament or that, and whenever Sandy heard Wes's laughter or caught a glimpse of the light glinting off his golden hair something went through her that left her breathless, a moment of suspended magic, and once she even caught herself humming along with the carols. She realized in amazement that for the first time since she was a child she was actually enjoying the annual tree-trimming circus. And she didn't have to look far for the reason why.

But still, she cautioned herself, it meant nothing. Wes brought cheer wherever he went; it was only natural that he should weave her family into his spell and make this holiday a little more special than others. And it was only natural that, after all he had meant to her, she should feel a little giddy upon seeing him again. But it didn't mean anything had to come of this semireunion. She would be a fool to let anything come of it.

Sandy helped clear the table, do the dishes, straighten up the boxes, and eventually she was drawn by persistent children into the ornament-hanging ritual. All of the grandchildren, and most of the children, had keepsake ornaments with their names on them already hanging on the tree. Sandy had had many of them in her life but was never able to keep up with them, so it usually became her job to trim the tree with the tacky glass balls and Styrofoam snowmen that always lingered at the bottom of the box. But now, as she dug into the box for something worth hanging, someone held another ornament before her face.

"How about this?" Wes said.

It was a wooden rocking horse with "Sandy" burned into the runners. She took it from him slowly.

"Your dad told me how you were always breaking yours," Wes explained with a shrug, watching her carefully.

"She always was a rambunctious child," put in Sandy's mother with an affectionate pat on her head in passing. "That's how we knew she would be an athlete."

"I'm sorry I didn't have time to paint it," Wes said, sounding casual but still watching her. "It wouldn't have dried, and I wanted you to hang it tonight."

She looked up at him in slow filling wonder. "Wes...did you make this?"

"Your dad gave me the pattern," he admitted. "It wasn't hard. Just took a few minutes down in the workshop."

So *that* was what he had been doing down there all that time. Making a gift for her. This man who had never done anything useful in his life had put his first energies toward making something with his own hands—for her. Unexpectedly she felt her eyes fill with tears, and she was too embarrassed for the sentiment to let him see. "It's beautiful, Adrian," she said huskily.

He grinned and lifted a dismissing shoulder. "It's not as nice as something your father could have done, and I was pretty clumsy—even burned my finger a little." She saw, through the haze of tears, the fat blister that was rising on the tip of his beautiful, unblemished finger. "But," he added cheerfully, "no good thing comes without sacrifice, they say.... Hey." Swiftly, his voice was filled with concern, and his finger touched her beneath her chin, gently turning her to face him. "Are you crying?"

Laughing a little, Sandy tried to blink back the betraying moisture, to little avail. "No, it's just that..." *That I love you. Lord, help me, but I think I really do....*

"Mistletoe, mistletoe!" Little Cindy, having just discovered the power mistletoe had to make adults act silly, was dancing beside them, a sprig of the plant held over Sandy's head. Sandy laughed through the sentimental tears and tried to duck, but Wes had caught her hand, guiding it to hang the ornament on the tree as he guided her face to his, and when their lips met all of Sandy's soul sank into the sweetness of it. Her arm curved around his neck, she lost herself in breathless wonder as they came together, as natural as a smile, as unpreventable as living, and as certain as tomorrow.

The overhead lights went off, the multicolored tree spread its aura of gentle loveliness over them, and Sandy did not know whether the applause and the cheers that were generated were for the tree or for the love-struck sight she and Wes made, staring so rapturously into each other's eyes. It didn't matter, because at that moment nothing and no one else existed except she and Wes, and she hoped the world kept applauding forever.

BILL AND CASSIE dropped them off in front of Sandy's apartment on their way home, and Sandy walked Wes to his car. It was bitter cold, and tiny little snowflakes were whirling through the air with little promise of accumulation. It was only natural that Wes should wind his arm through Sandy's for the brief walk through the parking lot, and he teased indulgently, "So tell me again about living in Disneyland. I confess, Sandy, I've been in some of the most lauded playgrounds in the world, and I've *never* had as much fun as I had tonight."

Sandy laughed a little. "My family is very strange. They work like maniacs, they play like maniacs." She shrugged. "I guess with a background like that it's no wonder I have trouble getting my priorities straight."

With great self-restraint Wes did not ask her what her priorities were. He kept to the subject at hand. "I really don't understand it, Sandy. How can you *not* like a Christmas like this? With your family, it's like being a kid again every year. What can be wrong with that?"

Again she shrugged. "Only that everyone has to grow up sometime."

"Ah, yes," he said softly. "Pinocchio wants to be a real boy."

She stopped and looked up at him. Tiny snowflakes fell in the dark between her face and his, and his eyes were very sober. He said nothing, but she knew what he was thinking as clearly as if he had written it down: she was not acting very grown-up now. She was running away from responsibility, turning her back on those who loved her, looking for satisfaction in nothing but her own selfish needs.

But she couldn't help it. She wanted this. She needed it. She had *earned* it. And not even Wes, as much as she wanted and needed him, could take this away from her.

Sandy turned away and, tugging a little on his arm, resumed their more-or-less aimless walk across the parking lot. "I guess," she said heavily, "when it comes right down to it, the thing I hate most about Christmas is that it reminds me of endings. You know, coming at the end of the year, and you're thinking about all the things you expected to have done by now and haven't.''

"Christmas should be about beginnings," Wes pointed out gently. "Isn't that the essence of it? Birth, life, hope?"

"Beginnings frighten me, too," Sandy said, very low, and Wes stopped.

Very lightly, his hands came up to cup her arms, turning her slightly to face him. His head bent to study her face, his eyes careful and filled with understanding. "Is that why I frighten you? Because it's so new?"

She had never thought of Wes in terms of fear before, but wasn't that basically what it was? Afraid to trust her own feelings, afraid to become involved, afraid to share her life with another person? She looked at him, with what seemed to be a great deal of courage, and replied, almost evenly, "Isn't that only natural? To be afraid of what you don't understand?"

"Ah, love..." With a slow breath, he drew her into his arms. "Why do you have to make it so complicated? There's no trick to it—only believing."

And as the warmth of his lips fell upon hers, it did seem that simple. She did not think about fear or responsibility or believing or selfishness. She only thought that she needed him, and she wanted to stay with him like this forever.

But then Wes drew away. Smiling, he brushed a light powdering of snow from her curls. "I promised myself I wasn't going to rush you." He lowered his eyes, and his next words seemed difficult for him to say. "I know at this point in your life you don't need pressure—you don't need interference from another person. I just want you to know that I'm here...if sharing would make things any easier."

So much love and need for him welled up inside Sandy that it almost choked her. But it was still too confusing, and she was not ready to reach out...not yet. She turned and looked without interest over the cold, dark parking lot. "My parents think my plan for the future is crazy and irresponsible. They think I should stay home and start a career and—" she swallowed hard "—get married and raise a family just like all of the other responsible, upwardly mobile Garrets."

"Being parents," Wes suggested gently, "what else could they think? But, Sandy, sometimes your first responsibility has to be to yourself. It's important for you to do this because *you* want to do it. And—" this was very hard to say "—if you have to do it alone, then that's important, too."

Oh, God, she thought, *how could I have been so wrong?* How could she have wanted to live her life alone when there was Wes, the other half of her, to share it with? Oh, she wasn't blind to the problems, for those hadn't changed. Still they came from different worlds, still they sought different things from life, still they had known each other for only a short measure of time and there was still the possibility that when this lovely afterglow of romance had faded into stark reality they would find they didn't belong together at all, and didn't want to. But for now, this moment, she wanted nothing more than to be with him as long as it lasted.

She turned, and laid her gloved hands very lightly upon his lapels. "Wes," she said carefully, "I can't promise you anything. Please understand that what I feel for you is so new and so hard to understand—just as my whole life is right now. That's why I need to move around for a while, and learn things, and just—explore life, before I make any major decisions. It wouldn't be fair to commit to anything right now, not even a job.... But..." And she looked up at him, her eyes filled with uncertainty and a little fear and, above it all, hope. "If you still want to come with me...we could give it a try for a while, and see how it goes."

Very gently, his hand cupped her face, unsteady fingers smoothing back her hair. He hardly breathed for fear she might change her mind. "Sandy, are you sure?"

As always, everything she felt was written in her eyes. "All I'm sure of," she said a little shakily, "is that I don't want you to go home tonight...."

And later as they lay tangled in the sheets of Sandy's bed, quiet and content and filled with the wonder that follows love, she was no more certain of the future, but much less frightened of it. She turned to him, smiling, and traced with the back of her finger the shadow of his chin. "Sometimes," she said softly, "I guess the beginning is the best place to start over."

Lovingly, he captured her finger with his lips. "That," he responded softly, "is exactly what I've been trying to tell you."

Sandy fell asleep in his arms thinking how easy it was to love him, when so little was required of her.

Chapter Twelve

Wes said, very quietly, "That's impossible."

They were sitting in the main parlor of the Wesley mansion, the three prestigious attorneys and the Wesley heir. A fire was crackling cozily in the grate, an elaborate tea cart complete with silver tea service stood nearby. Before the window was a feather-white Christmas tree decorated in perfectly matched blue glass balls and tiny blue lights. The packages—empty boxes, designed for effect only—under the tree were wrapped in color-coordinated blue foil. *Empty boxes,* Wes thought now, and the phrase rang through his head with distant fascination. What would Sandy say if she could see Disneyland now?

In the past five days it seemed as though not a moment had been spent apart from her—laughing, loving, making plans. Nothing had ever felt more right to Wes than being with Sandy, even if her commitment to him lasted only as far as the next town. Being with her, helping her discover life in her own way, growing with her and learning with her...he could spend the rest of his life doing nothing but that.

The lawyers had kept trying to postpone this meeting, but Wes was taking definite steps to put his affairs in order for another prolonged—perhaps permanent—absence from Philadelphia. He had no idea what the running of a financial empire entailed, but it had never seemed to take too much time out of his father's life, and Wes was confident that by delegating authority in the right places he could live with the same sort of freedom he had done before. He only hoped there were not too many complicated decisions to be made, for he was neither trained nor qualified for the business world.

He had never expected this.

Wes stared at the three unhappy-looking, very concerned replicas of a time gone by from his position behind his father's elegant Louis Quinze desk and thought, *This should be a portrait. Three wise men come to depose the heir to the throne.* Every muscle in Wes's body, every nerve ending and autonomic function, seemed slowly to be turning to stone, and he said, with an effort, "There must be a mistake. It can't be all gone, just like that, overnight."

Mr. Wilcox looked at him sorrowfully. "We've tried to explain, Mr. Wesley, that it wasn't overnight. The—er—dissipation of the family fortunes began almost a generation ago, and your father was—" he cleared his throat softly and uncomfortably "—with no disrespect intended, your father did nothing to improve matters. He was greatly concerned with, shall we say, enjoying life to the fullest? He had as little business or financial sense as any man I've ever known."

"Of course," put in Mr. Wilkins, giving tradition to the honor it deserved, "the Wesleys were never trained for great management decisions, which is why the family has always relied upon our firm and their investment brokers for counsel. Unfortunately, your father rarely saw fit to take our advice."

Wes was torn between an outraged defense of his father and a bitter acknowledgment of the truth the men were speaking. No, his father had never concerned himself much with where the money was coming from. Why should he have? No one had ever taught him that one day it might stop coming.

Wes took a deep breath. It hurt his chest. "All right." He folded his hands lightly atop the desk, composing his face into calm lines, facing this all with the equanimity expected of a Wesley. "The situation is bad, but not unsalvageable. We'll simply have to dispose of some property, that's all, and if absolutely necessary, some of the stocks. It will be a sacrifice, but we can survive it. I'm sure we've endured worse."

Mr. Wilkins the elder looked at him with all the pain of a father sacrificing a firstborn son. "Wes," he said gently, addressing him as he had since birth, "the property is long since gone. The stocks have been sold off more gradually, mostly to support your allowance these past few years. When your father was finally made to realize what was happening, his only determination was that you should not know. He always believed he would enter into one last grand venture that would recover it all—and his last venture cost him everything that was left."

Wes's tightly compressed lips grew even a shade paler. "Not everything."

Mr. Wilkins the elder dropped his eyes. It was his son who volunteered, reluctantly, "There is the house and its furnishings, and the automobiles, of course, which, including your mother's jewelry, have been assayed at an amount to cover outstanding debts and taxes. Am I correct in assuming that you have no major investments of your own?"

Wes did not answer. Of course he could never be bothered with complicated and troublesome matters like money management and investments. He could never be bothered with anything except enjoying himself.

Then it hit him, suddenly, fiercely, for the first time in the entire interview: *his mother's jewelry*. The stately mansion that had represented breeding and class for all of Philadelphia for half a century, the luxury automobiles in which Mitch took such pride, his mother's jewelry. Everything that was real and permanent in his life—heritage, tradition, the unquestionable truth of being a Wesley—was gone. It was truly gone.

Everything except his pride.

Wes stiffened his neck imperceptibly, even managed a vague replica of a smile. He made his voice light as he stood. "So, I am reduced to penury. How interesting."

The good gentlemen, as one, looked shocked. "Not penury," insisted Mr. Wilcox, and Mr. Wilkins the younger chimed in. "Certainly not!"

Mr. Wilkins the elder cleared his throat. "Whatever the present circumstances may be, we do not forget that you are, after all, a Wesley. And no son of Alex Wesley will ever be found wandering the streets. There is still the family name to uphold, you understand. There are certain legal steps we can take to allow you to keep this house—it is, after all, a monument to the Wesley tradition and shouldn't be allowed to fall into the hands of strangers. Most of the antiques, though, I'm afraid will have to go. And you will have no income of your own." The good man, whose father and grandfather before him had been upholding Wesley tradition for generations on end, found this fact almost too unhappy to relate. "And a great deal of output, I'm afraid, until this matter of taxes is settled."

Wes looked at him, hardly comprehending. "What am I supposed to do? Get a job?"

The three men looked uncomfortable. "A position," offered Mr. Wilcox, "is precisely what we have in mind."

"We have taken the liberty," continued Mr. Wilkins, "of discussing the matter with Geoffrey Madison, who, as you know, is an old and dear friend of your father's and, as his banker, is fully cognizant of the situation. He has quite generously made available to you a position within his firm.''

For a moment Wes only stared; then a harsh, incredulous laugh erupted. ''As what? An investment banker?''

Mr. Wilcox drew himself up to his full dignity. ''Hardly anything quite so—rigorous. Mr. Madison assures me that a gentleman as personable and as—well placed—as yourself would be quite valuable to his organization, yet the demands upon you would not be strict. The primary consideration, of course, is that it is a respectable position and the income would allow you to live—not luxuriously, but in marginal comfort.'' And then, the final words. ''I see no other options open at this point.''

It ripped through him suddenly, like a jagged piece of lightning, *Sandy. Oh, God, Sandy*. He wanted her, more desperately than he had ever thought he could want anything. Sandy, so levelheaded and practical; Sandy, who could make him laugh; Sandy, who was strong where he was weak; Sandy, just to stand beside him and hold his hand; Sandy, who could make this nightmare go away.

But Sandy did not belong here. She had no place in this discreet, spacious, elegantly furnished room with its centuries of taste and its sterile Christmas tree. Last night they had relaxed together in her tiny, homey apartment, she stretching out on the sofa while he rubbed her tired feet and told her of Paris, and afterward they had made love in her bed, which was too short to accommodate his frame, and he had thought that was reality. But it was another lifetime, and even the memory had no place in the face of what was, in fact, the final reality. He wanted her, briefly, intensely, with a fire in his soul, and then he let her go. She did not belong here.

He knew about the ''position'' he was being offered. A near necessity for firms that based their reputations upon respectability and tradition, it was a job for socially prominent but intellectually deficient unfortunates who had fallen on financial hard times but still, through long-dictated tradition, had a certain image to maintain. It required only that he be personable and charming, and act well-bred and responsible at all times, by his mere presence assuring the elitist clients of the Old Guard that their fortunes must be in good hands because, "after all, my dear, he is a *Wesley*." It was the only respectable option for a man of Wes's class, ornamental by nature, mutually advantageous by design. What else was to become of an unskilled, erratically educated, untrained young man with no money and three hundred years of tradition to maintain?

Wes said, very slowly, "I could sell the house and dispense with the debts. Or you can work whatever legal magic it is you work and I could keep the house and be in debt for the rest of my life."

A brief, somewhat stunned silence followed his speculation. And even as Wes spoke he knew he could not let go of the place. It would be like burying an era, like cutting the lifeline on an entire way of existence. The house itself meant nothing to him, but what it represented was all he had ever known.

"It's not just this house, you know," Mr. Wilkins replied carefully. "Even if we sold everything you own, down to the china and crystal, you would hardly have enough left over to keep body and soul together. You must think about a way to support yourself. I know it's difficult, but you must accept responsibility for yourself, Wes. There is no one left to do it for you."

Wes had nothing to say to that.

For a long time after they had gone Wes stood before the window, his thoughts chasing themselves around like automated toys until he became too weary to follow them anymore, too weary to do anything except to simply stand there and feel raw and empty and stunned, and older than he ever thought it was possible to get.

Poetic justice. He, who once had everything, now had nothing. He, whose life to this point had been empty and vain, was now reaping the rewards of his own intemperance. And the Wesleys, ancient and linked to the tradition of excellence through conservatism, were now brought to ruin by their own overconfidence. So went the reign of old kings and lavish empires.

How strange it all was. Money had never meant anything more to him than something one changed into tips and was careful not to carry too much of. Now that it was gone, it should have simply been gone, rarely considered, little missed. But somehow in its absence it had more power over him than it ever had with its presence. Its shadow was weighing down the rest of his life, changing it irretrievably. For it was more than the loss of a fortune. It was the loss of identity, of all he had ever stood for and known about himself, and he felt cut loose, suspended, floating somewhere between yesterday and tomorrow and not knowing where to turn.

Wes did not know how long Mitch had been in the room before he became aware of him, but he was not surprised to turn and find his faithful servant standing there. Mitch. Another part of a life that no longer existed, a ghost from the past, as solid and secure and as permanent as this house itself, but no longer affordable. God, the responsibility.

Wes said, quietly, "You knew about this, didn't you?"

Mitch faced him squarely, without arrogance, without shame. "I knew some," he admitted. "I had no idea it was this bad."

Wes nodded. Absently, he walked over to the desk, fingering a porcelain inkstand that was too valuable to contain real ink. The duties of the lord of the manor weighed heavily on his shoulders. He did not know whether he had the strength to execute them. "Mitch..." He turned slowly; he managed to smile. "Mitchell," he corrected himself softly, and saw the surprise register in the other man's face. "I want you to know that I'll do everything I can to see that you're taken care of. You shouldn't have to suffer for our mistakes, and you've—well, you've meant too much..." His voice thickened here, briefly, and he had to clear his throat with a determined effort. "You've meant too much to both my father and myself to be forgotten now."

Mitch looked at him for an implacable moment, and then he said, "I have sixty-three thousand dollars sitting around earning interest, a condo in Florida, and my army pension." He smiled briefly. "Your father paid me very well. Another one of his faults, perhaps." His expression sobered. "I know if I were any kind of friend, I would offer you some of that money, just to get you on your feet again. But it's precisely because I'm your friend that I'm not going to."

Mitch turned away from Wes, and for the first time in Wes's memory the great man in faded denim and scuffed sneakers looked uneasy. He clasped his hands behind him and spoke into the fireplace. "We always wanted the best for you, your father and me. But your dad, he couldn't teach you what he didn't know and I—well, you were such a cute little tyke, always could get around me or anything else on two legs." He looked at Wes, his expression strong through the distant hurt. "So we made mistakes. Ain't no use crying about them now. We let you grow up without ever having the faintest idea what responsibility was, or what it was to take care of yourself, or what would happen when the world stopped noticing your pretty smile and your winning ways.

"But let me tell you something, Adrian Wesley." Now Mitch's voice became fierce. "You come from a fine breed of men. Strong, honorable, decent men. It's time you started living up to your name, earning what's been yours so long you've forgotten what it means. You can build it all over again; you're smart enough, and you're strong enough to do whatever you have to. I believe that for a fact."

No, I'm not, Wes thought in distant pain. *I'm not strong enough to face this. I was never meant to be strong enough to face this.* Out loud he said, "In other words, it's time Peter Pan grew up."

Mitch looked at him, long and soberly. "Sometimes," he said, "the best way to get to the top is to start from the bottom."

There was a silence, and then Mitch said, more briskly, "I'll stay until you get things in motion and get yourself settled. But I've been looking forward to retirement for a long time, and I expect to be in Florida not too long after the first of the year."

Briefly, very vaguely, Wes smiled at him, grateful for the businesslike tone and his effort to put everything back on an even keel. "Sure," he said. "Thanks."

Mitch inclined his head, once more back into his butler role, and turned with a precise step to leave the room. At the door he stopped, and said, without looking around, "Good luck…" And he paused. "Wes."

Wes sank down behind the desk, leaning his head back against the smooth Corinthian leather of the chair, closing his eyes. *Time to grow up, Wes.* But he didn't want to grow up. He didn't want to worry about taxes and maintenance on this white elephant of a house, he didn't want to put on a suit every day and go to some bank and sit like a piece of furniture smiling prettily and keeping blue-haired, discreetly bejeweled old ladies confident and happy. He wanted to cast caution to the wind and see the world with Sandy.

But he wouldn't. He would stay here in Philadelphia and maintain the image and begin to build again because it was the honorable, responsible and respectable thing to do. Because he was a Wesley, and it was time he became a man.

Sandy. Oh, God, Sandy. He tightened his eyes against the sting of pain there. He had wanted to give her the world and now...he couldn't ask her to stay with him. He could not ask her to give up her dream, or even think of it. How could he turn his back on the legacy of responsibility that had come to rest, like a heavy mantel, upon his shoulders? This was what she had meant by real life. Only their realities, as they had always been, were two different things.

He stood abruptly, unable any longer to bear simply sitting there and letting the future press him down. He wasn't meant for this. How could this have happened to him? It couldn't happen, not to him, Adrian Wesley, who always had everything his way.

He stood restlessly beside the desk, his fingers absently stroking the porcelain inkstand, his eyes focusing, at last, upon the portrait of his father above the mantel. The handsome, slightly overbred face looked down at Wes with a touch of carefree arrogance and a twinkle in his eye—this man who loved life and lived every moment of it and never thought about the future. The man who had left his son his *joie de vivre* and the afterglow of a life well lived and nothing else. A rush of bittersweet resentment coursed through Wes, mixed heavily with confusion and he thought, *It's not fair.*

"It's not fair," he said out loud, and his fingers tightened around the inkwell until its delicate construction threatened to crack with the pressure. How could he tell Sandy? How could he let her go? Dear God, Sandy was the only thing he had ever really wanted in his life, and if it was only money that stood in his way it would have been easy. He had come so close to losing her, it had been so hard for her to let him into her life, and just when he was beginning to think they had a chance...

But she must go her own way, wherever her search for life took her, and he—he was bound here by a sense of honor he would never understand and a responsibility he had not sought and did not want.

He had to stay and make the best of what was left. For his father, and his father before him, and all the generations of Wesleys who were depending upon him.

And suddenly he hated it all, everything that he was and everything that he had to be, with a deep and burning intensity that flared through his veins and seared his brain, and he drew back his arm and flung the inkwell at his father's face. "Damn you!" he shouted. "Damn you for doing this to me!"

It was not until he had stalked coatless out into the dying day that Wes realized it was twenty-thousand dollars worth of irreplaceable antique porcelain that he had smashed against the mantel.

SANDY STRODE into the precinct house, her face a tight mixture of alarm and amusement. Rick's phone call had been rushed, and she still wasn't quite sure she had heard him correctly. If he had said what she thought he said, she had cause either to be very worried or very amused, but even after the twenty minute drive to the station she still wasn't certain which.

Sandy spotted her brother in conversation with another officer and went over to him immediately. "If this is your idea of a joke at six o'clock in the morning..."

Rick lifted a hand in self-defense, his expression a mixture of weariness and amusement. "I swear, honey, after the night I've had the last thing I'm in the mood for is jokes. And I'm sorry if I woke you up, but I waited until just before I went off shift. I thought you'd want to know."

Sandy carefully assessed his expression and his words and decided he was not joking. Then something was wrong. Very wrong. She should have known. Last night was the first time she had neither seen nor heard from Wes in almost a week.

She had excused him to herself at the time, for he had told her he had business to take care of yesterday and he was probably tied up with all those complicated things that went along with being rich. Besides, she didn't ever want to start feeling possessive toward him. The last thing she wanted was for either one of them to get possessive. But she *should* have been possessive, she berated herself now. She should have *known* something was wrong. She should have known Wes would have at least called her if he had been able....

Her heart was beating fast and there was a tight feeling in her stomach, and she demanded, with an urgency that she bitterly recognized as being too little, too late, "Is he hurt? Can I see him? Rick, are you sure he's all right?"

Rick's nonchalance made her feel like hitting him. She was in no mood to sympathize with the fact that a man who had been through two armed robberies, a shooting and a near kidnapping in the past ten hours would be wont to see Adrian Wesley's situation in a slightly different light than she did. "Sure." He shrugged. "I don't imagine he's feeling exactly on top of the world right now, but he'll live. Do you want to bail him out? The bondsman's getting ready to leave."

Sandy felt slightly ill. Adrian Wesley, so dignified, so confident, thrown in jail like a common criminal. She had a flash of that look in his eyes the last time he had been brought here and the nausea only tightened. *Oh, Adrian, how could this have happened?* She should have known. Was this the way she showed how much she cared for the man she loved—by assuming what he did with his own time was none of her business? She should have *known* he wouldn't just disappear like that without calling.

Her eyes went from the direction of the holding cells back to Rick, torn. Adrian would hate it there. The first thing she had to do was get him out. "Yes," she said, beginning to fumble through her purse. "Let's hurry. Do you have any money? I'm not sure I—"

Rick threw a comforting arm around her shoulder, leading the way toward the interrogation room where the bondsman was just beginning to close up shop. "Take it easy," he said. "It's not like he's on death row or anything. He'll wait a few more minutes." And then he grinned. "Hey, you'll never guess who else we have back there...."

WES OPENED HIS EYES foggily to a bleak green ceiling and heavy fluorescent lights, and a moment of disorientation would have been a blessing. But there was none. Adrian Wesley knew exactly where he was.

Dimly, his mind put together a picture of his life for the past three weeks: he had lost his father, been arrested, fallen in love, lost a fortune.... And now Adrian Wesley, who had been bred to hold his liquor like a gentleman, was sitting in jail for public drunkenness and disorderly conduct. He would have smiled if he had had the energy.

He sat up slowly, holding his face in his hands, feeling as if the bones of his skull were going to split in two. There was no way to tell whether it was daylight or dark, and Wes had no idea how long he had been there. Not long enough, he suspected. Right now, jail seemed to him like the safest place to be.

A gentle hand fell upon his knee, and an almost familiar voice inquired, "A minor reversal of fortunes, young man?"

Wes peered fuzzily through his fingers and was not at all surprised at what he saw. Santa Claus, who else?

Wes slowly straightened up, trying not to wince. Every part of him ached, and his mouth felt like something too filthy to describe. He said, a little hoarsely, "So, what are you in for, old man?"

Santa gave a dismissing wave of his hand. "Vagrancy, loitering—they have some fancy word for it." He smiled. "I suspect, however, that this was the nice young policeman's way of making sure I had a warm place to sleep. They don't understand I'm used to much colder temperatures than Philadelphia could ever produce!"

Very carefully, Wes eased his shoulders back against the wall, resting his head. The smile that twisted his face was barely a grimace. "Well, I suppose this means my name gets stricken from your list."

"Not necessarily. Everyone is entitled to one mistake a year, at least. And you've been so very good I hardly think this should count much against you."

Wes almost laughed. The light hurt his eyes, so he kept them closed. "I've been good, have I?" He wondered what his father would think if he could see him now. Or Mitch. Or Sandy...and then he didn't feel like laughing anymore.

"Oh, yes, indeed," replied Santa Claus confidently. "But then, you are one of those people to whom being good comes easily. It's in your nature. Oh, yes," repeated Santa, launching forth into what was apparently one of his favorite subjects. "You are an almost perfect example of the Christmas spirit, I think. Kind, considerate, putting others before yourself comes easily to you."

Wes opened his eyes then, to look blurrily at the old man. He wasn't kind or considerate. He was selfish and irresponsible, he always had been, everyone knew that. But what was he doing sitting here in jail listening to a crazy old man sum up his character? Wes closed his eyes again.

"And generous," continued Santa benevolently. "Not just with your material possessions, but with yourself as well."

Wes emitted a short, harsh laugh. "Good thing. Because I don't exactly have a lot of material possessions to be generous with anymore." And suddenly he was annoyed. He didn't want to be in this filthy cell with this pathetic old man. He would almost rather face Mitch. Didn't he get one phone call or something?

"Precisely." Santa's voice was soft. "It all depends, doesn't it, on where one's treasures are."

Wes looked at him again, surprised by the almost intelligent look in the faded blue eyes of the wizened old man next to him. This was getting spooky. If it had not required so much energy, Wes thought he would have called out for a guard, demanding his phone call. But then he thought of what was waiting for him outside the cell and decided it would be easier to put up with the demented ramblings of a harmless old man. Weren't there facilities for people like this, Wes wondered absently. Was this the best the city could do for the indigent and the insane?

"And of course, we mustn't forget the most important thing," declared Santa, settling back with a beaming smile of approval. "You believe. It's not easy to find people today who believe. Most people don't believe in anything but themselves, and you—" Santa's eyes grew briefly troubled "—well, I suppose the only thing you *don't* believe in is yourself. That's not good. Not good at all. But..." He brightened. "You're young, and you have plenty of time to learn, don't you? I would say, as a matter of fact, that the one thing you do have plenty of right now is time."

Sometimes the best place to start over is from the beginning....

There were footsteps in the corridor, shadows against the bars, and an officer swung the door open. "Okay, Wesley, you can go. Bond's been posted. Be sure to pick up your things at the desk. You, too, Kris. Time's up."

Wes started to get shakily to his feet, wondering vaguely who had called Mitch to post bond, and then he saw Sandy.

Her cheeks were rouged with cold, or excitement, and her hair was wind-tousled. She was wearing jeans and the bright red parka that made her skin glow like the reflection of a fire on the purest of porcelain, and she looked so young and fresh and alive that something in Wes's chest tightened and threatened to choke him, and he couldn't have moved then if his life had depended on it. All he could see was Sandy, walking through the snow, laughing up at him, her eyes like diamonds, her breath frosting in the air, and everything within him reached out to her, wanting her, wanting her so badly he thought his heart would break.

Let it go, Wes. Don't drag her into this. It's not fair.

"Well," declared Santa, rubbing his hands together with enthusiasm as he got to his feet. "I must be off. Busy time of the year, you know, and less than a week left until the big night." Smelling like gin and old clothes, he paused beside Sandy, his merry blue eyes quiet with the kindness of his voice, and he said, "Remember, little one, the only gifts of any value are those that are the hardest to give." Then, with a cheery wave to both of them, he added, "I shall see you both before I leave—I'll make a special point of it. Merry Christmas!"

And then Sandy was left there alone, looking at Wes.

It was a frightening sight. Adrian Wesley, alone in a jail cell, sitting on a sagging cot looking rumpled and unshaven and bleary-eyed—and defeated. His hair was dull and tousled, his expensive clothes wrinkled and mud-stained, his beautiful smile gone. This was not Adrian Wesley, perfect man. This was reality, and it scared her.

"Adrian…" she half whispered, and took a step toward him.

He held up a hand to ward her off. "No, don't come near me. I haven't shaved and I smell bad."

Her heart began to pound, fiercely, distantly, with a cold premonition of pain. He didn't want her. He wouldn't even look at her. *What had happened to him?*

There was a small shadow of a bruise on his gold-bristled cheek, and the alarm in her chest quickened. "Adrian, what happened? Were you in a fight?" Incredible, even to her own ears. "Are you hurt?"

He shook his head, still not looking at her. "No." His voice was terse. "I fell down, I think. I'm not hurt." And then his lips twisted into a bitter semblance of a smile. "I was very drunk."

Adrian, drunk? No. Something was very, very wrong. She wanted to go to him, to gather him in her arms, to hold him and to comfort him and to share whatever it was that had made him this way, that even now seemed to be tearing him apart inside. To share, as they always had, from the first moment. Adrian in a dim and trendy lounge, listening with compassion and understanding in his eyes as she told him about her lost career, sharing his own loss with her, making her see everything more clearly...Adrian, picking her up out of the snow and giving her a shoulder to cry on. Adrian, sweeping her into his arms and declaring that if she wanted to see the world, that was exactly what he would show her. Adrian, who had been there at every important crisis in her life, sharing, understanding, enlightening. Why wouldn't he let her be there now for him?

"Please," she said. Her voice was hoarse and her eyes searched his face. But she did not move closer. She would have given her life if only he had come to her. "What is it? Adrian, tell me what's wrong."

Wes leaned his head back against the wall, closing his eyes, and the bitter smile deepened a fraction. "A minor reversal of fortunes," he quoted smoothly, and then the smile faded. It suddenly sounded self-pitying, childish and petty, and a minor detail indeed when Sandy was standing there, close enough to touch, and all he had to do was sweep her into his arms and everything would be the way it was before.

But no. Nothing would ever be the way it was before. He didn't know if he could live with that yet. He had no intention of asking Sandy to.

He opened his swollen eyes, looked at her soberly. *Grow up, Wes. Face it.* "Sandy," he said quietly, "it's too complicated a story to go into, but the money's gone, and I've been offered a job here in Philadelphia. I have to stay and take it."

Sandy's first thoughts were incoherent. *Money? What money? What does he mean—job?* But as she stared at him, one thing slowly became clear: something had changed. No, everything had changed.

Wes looked at her, and he thought suddenly how silly it all was—how incredible that one small twist of circumstance like this could keep them apart. One day he was free to be with her and the next he wasn't, and why? Because of money? No, because they both had outgrown Disneyland. Because miracles and magic and make-believe could only work for so long and eventually you had to wake up in the real world. And in the real world things were different.

His smile gentled and he said, "I know it doesn't make sense. I don't even understand it myself. Maybe when I do I'll explain it to you, but right now I have a lot of responsibilities to take care of." He made a small sound that could have been an echo of a sad, wondering laugh. "Funny," he said, but there was no amusement at all in his eyes. His eyes, in fact, looked bleak. "The only thing in my life I ever wanted to be responsible for was you."

And she wanted to be responsible for him. She knew that suddenly, and instinctively, without thinking about it at all, simply because he belonged to her, was an indelible part of her. And even as she knew it she could feel him slipping away.... "Adrian," she said swiftly, torn with confusion and creeping desperation, "I don't understand. If you're in some kind of trouble, let me help." And then she understood, quite suddenly, quite indisputably, and it took her breath away. Wes had to stay here, and she had to go. It was as simple as that.

Oh, God, he thought, *how can I do this? How can I do this without her?*

But there were some things a man had to learn for himself.

Wes got to his feet slowly. "Sandy," he said gently, and with great difficulty, "we both have important things to do with our lives now. Only they're taking us in different directions. It's important for you to go through with your plans." He didn't give her a chance to object. "It's right for you, it's *necessary* for you, just as it's necessary for me to fulfill the obligation of being who I am. I know it sounds corny, but that's the way it is. I suppose you were right before...when you said we come from two different worlds. It never made any difference, I guess, until I suddenly realized how strongly I was tied to mine."

But was he really? The thought came out of nowhere. What was there left to be tied to? Nothing except vague concepts like honor and nobility and responsibility.

He wanted it to be different. He really did. But he was a Wesley.

Sandy, white-faced, said, "And so all along we were just playing at love, right?" What was wrong with that? Wasn't that what she wanted? No commitments, no involvements.... "And the first little thing that comes along..." Her voice almost broke and she clamped down on it rigidly, refusing to let her gaze waver from his. What she saw in his eyes broke her heart, slowly, piece by piece.

"Not a little thing." His voice was thick, and it hurt to speak. Was he really going to walk away from her and never look back? But how could he ask her to come with him?

Where are your treasures?

He took a deep, painful breath, steeling himself for the last. "Only," he said, "what I'm going to do with the man called Adrian Wesley, now that I'm beginning to find out who he is... I've got a lot of decisions to make, Sandy," he said tiredly. "I don't know what else to tell you except that I have to make them on my own."

Just as he had allowed her to make her decisions on her own. She had never extracted any promises from him, or offered any. They had known each other for such a short time. It had all been carousels and cotton candy, carefree and easy, loving each other when it cost them nothing. She should have known. She should have known it wouldn't be that simple in real life.

Wes stopped beside her and lightly, with infinite gentleness and a heart filled with care, touched her face. His beautiful eyes, bloodshot and puffy, were filled with so much love and so much pain that Sandy couldn't help it— the tears that had been clogged in her chest, sluggishly filling her heart and impairing her breathing, began to slowly creep upward. *Please, Adrian,* she thought, *don't do this.* But how could she stop him? How could she ask him to give to her what she had never, ever, been willing to give to him— herself, complete and without reservation, at whatever cost.

"I want you to have a good life," he said huskily. "That's all."

And then he dropped his hand and Sandy turned quickly away, refusing to tie him down with tears when she refused to tie him down with promises. *This is what you wanted, isn't it? One less person on your Christmas list?* Then she almost did sob. She had to hug her arms very tightly to her chest to stop it.

She heard his footsteps moving away, and at the door he paused. "Thanks for bailing me out," he said. "I'll pay you back." She turned and through a fog of moisture saw the slight bitterly reflective smile tug at his lips. "Wesleys always pay their debts," he said.

He turned and was gone.

Chapter Thirteen

For the first two days Sandy didn't believe it. She went to work, she came home, she ate, she slept. She kept a bright smile painted on her face for the grouchy, rushed, last-minute Christmas shoppers whose incredible demands and increasingly bad temperaments would have made a saint swear on his best day, and every time she looked up and caught a glimpse of a blond head her heart would stop.

She told herself it didn't matter. So she had been disappointed in love—wasn't that all part of growing up? There was no law that said one's first lover had to be the last. She had known it wouldn't work; from the beginning she had expected this, that was why she had been so determined to keep it light. It was just never meant to be. She had known that. She shouldn't be hurt. And every time the doorbell rang she stopped breathing, and this awful surge of hope would flare to her chest.

Sandy told no one what had happened, and if she was a little too cheerful, a little too helpful, maybe even a little too brittle, her family was too busy with the frantic preparations for the holiday to notice, or they attributed it to the Christmas spirit and enjoyed Sandy's equanimous temper while they could. Mostly, Sandy avoided seeing her family. Mostly, she tried to convince herself that she was too busy with her own plans to mourn the loss of a man she had known less than a month. Look at the way Midge went through boyfriends. She had the right idea. Don't get too attached to anyone; just enjoy them all while you can. Yet every time the phone rang Sandy leapt for it, her heart exploding in her throat. But it was never Wes.

Wes kept himself very busy. His lawyers worked overtime, drawing up papers for his signature, consulting with various financial experts, pushing the estate through probate. Wes called Mr. Madison and talked with him about the job, and all the while he was thinking, *Why am I doing this? Why am I doing this thing I don't want to do? Why am I turning my back on the only real chance for happiness I've ever known?*

Because his father would have expected it of him. Because everyone expected it of him.

So he consulted with estate auctioneers and financial planners, and listened intently to all the advice his attorneys had to give, and there was not a minute of any day that he did not wonder what Sandy was doing now....

BY THE THIRD DAY, Sandy had gotten angry. How could he do this? How could he just walk away from her after all they had shared? He had been her first lover, for heaven's sake; didn't he have any idea what that had meant to her? How could he just forget about her because he had something better to do? She had *trusted* him, she had depended upon him, she had let him into her life. How dare he come sweeping down upon her and rearrange her thoughts and feelings and even her plans and then just leave her with nothing but a memory for the good times. She hadn't *wanted* to love him. She had told him it wouldn't work. But he had made her love him, he had insisted upon becoming a part of her life. And then he just tossed it all away.

What did he expect her to do? He knew what she wanted from her life. She had an opportunity to find it, to explore all the options open to her, to do and discover the things she had always wanted to. Did he expect her just to drop everything and hang around Philadelphia, on the off chance that he might some day decide to notice her again? What was so damn important about taking a job, anyway? *She* wouldn't have a job after the first of the year, and was she worried? Damn it, she had never cared about his money. Why did he think he had to leave her just because he didn't have it any longer? Did he think she was that shallow, that selfish?

And why didn't he call?

WES WANTED EVERYTHING that could possibly be done well on its way to completion before the first of the year. He did not know why he felt such an urgency, except that there were years of uselessness to make up for, and as long as he kept busy he didn't have to think so much.

But he couldn't help thinking of Sandy, with her quirky sense of humor and her determined independence, and her wide-eyed love of life that glowed like a beacon through the veil of cynicism she tried so hard to wrap herself in. How much she had taught him. From the very first moment they met, she had brought into his life a taste of the unknown, when he thought he knew everything. She had brought him challenge when he thought there were no challenges left. She had taught him to care when he knew nothing of caring. With everything she did, she had made him stronger, better, wiser, more aware, almost as though by design, knowing that one day he would need everything he had gained from her, preparing him for this time in his life that he never would have survived without relying upon characteristics she had taught him. And now she was gone, but what she had brought into his life lingered...would always linger.

He did not know how he was going to make it without her, but he would never ask her to stay with him. All her life she had been tied to achievement, obligation, discipline, and she had earned the right to live her life the way she pleased. He would not, even if she insisted, allow her to sacrifice her dream for a life with him—a life that even he did not like. He had nothing to offer her except her own freedom.

And at night, when he lay sleepless and alone in bed, he could not understand why the only things worth having were so suddenly and inescapably beyond his reach.

ON THE FIFTH DAY, Sandy started to cry. It came upon her suddenly and without warning, and once she started she could not stop. She was having dinner at her parents' house, determined that the only way she could ever stop expecting Wes to call was to get out of her apartment and away from her telephone, when suddenly she caught a glimpse of the wooden rocking horse with her name carved on it hanging on her parents' Christmas tree. The tears, big and sluggish and painful, coursed out of her eyes, and neither her mother's alarmed flutterings nor her father's stern comforting could stop them.

She knew then that it was over. Wes had given her everything—his love, his tenderness, his patience and his determination in the face of all odds. He had come back to her when she said she didn't want him, he had stood by her though she refused to make a commitment. He had told her he would love her forever and she had never told him she loved him at all.

And what had she given him? Careless affection, a few good times, and a warning not to get too close. She had used him, she had taken from him, she had never once thought of anything or anyone but herself. *She* was the one who was important, *she* was the one who had to take care of herself, and when he had wanted to share with her, to make it easier for her, she had agreed only at great length and then conditionally. All she had ever cared about was her own indulgence, her own pleasure, *herself*, and she had allowed

Wes to come into her life only as long as he didn't cause her too much inconvenience. He had loved her, totally and without reservation, enduring rejection, uncertainty and her own self-involvement, and he had never once demanded more of her. But when he needed her—when he was in trouble and he needed reassurance, comfort, strength—what had she done but let him walk out to face it on his own? She had her own plans, her own life to live. She couldn't be bothered.

Oh, yes, it was easy to be in love with Adrian Wesley. But loving him required strength, commitment, even sacrifice—all things she had never known anything about.

What was it Bill had said? That loving had to do with when you stopped thinking about what you can do for yourself and started thinking about what you could do for the other person.

But what *could* she do? Sandy, who had grown up with the strict values of responsibility and stability and goal achievement embedded into her consciousness, knew too much about what Wes was facing now not to understand why he had to do it. She could not ask him simply to turn his back on everything he stood for, and everything his family had stood for, for generations, and come away with her.

She thought she was so mature, so practical and so well oriented to life and what it required of her. But she was a child, self-centered and self-concerned, and she would remain so until she learned the most important lesson: that love is not a passing fancy, to be played with at leisure and put aside when one grows bored or the game gets too complicated. It requires all of you, heart and soul and without reservation, for all time.

The only gifts of any value are those that are the hardest to give. Who had said that? Sandy couldn't remember, but she knew the truth of it in a rush of overwhelming sorrow that started the tears afresh. The only thing she had to give

Wes now was herself, and she was very much afraid that that was the one thing he no longer wanted.

WES WAS GOING through his mother's jewelry, in the company of two security guards and a bank official, making arrangements for its disposition. He had no sentimental memories of the pieces—his father had shown it to him only once, when he had told Wes that it would all belong to him, someday, to give to his wife—but it was all quite beautiful. And there was a pang when he imagined the emerald necklance around Sandy's neck, or how her skin would add luster to the pearls, or how the diamond earrings would sparkle in her ears.

Several pieces, the most valuable, were quite old, but most were modern-day replicas of what various former Wesleys had listed in their inventories and had lost through war or theft or gambling. Wes believed it was his grandfather, or perhaps his great-grandfather, who had taken it upon himself to refill the Wesley coffers with newly designed family jewels. Even without the antique value, every item was a masterpiece and incredibly valuable. It was difficult for Wes to imagine anyone losing as much money as this jewelry was worth.

There was one piece, a strange onyx-and-silver necklace, that was designed after what was reputed to be a fifteenth-century original, owned by one of the first Wesleys to distinguish himself at court. As Wes held the heavy silver ornament in his hand, he wondered what they must have been like, those first Wesleys, the founders of the dynasty. Savage brutes, most likely, vicious in battle, pillaging and plundering and laying claim to all that they could conquer. Men of strength and determination, men of little vision but great greed who saw what they wanted and took it.

But this is not what I want, Wes realized slowly. He sat there with the exquisitely ornamented silver necklace in his hand and thought, *It's only metal.* Someone, somewhere back in history, had no doubt died for what this represented, but to Wes it was only metal.

Where are your treasures, Wes?

Wes had no doubt now that, if he wanted to, he could build again just as surely and just as firmly as those long-ago dukes and earls of an untamed empire had done. He could preserve what they had begun without having ever intended to begin anything at all...or he could leave the ways of the Old World and start anew.

Endings and beginnings. Even those old-time heroes had begun with nothing more than a belief in themselves and knowledge of what they wanted. Everyone had to start somewhere.

Wes left the jewelry in the astonished hands of the security guards—all except one piece, which he cheerfully pocketed—and strode out of the bank. The first thing he did when he got home was telephone Mr. Madison, with regret in his voice that was somewhat less than sincere, and informed him that while his offer was appreciated, it was no longer necessary. The second thing he did was to shout imperiously for Mitch. They had plans to make.

BY CHRISTMAS EVE Sandy had stopped crying. She covered her puffy eyes and red nose with enough powder to guarantee that a resemblance between herself and Rudolph would be purely superficial, and even added a little lipstick for the occasion. She bundled up in hat, scarf, mittens and coat, and then with one final deep breath meant to ward off quaking nerves, she set off.

The Wesley mansion wasn't all that hard to find, but the traffic was terrible and the snow was coming down in thick foggy sheets. Even the gay green and red Christmas lights were muted, blinking on and off like distant beacons to a half-remembered dream. The drive was not lit, and Sandy left her car in the street, trudging up the slippery snow-layered path in the dark and wondering whether, now that she had found the courage, the effort would be wasted, whether he was even home or would want to see her.

Sandy tried not to be intimidated by the sheer size of the place, or by the discreet echoing of musical chimes that responded to her push on the bell. But the door was opened by the largest, unfriendliest-looking man Sandy had ever seen, and there was no point in denying it anymore. She was intimidated.

In a rush of sheer cowardice she started to stammer some apology and flee into the night. This was crazy. Wes wouldn't want to see her. Why would he want to see her? He had enough problems, and after the way she had treated him...

But then she heard Wes's voice from some distant room, "Damn it, Mitch, if that's Wilkins again tell him—" He appeared behind the huge man at the door. He saw her.

He was wearing that same lovely gray-and-black sweater he had worn on that morning so long ago when he came to sweep her away to a mountain paradise. His hair was shiny and bouncy and his eyes were so blue they looked as though they could burn. He stood poised, not speaking, not moving, just looking at her, and Sandy could read nothing from his face. Everything within her stopped, waiting, aching for some sign of recognition or welcome but not expecting any. She wanted to run and fling herself into his arms, to press her wet, cold body into his and accept his shelter, to beg his forgiveness, to promise him...everything. But she did not move, because she knew if he did not want her she would go. But not before she told him.

Then Wes breathed, "Sandy. I was just trying to..." He had been trying to call her for the past hour. He had only just realized it was Christmas Eve, and that she was probably with her parents. He had thought about calling them, but then decided he would go there instead, and he had just come to get his coat when he heard the door chimes and she was there, standing on his threshold, dusted with snow and looking small and cold and very uncertain.

''For goodness' sake, Mitch,'' he said impatiently, striding to the door, ''move. Sandy, come in, you look half frozen. Mitch, get us something hot to drink, will you?'' And all the while something inside him was singing, *My God, it is her. She's here. Miracles do happen.*

The huge man gave a little bow, which seemed ridiculously incongruous with his combat-fatigue attire, and moved away. Then Wes had caught her wrist, pulling her inside, closing the door, and his eyes were going over her, through her, with wonder and welcome and a small measure of disbelief. Feelings of joy began to explode inside Sandy just because he was there and looking at her.

Wes wanted to pull her into his arms, to feel her real and solid against him, to inhale her fragrance and touch her hair and then to hold her some more. But the moment between them was suspended, fragile, and neither one of them seemed capable of putting his or her feelings into action. All Wes seemed able to do was to go through the motions, hanging up her coat, taking her hat and her scarf and her mittens, leading the way into the main parlor and seating her before the fire, and then he could only look at her, absorbing her, waiting for he knew not what.

He looked tired, Sandy noticed. There were little lines around his eyes that she did not recall seeing before, and there was a certain tenseness about his shoulders that should not have been there. She wanted to make it better for him. She wanted his eyes to laugh again; she wanted to ease his tension and take all his worries away. She knew she could not do that, but she could be there, to share and to comfort.

After a long time when only the crackling of the fire and the gentle brush of the wind against the windowpanes could be heard, Sandy said, "I guess you're wondering why I'm here."

Wes did not care. It only mattered that she *was* here.

She reached into her purse and drew out a small wrapped box. "We have a tradition," she said and then, with all the courage she possessed, she held the package out to him. "We always open some little something on Christmas Eve. I hope you don't mind."

Wes took the package with a questioning look, but her face gave him no answers. He tore off the wrapping with shaking fingers and lifted the lid. It was a key.

"It's to my apartment," she explained in a rush, watching him anxiously, searchingly. But his head was lowered, his eyes fixed upon the key, and she could see nothing in his face. "I was...going to give it to Bill, as, you know, kind of a gag Christmas gift because he's been so good about letting me live there so cheaply and I thought I would be leaving, but... Well, I've decided to stay a while after all, and I wanted you to have a key in case...in case you needed me for something...." Her voice faded off then, into the ringing silence, the ticking of the clock and the crackling of the fire, and Wes said nothing. He did not even look up.

And then, abruptly, he moved. He walked over to the fake white Christmas tree with its blinking blue lights and its color-coordinated packages, and he picked up a small square box wrapped in blue foil. He brought it over to her. "I have something for you, too," he said, and his voice sounded funny, almost choked. There was a strange look in his eyes.

Hesitantly, Sandy unwrapped the box, her heart pounding, hardly daring to look at him. It was a simple cardboard box, stuffed with tissue paper. And inside the tissue paper was nestled another key.

Sandy looked up at him, confusion and uncertainty fogging her eyes, and she said, "What—what does it go to?"

Wes's eyes were dancing. He put his arm around her shoulders, leading her to the window, and Sandy could feel the electricity of excitement and the coursing of joy that pulsed through him like a living thing. It caught something within her, which grew into a cautious yet shimmering wonder as he lifted his hand and rubbed a clear spot on the foggy windowpane. "This," he said.

Sandy, looking out, could just discern beyond the curtain of snowflakes the shape of a large vehicle parked close to the house. She said, glancing at him hesitantly, "A van?"

He nodded. "It's seven years old but in good shape— Mitch picked it out, and if there's one thing he knows it's automobiles. And the best part is, it only cost twelve hundred dollars." He looked briefly amazed. "I didn't know you could buy *anything* on wheels for that price."

Torn between the urge to laugh out loud and hug him hard and the still-questioning, almost overwhelming disbelief, Sandy said, "You mean—it's yours?"

Gently, Wes closed her fingers over the key. "Ours." Then, in a rush, holding both her hands tightly in his, he said earnestly, "Oh, Sandy, I don't want you to stay here with me. *I* don't want to stay here. It's all a matter of values, don't you see, and the only people we have to be true to are ourselves. Nothing I could do, nothing I could accomplish here, would be worth anything if I lost you."

All the love and wonder she felt for him filled her and bubbled over; she felt like crying, she felt like laughing, she felt like holding him tightly and never letting him go. Her hands tightened beneath his and she said, "Wes, it doesn't matter. I can't let you turn your back on everything because of some silly idea of mine. We can stay here, and we'll work together."

He shook his head firmly. "There's nothing here I want to work for. I want to start over, from the beginning, and build my own dynasty, in my own way...with you."

And then the power that had been drawing them ever closer met in one long, intense, searing kiss. Sandy felt the world slowly tip and right itself again, a world that was as new and as fresh and as filled with possibilities as it had been on the first day of creation, waiting for the two of them to explore and to savor and to do with it what they must, together.

When they parted, they both were flushed, and a little breathless, and very unsteady. Wes's eyes were bright, and dazed with love, but very sober as he said, "I can't keep living my life tied to the past, Sandy, doing what everyone expects me to do, any more than you could. Maybe I will never achieve greatness, or accomplish anything useful, or live up to the Wesley name—whatever that means—but maybe I wasn't meant to. Maybe the only thing I was ever meant to do was to love you."

Tenderly, Sandy reached up to stroke his heated, beautifully planed face. "Aren't you afraid of abandoning your heritage? Of turning into—" and her eyes teased him briefly "—a nobody?"

He shook his head. "I've got a lot to learn about life, too, Sandy. And I can't think of any better way to do it than to experience it with you. Not," he assured her, "that I can't be useful. I'm not going to let you support me entirely, and I can find work just as well as you can. There are a lot of things I'm sure I could do if someone would only show me how—and I need to learn those things. I already have a head start." He grinned. "I'm good with my hands, remember?"

Sandy, loving him more intensely than she ever thought was possible to love anyone, looked up at him gravely. "Show me," she whispered.

He did.

CHRISTMAS MORNING at the Garret house: children and wrapping paper were tangled everywhere. Battery-powered toys ran rampant over the carpet, and laughter and delight and surprise mixed with the background sound of carols from the stereo and the warm scents of coffee, evergreens and cinnamon breakfast rolls. O.J. was home from the Philippines with exotic gifts for everyone and enough wild tales to keep gullible children dreaming the dreams of the high seas for a year. The high point of the morning was when Linda arrived, looking somewhat abashed and greatly defensive, with a bedraggled, ancient Santa Claus in tow. "Well," she asserted, during the momentary astonished silence that followed her entrance, "he was just standing out on the street corner in the cold—what was I supposed to do? It's Christmas, after all!"

The children, having no doubt in their innocent little minds that this was indeed *the* Santa Claus, ran to welcome him, and Wes and Sandy fell, laughing, into each other's arms. The Christmas spirit had even gotten through to the staunch and conservative Linda and not a moment too soon.

Sandy opened boxes filled with woolen scarves, leather gloves, luscious perfumes, frilly blouses, candy, exclaiming over each gift with more enthusiasm than the last. Her eyes filled with tears of love and gratitude when her parents brought out their gift to her—a set of matched luggage. "Well," her father explained gruffly, "if you're going to travel, you might as well do it in style." From Rick there was a hand-painted gift certificate for a custom paint job on the van. Linda's offering to the state of Sandy's wardrobe this year was a sheer and lacy negligee, and when Sandy saw the glint in Wes's eyes as she held it up to herself she knew that this was one of Linda's extravagances that would be well used. But to her it was the best Christmas ever because whenever she glanced up she saw Wes's twinkling blue eyes or the shape of his profile or the gleam of his hair, or heard his laughter, and no gift could compare with that.

A necessary lull in the excitement fell as the breakfast buffet was set out, for not even the children would miss Grandma's famous cinnamon rolls. Sandy was helping her father gather up the last of the wrapping paper for the fire before joining Wes for orange juice and sweet rolls and a well-deserved moment alone when her father said, "Oops, we missed one." He pulled out a medium-sized package and examined the tag. "For you, sweetie."

Sandy took the package and opened it without cere-mony. She discarded the lid and pushed aside the tissue pa-per, then slowly pulled out the gift.

It was a rhinestone-studded, garishly painted mother-of-pearl seashell, with two glittering sea horses inside, sitting on a base inscribed "Florida." The attached card read sim-ply, "Believe—Santa."

Sandy stared at it for a long, long time.

"It's—pretty," Wes said hesitantly, beside her.

Sandy's eyes jerked around, searching the room urgently for the familiar figure in the torn and stained red suit, but even as she looked she knew he wouldn't be there. She searched once, twice, and then she turned back to Wes, the excited, curious, amazed incredulity in her eyes turning slowly to gentle wonder. Impossible. But hadn't more im-possible things been brought to earth these past few weeks? Wasn't Wes, standing here beside her, proof of that?

"No, it's not," she said, slowly, holding on to the sea-shell. Laughter bubbled inside her and she wanted to fling out her arms and embrace the whole world. What did she know about impossible? She was only beginning to learn. "It's the ugliest thing that was ever designed," she de-clared, hugging the souvenir to her chest. Her eyes were dancing with joy. "But I love it!"

Wes gave her a smile that said he loved her because of her eccentricities, not in spite of them, and then he reached into his pocket. "I have something for you that's not quite as tacky," he said, "but almost as pretty." He took her hand, and, as she held her breath in cautious disbelief, he slipped a diamond solitaire on her finger. "It was my mother's," he explained simply. "One thing that I thought was worth saving from the past. There's a wedding band that goes with it."

With a muffled cry, Sandy threw herself into his arms, wrapping her arms around his neck, receiving his startled laughter and his reciprocal embrace as a dim background to the soaring joy of Christmas miracles come true. With her eyes squeezed tightly shut against the tears of sheer happiness that threatened to break through, the seashell clutched in one hand and the diamond gleaming on the other, Sandy's lips moved to form two simple words.

They were: _I believe._

Epilogue

The great rooms and corridors of the Wesley mansion were transformed. Most of the more valuable furnishings and artwork had already been removed into the estate agent's safekeeping until an auction could be arranged; the mansion itself would go on the market within the week. Tonight the great empty house was filled with people, with noise, with music, with the smells of rich food and the sounds of boisterous laughter and untutored accents. The street people of Philadelphia—the poor, the hungry, the aged and the homeless—were feasting upon all the lavishness of the world-renowned Wesley hospitality with imported wines, a string orchestra and the finest catering service Philadelphia had to offer. Adrian Wesley was finally playing the lord of the manor and, in his opinion, neither the house nor his bank account had ever been put to better use.

After the final sales were made, Adrian would have less than eight thousand dollars left to his name. Deducting from that the cost of the party and the van left just under two thousand dollars with which Sandy and Wes would begin their odyssey. Wes would have preferred to dispose of the remaining money and be free of it, but Sandy was too practical to carry Thoreau's policy to the extreme. They would be living simply enough even by Walden Pond standards; there was no sense in overdoing it.

Sandy stood near the fireplace, looking out over the crowds of strangers whom Wes, with this single act of generosity, had made so happy, and she thought how typical this was of him. And how lucky she was to have found him. And how very, very obvious it was who was going to have to hold the purse strings in their family.

Wes brought her a refilled glass of champagne, and she sank happily into the circle of his arm. "Have I told you lately how much I love you?"

"Hmm…" He pretended thoughtfulness. "Not within the past half hour, I believe."

"I love you."

"The sentiment is reciprocated."

Their lips touched in a light, lingering, caressingly familiar kiss, and then the clock in the corner began it's slow ponderous chiming toward the stroke of midnight. Sandy straightened, her eyes sparkling, and Wes stood soberly by her side as the rush of excitement grew through the crowd, plastic glasses hurriedly filled with champagne, scrambling for places next to familiar faces, counting out loud the remaining seconds.

Wes turned toward the fireplace, eyes twinkling, and lifted his glass toward his father's portrait. "To my dad," he said, "who made all of this possible."

Sandy, likewise, lifted her glass and offered grandly, "To Santa Claus, who brought us together!"

They turned to each other, their eyes filled with laughter and joy, and said in unison, "To us!"

"Three…two…one…"

The cheers and the laughter of the wild celebration of "Auld Lang Syne" surged and faded around Wes and Sandy, for already they were lost in each other's arms.

They parted at last, with great reluctance, and spent a long time simply looking into each other's eyes. Then they toasted each other with the only two pieces of real crystal remaining in the house and, in a single motion, turned and tossed the glasses over their shoulders into the fireplace. Laughing, they came together again.

"Out with the old, in with the new," said Wes, drawing her close. "Happy New Year, darling."

And it was.

Six exciting series for you every month... from Harlequin

Harlequin Romance®
The series that started it all

Tender, captivating and heartwarming...
love stories that sweep you off to faraway places
and delight you with the magic of love.

◆

Harlequin Presents®

Powerful contemporary love
stories...as individual as the
women who read them

The No. 1 romance series...
exciting love stories for you, the woman of today...
a rare blend of passion and dramatic realism.

◆

Harlequin Superromance®
It's more than romance...
it's Harlequin Superromance

A sophisticated, contemporary romance-fiction
series, providing you with a longer,
more involving read...a richer mix of complex plots,
realism and adventure.

Harlequin
American Romance™
Harlequin celebrates the American woman...

...by offering you romance stories written about American women, by American women for American women. This series offers you contemporary romances uniquely North American in flavor and appeal.

◆

Harlequin Temptation™
Passionate stories for today's woman

An exciting series of sensual, mature stories of love...dilemmas, choices, resolutions... all contemporary issues dealt with in a true-to-life fashion by some of your favorite authors.

◆

Harlequin Intrigue™
Because romance can be quite an adventure

Harlequin Intrigue, an innovative series that blends the romance you expect... with the unexpected. Each story has an added element of intrigue that provides a new twist to the Harlequin tradition of romance excellence.

Harlequin Books®

PROD-A-2

WORLDWIDE LIBRARY IS YOUR TICKET TO ROMANCE, ADVENTURE AND EXCITEMENT

Experience it all in these big, bold Bestsellers— Yours exclusively from WORLDWIDE LIBRARY WHILE QUANTITIES LAST

To receive these Bestsellers, complete the order form, detach and send together with your check or money order (include 75¢ postage and handling), payable to WORLDWIDE LIBRARY, to:

In the U.S.
WORLDWIDE LIBRARY
Box 52040
Phoenix, AZ
85072-2040

In Canada
WORLDWIDE LIBRARY
P.O. Box 2800, 5170 Yonge Street
Postal Station A, Willowdale, Ontario
M2N 6J3

Quant.	Title	Price
_____	**ANTIGUA KISS,** Anne Weale	$2.95
_____	**WILD CONCERTO,** Anne Mather	$2.95
_____	**STORMSPELL,** Anne Mather	$2.95
_____	**A VIOLATION,** Charlotte Lamb	$3.50
_____	**LEGACY OF PASSION,** Catherine Kay	$3.50
_____	**SECRETS,** Sheila Holland	$3.50
_____	**SWEET MEMORIES,** LaVyrle Spencer	$3.50
_____	**FLORA,** Anne Weale	$3.50
_____	**SUMMER'S AWAKENING,** Anne Weale	$3.50
_____	**FINGER PRINTS,** Barbara Delinsky	$3.50
_____	**DREAMWEAVER,** Felicia Gallant/Rebecca Flanders	$3.50
_____	**EYE OF THE STORM,** Maura Seger	$3.50
_____	**HIDDEN IN THE FLAME,** Anne Mather	$3.50
	YOUR ORDER TOTAL	$_____
	New York and Arizona residents add appropriate sales tax	$_____
	Postage and Handling	$ .75
	I enclose	$_____

NAME _____

ADDRESS _____ APT.# _____

CITY _____

STATE/PROV. _____ ZIP/POSTAL CODE _____

WW2

What readers say about Harlequin romance fiction...

"I absolutely adore Harlequin romances!
They are fun and relaxing to read, and
each book provides a wonderful escape."
  –N.E.,* Pacific Palisades, California

"Harlequin is the best in romantic reading."
  –K.G.,* Philadelphia, Pennsylvania

"Harlequins have been my passport to the
world. I have been many places without
ever leaving my doorstep."
  –P.Z.,* Belvedere, Illinois

"My praise for the warmth and adventure
your books bring into my life."
  –D.F.,*Hicksville, New York

"A pleasant way to relax after a busy day."
  –P.W.,* Rector, Arkansas

*Names available on request.

What the press says about Harlequin romance fiction...

When it comes to romantic novels...
Harlequin is the indisputable king."
—*New York Times*

"...always with an upbeat, happy ending."
—*San Francisco Chronicle*

"Women have come to trust these
stories about contemporary people,
set in exciting foreign places."
—*Best Sellers*, New York

"The most popular reading matter of
American women today."
—*Detroit News*

"...a work of art."
—*Globe & Mail*, Toronto